Macbeth

麦克白

原　　著：（英）威廉·莎士比亚
丛书主编：彭　萍
丛书副主编：（按姓氏拼音排序）
　　　　　胡钰翎　沈忆文　徐　阳
本书导读与注释：胡钰翎

中国宇航出版社
·北京·

专家寄语

看到中国宇航出版社"我的心灵藏书馆"导读注释丛书，这些颇为久违的书目在心里激发出一种十分亲切的感觉。这其中很多是当年我们做学生时读过的，不少记忆犹新。记得在上海外国语学院（现上海外国语大学）读书时，老师常对我们说，学习英语离不开文学，建议我们阅读英美文学经典著作。

各国的经典著作是人类共同的宝贵文化财富。由于历史条件等原因，这些文学巨匠的作品是无法超越的。这些巨著所描绘的绚丽多彩的生活画卷，扣人心弦的情节，栩栩如生的人物形象，深入透彻的内心精神分析，脍炙人口，令人赞叹，不但从文学角度本身来说有极高的价值，还能帮助我们了解政治、历史、哲学、经济、文化、宗教、风土人情、风俗习惯等英美社会的方方面面，因为文学是反映社会现实的，是生活的百科全书。此外，英语中的许多成语典故乃至谚语都出自这些经典著作，作为英语专业的学生或英语自学者，这些都是不可或缺的。

学英语应该对英美文学有相当的了解，尤其是传世的经典著作。但是英美文学经典著作浩瀚如烟，而且很多是厚厚的大部头，只能选读一部分，这次中国宇航出版社"我的心灵藏书馆"所选的书籍都是经过精心挑选的，决定这份书单，参考了大量的材料，做了大量的调查，因此可以说所选之书都是精品中的精品。这些书的语言文字十分优美，不少精彩的段落适合反复吟读，也值得背诵。

针对中国学生的导读注释本会提供很多帮助。导读就作者情况、作品的背景、作品的情节、主要人物、其在文学史上的地位和社会意义等作了介绍，引导读者进入英美文学的神圣殿堂。注释部分对语言难点、文化社会背景、典故、历史事件、历史人物和地点等作了详尽的解说，指点迷津，指出许多成语典故的出处和习惯用法，可以帮助读者除掉许多文字方面的拦路虎，大大方便英语学习者，从而能帮助读者正确理解故事情节，提高阅读的速度。笔者的经验表明，经典著作精练的语言本身能保证所学英语的语言质量，但是要有一定量的阅读才能提供数量上的保证，只有质和量双管齐下才能保证英语较大的提高。

十年动乱之后高等学校复课时，很多出版社都出版了一批经典名著和一批当代和现代的优秀作品，深受广大学生的欢迎，对教师的英语教学和学生们的英语学习作出了很大的贡献。可是现在学英语往往强调时代性和实用性，各种实用英语很多，还有许多时髦的读物，相对而言，经典著作出版得反而很少，书店的书架上很难寻觅到它们的踪影。笔者觉得这是一种方向上的偏离。即使在外事活动、经济交流中，掌握必要的英美文学方面的知识也是十分有用的。我国领导人与外国政要会晤时也常常引用外国文学作品中的名言，这对建立和增进友好气氛有很大的作用。

经典著作的作用是其他作品取代不了的。中国宇航出版社推出这套名著注释版丛书是很有眼光的，可以说是填补了一个空白。他们请北京外国语大学骨干教师彭萍博士担任这套书的主编也是非常适合的，而诸位导读和注释者在英语教学方面都有着丰富的经验，不仅指出作品中英语特有的成语和习惯用法，有的还详细举例说明，让读者更好地理解如何应用，尤其着重指出一些与文化有关的背景知识。不仅如此，注释还指出了作品布局、前后照应、句式结构以及修辞等方面的许多特点，有些很难翻译的词句还提供了参考译文。这些视角很有创新意识。作为一个学英语、教英语几十年的过来人，笔者愿意热情地向大家推荐这套丛书，相信广大学生和英语学习者一定会从中获益匪浅。

陈德彰
2010 年 10 月

丛书总序一

那是一个春寒料峭的日子，中国宇航出版社的策划编辑战颖找到我，要我负责主编一套世界经典名著的导读和注释丛书，想请我邀北外的一些老师加入到这一工作中来。我看了她给我的书单后，心中不由地一动，多么熟悉的书名啊，这些经典名著的英文版和中文版是伴我度过大学时期的重要精神食粮之一。因为在我的大学时代，校园里不像现在这样充斥着浮躁的气氛，而是一种宁静的读书氛围，我们读古诗词、现代抒情诗、三毛的散文、席慕蓉的散文和诗歌、罗兰的小品文等，而我们这些英语专业的学生当然还要阅读英文经典名著，不是老师布置的作业，而是主动为之。时至今日，这些经典中的主人公形象依然留在自己的脑海中，这些经典中的故事情节依然让人心潮澎湃。所以，我禁不住想答应下来。可是，经验告诉我，为英语读物作注释，尤其是为英文原版小说作注释，看起来或听起来是一件简单的事情，而真正做起来却是耗时、费力的工作，因为文学著作的注释不是简单的单词注释，还有很多地名、人名、历史事件、文化典故等诸多百科全书式的东西要为读者解释出来。作长篇巨著的注释更是很多人望而却步的事情，所以对能否邀请到一些同事从事这一工作我有些不敢确定。虽然我本人愿意为经典的传播、为读者的阅读提供自己的一点见解和帮助，可个人的力量毕竟是有限的。因此，当时我犹豫了，但对经典名著的情结又让我对这一工作难以割舍。于是，我跟战颖编辑说，我先询问一下看有多少人愿意去做这件事。让我欣慰的是，我找到了几个如我一样热爱文学的同事，他（她）们表示愿意承担这样的工作。于是，"我的心灵藏书馆"丛书的导读和注释工作从此拉开序幕。而现在，就在我写这篇总序的时候，北京正由深秋迈向寒冬，外面刚刚下过一场秋雨，天还是阴阴的，冷冷的，可面对完成的一本本书稿，我心里依然是春天般的温暖。

　　文学是人性和社会的一面镜子，又是滋养人心灵的沃土，优秀的文学作品又给人以思想的启迪和审美的愉悦。无论哪个年代，阅读文学的人都不会孤独，不会空虚。具体说来，文学首先具有审美价值。阅读一部文学作品，读者首先是通过各种风格的语言、曲折的情节和人物的艺术形象等获得一种审美体验。读者可以融自己的想象于阅读过程当中，从而使自己的体验得到美的升华。其次，文学具有社会现实价值。任何文学作品的创作都离不开其所在的时代和社会，是时代和社会现实的重要体现。通过阅读文学作品，读者从其中的人物性格、命运及家庭、社会环境的发展脉络可以窥见人的本质和社会现实。第三，文学具有文化意义。通过阅读经典名著，可以领略到作品透射的文化背景，从而丰富历史、地理、宗教、风俗等百科全书式的知识。尤其是一些经典名著，无论从上述哪个方面讲，都是人类不可或缺的精神食粮。

　　中国宇航出版社之所以选择《简·爱》《呼啸山庄》《飘》《傲慢与偏见》《老人与海》《欧·亨利短篇小说精选》《鲁滨逊漂流记》《瓦尔登湖》《理智与情感》《了不起的盖茨比》等作为"我的心灵藏书馆"系列的第一批入选书目，是基于这些经典不朽的主题和魅力。可以说，以上名著是对世界各国读者影响最为深远和最为广泛的经典作品，其形象塑造、语言艺术、情节设计、思想意义等从著作诞生那时起时至今日，已经影响和启迪了一代又一代的读者，这些著作的情节和人物塑造在中国读者群中享有很高的赞誉，给中国读者留下了深刻的印象。《简·爱》通过简·爱与罗切斯特的爱情故事，塑造了简·爱这样一个追求个性自由、主张男女平等的独立女性形象；《呼啸山庄》使用现实主义、浪漫主义、象征主义等表现手法讲述了希刺克厉夫和凯瑟琳的真挚而最终走向悲剧的爱情故事，塑造出希刺克厉夫这样一位由爱生恨、具有极度反叛精神的人物形象；《飘》以美国南北战争前后的南方佐治亚州为背景，以一个种植园主的女儿郝思嘉为核心人物，通过几个家族的兴衰变化反映了美国南方各州在这一重要历史时期的社会现实；《傲慢与偏见》通过伊丽莎白和达西的故事以及其他几个人的爱情故事，揭示出傲慢与偏见是生活中常见的弱点，只有加深了解，才能有更客观的认识，以及婚姻应以爱情为基础这样看似平凡却又非常深刻的道理；《老人与海》用简约的风格塑造出一个真正的硬汉形象，告诉人们"人可以被毁

灭，但不能被打败"的人生哲学；欧·亨利的短篇小说亦庄亦谐，
很多故事从小处着眼，却塑造出不同阶层的人物形象，尤其是下层
人民的形象，读来不免发人深思；《鲁滨逊漂流记》通过写实的手法
塑造出鲁滨逊这样一位理想的资产阶级英雄形象；《瓦尔登湖》用幽
默、睿智、优美的语言揭示出深刻的人生和社会哲理；《理智与情感》
通过两位女主角的婚事波折揭示了当时英国社会中以婚配作为女子
寻求经济保障和提高社会地位，却不重视女子情感和权利的陋习；
《了不起的盖茨比》描写了主人公盖茨比与黛西的爱情悲剧，揭示了
"美国梦"的破灭。当然，这些经典名著的意义不是一两句话就能
概括出来的，只有真正走进去，沉浸其中，才能真正感受到文学的
魅力。

通过阅读英语名著学英语一直以来被公认为行之有效的学习方
法，也是经过了数代人的实践得出来的真理。因为名著的语言一般
比较规范和地道，即人们经常说的"原汁原味的英语"。因此，阅读
这些著作对形成英语的语感大有裨益。同时，阅读名著可以扩大词
汇量，丰富百科知识，有助于增进对英语国家的了解。而本套丛书
可谓"精华中的精华"，阅读这些书籍，读者一方面会沉浸于文学的
殿堂中，感受书中的情节美、人物形象塑造美以及语言艺术美，提
高文学的素养，同时又在不知不觉中浸染在"原汁原味"的英语当
中，提高英语的表达能力和丰富英语文化知识。当然，对有些读者
来说，阅读名著很多时候会存在一定的难度或遇到一些词汇、句法
或背景知识的障碍，这时读者不免会产生一种"受挫感"。而本套丛
书的注释正是为了帮助读者克服这样的"受挫感"，使读者不必阅读
简易读物就能直接进入到原著气势恢宏的"殿堂"当中，定会愉快
地将文学欣赏与英语学习有效地结合在一起。

本套丛书的原文大部分参考美国企鹅出版集团出版的"企鹅经
典丛书"（Penguin Classics）和英国华兹华斯出版公司出版的世界
名著系列（Wordsworth Classics）两种版本进行校对。本套导读与注
释丛书的目的是想帮助读者更好地阅读和理解原版英文名著。具体
说来，一方面可以使读者在阅读原著的过程中提高自己的英文语言
水平，另一方面可以拉近读者与英文原著的距离，使读者更好地体
会英文原著所传达出的各种信息，从而更好地欣赏原著。注释的原
则和内容如下：（1）生词。本套丛书注释的单词基本为大学英语四
级以上的词汇，同时各位注释作者也会根据自己的教学经验适当地

进行取舍，但总体原则是注释的单词"宜多不宜少"。同时为一些常用单词提供一个短语或句子做例子，并给出了这个短语或句子的翻译，从而更好地说明单词的用法。考虑到读者第二次遇到一个生词后，可能会忘记前面已有的注释，所以一些单词有重复注释的现象。（2）短语。英语短语的掌握对应用这门语言起着非常重要的作用，因此本套丛书的注释中没有忽视短语的注释，有些短语是读者熟悉的，有些是不熟悉的，读者通过这些短语的注释能够做到"温故知新"。重要和常见的短语后面一般均提供例句及其翻译，便于读者进一步巩固和学习这些短语的用法。（3）专有名词。由于丛书所包含的著作涉及不同国家（尤其是英美国家）的不同历史时期和不同地点，因此注释也考虑到了其中的地名、人名、历史事件名等（个别虚构的地名和人名除外），对这些名称一般提供简短的说明。可以说，这一部分对丰富读者的地理和历史知识很有帮助，同时能帮助他们更好地把握著作的内容和写作背景。（4）文化知识。这部分主要包括成语典故、宗教知识、引用等，对这些文化知识一般先注明其来源，然后提供简短的说明，从而使读者在阅读名著的过程中对英语的成语典故、宗教知识、名言警句等有一定的了解。（5）复杂句。本套丛书中的著作有的风格简约，句式比较简单，有的则包含很多长句或复杂句。注释者根据自己的经验，对一些可能会让读者费解的句子首先稍作分析，然后提供译文。为有效利用已有的名著翻译成果，这些长句的译文大多数参考了现成的权威译文，标明出处；有些译文由注释者进行了改动，以使其更加忠实和通顺。（6）黑人英语和非标准英语。名著中必然会出现一些对话，为了刻画人物的形象，一些作者会根据人物的身份或阶层使用非标准英语或黑人英语。注释中原则上提供这些非标准英语或黑人英语的标准表达法，个别地方给出了中文。除以上几点外，注释中还对一些精彩句和话语的隐含意义进行了注释，提供了汉语译文，同时还有个别地方注释了与上下文的联系。

值得一提的是，本套丛书导读和注释的团队成员均来自北京外国语大学，是教学经验极其丰富的一线骨干教师，长期从事英语精读、泛读（其中很重要的一部分就是指导学生阅读英语名著）、文学、翻译、语言学等教学和研究工作，均有着深厚的文学和语言功底。可以说，团队的每个成员都是读着这些以及更多英语名著成长的过来人，而且不少还都在继续研读这些经典著作。正如我在开篇所说，为名著作导读和注释是一件听起来容易、做起来相当耗神和耗时的工作，但是各位同仁本着对文学的热忱和对读者负责的态度，按预期的速度高质量地完成了这项工作，在此对他（她）们谨致谢意！

在本套丛书完稿之际，北京外国语大学陈德彰教授欣然提笔，为本套丛书撰写了寄语，这是对我们这个团队莫大的鼓励。同时，感谢中国宇航出版社为我们提供了这样一个为读者服务的机会，感谢策划编辑战颖女士提供的各项协助工作！

希望本套丛书提供的导读和注释能给广大的英语爱好者、英语学习者、英语文学爱好者和英语文学学习者提供一定的帮助，使读者朋友更轻松、更有信心地穿越时空，与经典名著进行心灵的对话和沟通。当然，由于时间紧迫，任务繁重，导读和注释中难免出现纰漏或疏忽之处，敬请广大读者予以谅解，并不吝赐教！

彭萍

2010 年深秋

于北京海淀世纪城平心斋

丛书总序二

　　"我的心灵藏书馆"导读和注释丛书第一批10本面世以来，受到了读者的热烈欢迎。读者普遍反映，这套丛书不仅汇集了真正的经典名著，更重要的是降低了中国学生阅读国外原版名著的门槛。每当阅读到困惑之处时，这个版本都给出了恰到好处的注释，就好像一个耐心的老师随时等待亲爱的读者提出疑问并作出回答。而且，整套丛书无论是封面设计还是装帧工艺都堪称一流。可以说，本套丛书不仅具有帮助读者学习英语、提高文学修养的实用价值，还具有特别的文学收藏价值。在这个人人谈论和阅读电子书的时代，"我的心灵藏书馆"真正是一套可以带给读者阅读享受的好书，是世界名著纸本书的经典呈现，是值得收藏的珍贵版本。每当在网络上或者书店中看到、听到读者对该套丛书的青睐与好评，我们这一导读和注释团队就会感到读者的巨大热情与信任。为了让广大读者能走进更多的名著，熟悉更多的作品，后续15部英文经典名著经过10余名老师近一年的努力，现即将出版。希望这15部英语经典名著及其导读和注释能一如既往地给予读者阅读上的愉悦和学习上的帮助。

　　此刻，我审阅着一本本的书稿，回忆着这些经典名著的情节，一个个鲜活的人物形象在我的脑海中逐渐清晰起来，向我展示着不同时代、不同背景下的人性及社会生活。优美的语言，错综复杂的故事情节，注释者细致的注释和讲解，使我在心中油然升起一种美的享受，犹如窗外的秋叶、湛蓝的天空和午后的暖阳，让我的心变得越来越温暖……

　　第二批丛书包括《名利场》《莎士比亚故事集》《一九八四》《查泰莱夫人的情人》《小妇人》《马克·吐温短篇小说精选》《杰克·伦

敦小说精选》《嘉莉妹妹》《红字》《泰戈尔作品集》《茶花女》《苔丝》《格列佛游记》《永别了，武器》和《夜色温柔》。这些著作都是脍炙人口的作品，在世界文学中占据着重要地位。其主题分别可以概述如下：《名利场》通过蓓基·夏泼的钻营史和爱米丽亚与乔治的罗曼史，真实地描绘了1810—1820年摄政王时期，英国上流社会没落贵族和资产阶级暴发户等各色人物的丑恶嘴脸及弱肉强食、尔虞我诈的人际关系。《莎士比亚故事集》是英国散文家查尔斯·兰姆和姐姐玛丽·安妮·兰姆两人用叙事体散文编写的20个莎士比亚戏剧故事，希望读者通过这20个故事对原著产生兴趣，从而走进莎士比亚的戏剧世界，领略其中独一无二的丰富宝藏。《一九八四》通过对大洋国一名英格兰社会主义党的普通外围党员温斯顿·史密斯个人生活的细致入微、栩栩如生的刻画，向世人展示了一个令人感到窒息和恐怖、以追逐权力为最终目标的假想未来社会的景象。《查泰莱夫人的情人》讲述了贵族阶级的康斯坦斯·查泰莱夫人和在她丈夫领地上的守林员麦勒斯之间的爱情故事，反映出劳伦斯对阶级、人性和情感关系的思考。《小妇人》以美国南北战争期间马奇一家及其四姐妹的生活为描写对象，讲述了她们对自强自立精神的追求、对于家庭的眷顾和对爱情的忠诚。《马克·吐温短篇小说精选》汇集了美国讽刺小说家马克·吐温优秀的短篇小说，读者可以从作品轻松嬉笑的外表下，窥见作者对社会和人性的严肃批判。《杰克·伦敦小说精选》描述了人与自然之间的严酷搏斗，以及人与人之间错综复杂的社会关系，体现了杰克·伦敦对达尔文的"适者生存"，以及斯宾塞的社会达尔文主义的推崇。《嘉莉妹妹》通过农村姑娘嘉莉在大城市的经历，揭露了20世纪初美国人狂热追求美国之梦的悲剧事实，说明在以金钱为中心的资本主义社会里人们不可能有真正的幸福。《红字》一书以17世纪中叶的新英格兰为背景，通过对三个主要人物的思想矛盾和生活悲剧的描写，揭示了人性、社会、宗教压迫等各方面的图景。《泰戈尔作品集》共包括六个诗集：《飞鸟集》《新月集》《园丁集》《采果集》《吉檀迦利》和《流萤集》。这些诗集或讴歌灵魂，或赞颂生命，或描叙爱情，或充满宗教和哲学的精神，或表达赤子之情，其文字清澈隽永，描写细腻深刻，意象奇崛美妙，对20世纪世界文坛产生过深远而广泛的影响。《茶花女》通过阿尔芒和玛格丽特的爱情故事，使读者看到了浪漫主义的背后是现实的冷酷无情。《苔丝》通过农村姑娘苔丝曲折多变的命运和连连受挫的爱情，揭露了资产阶级虚伪的社会道德，强烈谴责了19世纪末资本入侵农村给农民带来的毁灭性打击。《格列佛游记》假托主人公格列佛医生自述他数次航海遇险，漂流到小人国、大人国、飞岛国和慧骃国几个童话式国家的遭遇和见闻，全面讽刺、揶揄了英国的社会现实。《永别了，武器》通过一个美国青年和一个英国女护士在一战中的恋爱悲剧，真实地描绘了战争的残酷和罪恶，以及战争给人造成的难以愈合的心理创伤。《夜色温柔》描写的是一位出身寒微但才华出众的青年对富有梦幻色彩的理想的追求，但他最终遭到失败，从而变得颓废消沉，暗示了"美国梦"的破灭。

　　以上15部经典名著的导读和注释一如从前，其主要目的就在于帮助读者更好地阅读和理解英文原版名著。同时，我们在第一套书重印、再版时又进行过认真审读，也经常关注网络上读者对这套书的评论。在编写第二套书时，将从第一套书中获得的实践经验和读者的宝贵意见融入编写过程，使第二套书达到了更好的服务读者的效果。时刻想着读者，让广大英语文学爱好者能够从我们的注释版名著读物中真正学到实用的知识，轻松读懂大部头文学佳作，是我们衷心的希望。

　　本次导读和注释的团队成员均来自北京外国语大学，在第一套丛书导读和注释队伍的基础上增加了四名教师，和原有的队伍一样，她们都是北外的骨干教师，有着极其丰富的教学经验，长期从事英语精读、泛读（其中很重要的一部分就是指导学生阅读英语名著）、文学、翻译、语言学等教学和研究工作。可以说，团队的每个成员都是读着这些著作以及更多英语名著成长的过来人，而且不少还都在继续研读这些经典著作。当然，为名著做导读和注释是一件听起来容易、做起来相当耗神和耗时的工作，但是各位同仁本着对文学的热忱和对读者负责的态度，按预期的速度高质量地完成了这项工作，在此本人对他们谨致谢意！感谢北京外国语大学陈德彰教授为本套丛书撰写寄语，这是对我们这个团队莫大的鼓励，感谢中国宇航出版社为我们提供了这样一个为读者服务的机会，感谢中国宇航出版社外语编辑二室提供的各项协助工作！

　　希望本套丛书提供的导读和注释能一如既往地为广大的英语爱

好者、英语学习者、英语文学爱好者和英语文学学习者提供一定的帮助，使读者朋友更轻松、更有信心地穿越时空，与经典名著进行心灵的对话和沟通。当然，由于时间紧迫，任务繁重，导读和注释中难免出现纰漏或疏忽之处，敬请广大读者予以谅解，并不吝赐教！

彭萍
2011 年仲秋
于北京海淀世纪城平心斋

丛书总序三

2016 年 4 月 23 日是莎士比亚去世 400 周年、诞辰 452 周年的日子，世界各地都在举行这样或那样的纪念活动，莎士比亚的故乡尤甚。英国王储查尔斯王子亦到斯特拉福德观看表演，并向莎士比亚的墓地敬献花环。莎士比亚环球剧院全年排演莎翁经典剧目，从 4 月起至秋季，剧院会陆续上演《仲夏夜之梦》《驯悍记》《麦克白》《辛白林》《维洛那二绅士》《威尼斯商人》等剧目，据说该剧院 2016 年将举办 30 多场莎翁纪念活动。另外，全球 140 多个国家将参与由英国文化协会（British Council）与"GREAT 英国推广活动"（GREAT Britain Campaign）组委会推出的"永恒的莎士比亚"（Shakespeare Lives）纪念活动。就在莎士比亚的故乡为这位伟大的戏剧家举办纪念活动时，中国也毫不例外。话剧院、出版社、莎士比亚的读者都以自己的方式纪念着这位剧作家。一切的纪念活动进一步显示了莎士比亚在英国文学史乃至世界文学史上的地位。而"我的心灵藏书馆——莎士比亚系列"导读与注释丛书也正是对莎士比亚的献礼，也为广大读者纪念莎士比亚、阅读他原汁原味的作品提供了一定的帮助。

威廉·莎士比亚（William Shakespeare）于 1564 年 4 月 23 日出生于埃文河畔的斯特拉特福（Stratford-upon-Avon），其父曾任斯特拉特福镇的民政官和镇长。威廉作为长子，曾被送到当地的文法学校学习拉丁文和古代历史、哲学、诗歌、逻辑、修辞等，但 13 — 14 岁左右，由于其家道中落，威廉曾辍学帮助父亲料理生意。1582 年，也就是 18 岁那一年，莎士比亚与比自己大八岁的安妮·哈瑟维（Anne Hathaway）结婚，两人共生育了三个孩子：苏珊娜、双胞胎哈姆雷特和朱迪思。1590 年至 1613 年这 20 多年的时间里，莎士比亚在伦敦开始了跟戏剧相关的职业生涯。当时，他既是演员，更是剧作家，还是宫内大臣剧团（Lord Chamberlain's Men）的合伙人之一，宫内大臣剧团后来改名为国王剧团（King's Men）。这一时期也是莎士比亚创作的黄金时期，大量的作品就在这一时期问世。1613年左右，莎士比亚退休回到埃文河畔斯特拉特福，于1616年4月23日逝世。

莎士比亚是英国文学史上最杰出的戏剧家，也是全世界最卓越的文学家之一。他流传下来的作品包括37部戏剧、两首叙事长诗（《维纳斯和阿都尼》和《鲁克丽丝受辱记》）和154首十四行诗。其中，两首叙事诗为莎士比亚在上流社会和文坛赢得了重要的名声，也为他的进一步创作做了最好的准备。154首十四行诗中，前126首是献给一位年轻的贵族（Fair Lord）的，诗人热烈地歌颂了这位朋友的美貌以及他们之间真挚的友情；第127首至最后是献给一位"黑女士"（Dark Lady）的，描写了热烈的爱情。《十四行诗》出版于1609年，但每一首诗的写作年份并不确定，但评论家们认为这些诗歌是对爱、性欲、生殖、死亡和时间的深刻思索。

当然，莎士比亚影响力最大的文学成就还是他创作的戏剧。莎士比亚的戏剧创作可分为三个时期。第一个时期是1590—1600年，这一时期称为历史剧、喜剧时期，代表作包括历史剧《亨利四世》上下篇和《亨利五世》、喜剧《威尼斯商人》《皆大欢喜》《第十二夜》。这些戏剧的基调都是明朗、欢快和乐观的。其中历史剧的核心是主张国家的统一，歌颂开明的君主。喜剧主要在于歌颂爱情和友谊，歌颂人文主义理想，其中人文主义的代表人物形象大都性格开朗，对人热情，表现勇敢，故事的结局往往是恶人悔过自新，好人宽宏大量，最后皆大欢喜。第二个时期是1601—1607年，这一时期是悲剧创作时期，其中《哈姆雷特》《奥赛罗》《李尔王》《麦克白》这四大悲剧以及《雅典的泰门》等就是在这一时期创作完成的。当时，由于英国社会的变化，尤其是随着伊丽莎白一世与詹姆士一世之间的政权交替，英国社会的矛盾和丑恶现象日益暴露出来。时代的变化以及莎士比亚本人思想和艺术的日渐成熟，使其人文主义理想同社会现实发生激烈的碰撞，于是其创作由早期的赞美人文主义理想转变为对社会黑暗的揭露和批判，作品充满了悲愤、阴郁的情绪，对现实的严峻批判成为主要脉络。以上四大悲剧无不显示了这一点，其中牺牲、复仇、嫉妒、争斗、阴谋成为最明显的主题。当然，虽然这一时期莎士比亚戏剧的基调是阴郁悲愤的，但其中塑造的形象却更加丰满，运用语言的技巧也更加成熟。第三个时期是 1608 — 1612 年，这一时期是传奇剧创作时期，代表作包括《辛白林》《冬天的童话》《暴风雨》等，也许正是剧作家对现实的认识愈加深刻，其理想与现实的矛盾就愈发尖锐和激烈，于是其创作就从现实世界转入了幻想的童话世界，试图借助超自然的神奇力量来解决理想与现实之间的矛盾。这一时期的作品洋溢着宽恕与和解的精神，充满了美丽的幻想和浪漫的情调。

　　400 多年来，莎士比亚作品的影响力经久不衰，究其原因，主要有以下几点。首先，莎士比亚通过多样的体裁和题材塑造了多样的人物。从喜剧到悲剧，从历史剧到传奇剧，从叙事诗到抒情诗……都成为莎士比亚显示天才的文学范式。从宫廷和贵族生活写到市井民间的生活，从国内各阶层的现状以及各种斗争写到国与国之间的关系，从凡尘俗世写到大自然乃至仙灵境界，从浪漫的爱情和人的七情六欲写到战争与哲理……所有这一切都显示出莎士比亚广阔的视野。莎士比亚戏剧中塑造的人物形象涵盖了社会各个阶层，从帝王将相到凡夫俗子再到才子佳人，各种形象栩栩如生。剧中的主人公们有的哀叹，有的高歌；有的沉郁，有的乐观；有的高尚，有的卑鄙；有的富有智慧，有的懵懂无知……不仅在舞台上让人感觉"大千世界，无奇不有"，就连读者在阅读脚本时也会在眼前浮现出各种各样的人物形象，让人禁不住拍案叫绝。其次，莎士比亚的语言极其生动，富有感染力。莎士比亚的戏剧大多以诗的形式写成，但又不是枯燥乏味的抒情、叙述或说教，而是具有极高的娱乐性和良好的舞台效果，同时也具有启发意义和怡情的作用。这是莎士比亚善于使用各种表达方式所产生的奇特效果，莎士比亚的词汇非常丰富，有学者用电脑统计其用词量高达 43 566 个，涉及天文、地理、动植物、历史、神话、典故、生活、心理活动等各个方面。同时，莎士比亚还善于使用各种修辞手法，包括比喻、拟人、夸张、设问、反复、头韵等，这些修辞手法生动地塑造了人物形象，恰当地描述了当时的情景，细致入微地剖析了人物的内心世界。庞杂的词汇，多样的修辞，至今依然让读者和作家们顶礼膜拜。而且，莎士比亚使用的句式结构也相当灵活，充分显示了剧作家的语言功底。第三，莎士比亚的戏剧在很大程度上传达出了当时的文化精神。莎士比亚生活在西方社会从中世纪的禁欲时代走向文艺复兴思想解放的重要时期，这一时期正是西方思想发生重大变化的时期。欧洲的中世纪是个"黑暗的时代"（Dark Age），基督教教会是人们唯一的精神支柱，它建立了一套严格的等级制度，把上帝当成绝对的权威。所有的人文学科，包括文学、艺术、哲学，均要遵照《圣经》的教义，否则就会招致宗教法庭的制裁，甚至处以死刑。在这样的背景下，文学艺术死气沉沉，科学技术停滞不前，黑死病又在欧洲蔓延。但从11世纪开始，随着资本主义在意大利的萌芽，经济得到一定的发展，城市逐渐兴起，人们的生活水平得到提高，不少人开始改变以往对现世生活的悲观绝望态度，转而追求世俗人生的乐趣。14世纪意大利最先出现了对基督教文化的反抗，表达对基督教神权的厌恶和对禁欲主义的不满，一批知识分子希望借助复兴古代希腊和罗马文化来表达自己的文化主张，摆脱教会对文化的束缚，"文艺复兴运动（Renaissance）"应运而生。"文艺复兴运动"的核心概念就是人文主义精神（或叫做人本主义）。在人文主义概念中，人是万物的中心，是现实生活的创造者，拥有自己的价值和尊严，人生的目的在于追求现实生活的幸福和个性解放。这时的欧洲摆脱了几百年的禁欲束缚，社会犹如决堤的江河，欲望的闸门一旦打开，就有一发不可收拾之势。而莎士比亚正是这个时代的弄潮儿，他迎合了当时人们对娱乐的追求，歌颂人的智慧与善良，主张重用智勇双全的新贵，反对贵族、教会势力和对权力的贪欲，提倡国家富强、百姓安居乐业。这一切也正如莎士比亚本人所说："仿佛要给自然照一面镜子，给德行看一看自己的面貌，给荒唐看一看自己的姿态，给时代和社会看一看自己的形象和印记。"由于莎士比亚的创作题材极其丰富，对后来的启蒙主义、浪漫主义、现实主义等都产生了不同程度的影响。马克思也称莎士比亚是"人类最伟大的天才之一，人类文学奥林匹斯山上的宙斯"！恩格斯甚至指出："单是《温莎的风流娘儿们》的第一幕就比全部德国文学包含着更多的生活气息。"所有这一切也都进一步加强了莎士比亚对后世的影响。

　　"我的心灵藏书馆"本次收进的九部莎士比亚戏剧正是莎士比亚最具影响力的代表性戏剧，包括了四大悲剧《哈姆雷特》《奥赛罗》《李尔王》《麦克白》和四大喜剧中的《威尼斯商人》《仲夏夜之梦》《第十二夜》，另外选取了为中国人所熟悉的爱情悲剧《罗密欧与朱丽叶》和有时也被列为四大喜剧之一的《无事生非》（通常将《皆大欢喜》和前面三大喜剧列为四大喜剧）。其中，《哈姆雷特》的主要情节是：叔叔克劳狄斯谋害了哈姆雷特的父亲，篡取了王位，并娶了国王的遗孀乔特鲁德，而哈姆雷特王子因此为父王向克劳狄斯复仇。《奥赛罗》的主要故事情节是：威尼斯的勇将奥赛罗与元老的女儿苔丝狄梦娜相爱，在婚事受阻的情况下两人只好私下成婚，奥赛罗手下阴险的旗官伊阿古一心想除掉奥赛罗，便向元老告密，却不料促成了两人的婚事，但伊阿古又挑拨说另一名副将凯西奥与苔丝狄梦娜关系不同寻常，并伪造了所谓定情信物等，这让奥赛罗信以为真，在愤怒中掐死了自己的妻子，可后来他得知真相，便悔恨自刎，倒在苔丝狄梦娜身边。《李尔王》讲述了年事已高的国王李尔王退位后，被大女儿和二女儿赶到荒郊野外，成为法兰西皇后的三女儿率军救父，却被杀死，李尔王伤心地死在她身旁。《麦克白》的主要情节是：麦克白在夫人的怂恿下谋杀国王邓肯之后做了国王，为掩人耳目和防止他人夺位，他又杀害了邓肯的侍卫以及有关的一些人物，可是恐惧和猜疑使麦克白心里越来越有鬼，也越来越冷酷，这时麦克白夫人因精神失常而自杀。在众叛亲离的情况下，麦克白面对邓肯之子和他请来的英格兰援军的围攻，落得被杀头的下场。在《威尼斯商人》中，威尼斯商人安东尼奥为给朋友巴萨尼奥的婚事凑钱，便向犹太高利贷者夏洛克借钱，于是二人之间围绕割一磅肉的诉讼产生冲突，最后由巴萨尼奥的未婚妻鲍西亚女扮男装英明地判决了这一诉讼案件，夏洛克害人不成反而失去了财产，还被迫改变宗教信仰。《仲夏夜之梦》的故事发生在仲夏夜晚，两对恋人为了对抗一道荒谬无比的律法而出逃，当他们逃往林子后，精灵的介入使彼此爱的对象混淆，但一阵混乱之后，众人终于恢复理智与和谐。《第十二夜》中，伊利里亚公爵奥西诺向奥丽维娅小姐求爱屡遭拒绝，一对孪生兄妹航海到伊利里亚时在附近海上遇难，妹妹薇奥拉改扮男装，到奥西诺公爵家中做侍童，并充当了代奥西诺向奥丽维娅小姐求爱的使者，奥丽维娅对女扮男装的薇奥拉一见钟情，而薇奥拉却偷偷爱上了公爵。后来，奥丽维娅碰巧遇上薇奥拉的孪生兄长西巴斯辛，两人将错就错地结成夫妇，而公爵和薇奥拉也终成眷属。《罗密欧与朱丽叶》的故事对我国很多读者来说都是非常熟悉的，讲述的是罗密欧与朱丽叶因家庭矛盾而遭遇的爱情悲剧，最后双方殉情而死。《无事生非》的主要故事情节是：克劳狄奥向希罗求婚，得到希罗父亲的许可，但在婚礼上，阿拉贡亲王的庶弟约翰由于嫉妒和无聊捏造谗言，致使克劳狄奥上当受骗，以为希罗是不贞洁的女子而当面侮辱希罗，差点致希罗于死地。希罗的堂姐贝特丽丝想出计谋，让希罗假死然后查出真相，后来骗局被揭穿，克劳狄奥与希罗重归于好。以上戏剧故事情节大多错综复杂，引人入胜，每一个故事都塑造了多个主要形象，表现出不同的人对爱情、金钱、权力、物质的不同态度，更表现出这些不同态度对人生走向产生的影响。总之，四百年来，莎士比亚的戏剧在世界范围内的影响无法估量。许多领袖、作家、导演、艺术家、作曲家和演员都曾拜读过莎翁作品，从中汲取灵感并思考自己的人生与所处的时代。

　　总之，莎士比亚是英国文艺复兴时期最重要的文坛巨匠，他的戏剧自诞生之日起就受到读者和观众青睐，400多年一直未曾离开人们的阅读和观赏视线，更没有离开过文学评论家和戏剧研究者的研究视线，因此流传着"说不尽的莎士比亚"这一说法。在中国，莎士比亚的译介主要开始于20世纪初期。早在1903年，上海达文社出版《英国索士比亚澥外奇谭》，包括10个莎剧故事；1904年，林纾与魏易合作译出《英国诗人吟边燕语》（下文简称《吟边燕语》），包括莎剧故事20个。上述二译本皆为兰姆姐弟著的《莎士比亚故事集》的故事梗概。五四运动以后，田汉是第一个翻译莎士比亚原作的人，分别于1921年和1924年译出《哈孟雷特》和《罗密欧与朱丽叶》。梁实秋于1930年开始翻译莎士比亚，到1967年译完并出版《莎士比亚全集》（戏剧37卷），三年后，又翻译出莎士比亚诗集三部。提到莎士比亚翻译，不得不提的便是朱生豪。他于1935年春开始收集和研究莎剧各种版本、诸家注释和有关资料，到他生命终结的1944年底，以顽强的精神译出莎剧31部半。20世纪30—50年代，曹未风、孙大雨、卞之琳、吴兴华、方平等都曾翻译了莎剧。法国作家纪德（Gide）是最理解莎士比亚的法国作家之一，他认为"没有任何作家比莎士比亚更值得翻译"。为纪念莎士比亚逝世400周年，北京大学辜正坤主持了莎士比亚第一对开本的翻译工作，许渊冲、彭镜禧等目前华语翻译界和莎剧研究界的诸多知名学者也参与了翻译。该对开本的原文以英国皇家莎士比亚剧团（Royal Shakespeare Company）对莎士比亚第一对开本300多年来首次全面修订后的版本为蓝本。与众多莎士比亚中译本相比，全新的译本尽量呈现给读者原作的整体风格，以诗体译诗体，以散文体译散文体，并在传承现有中译本的基础上，根据新时代读者的审美趣味增强中译本的可读性。辜正坤在提到新译本时说，要将莎士比亚还原成一个诗人。

"我的心灵藏书馆"本次收进的九部莎士比亚戏剧导读与注释版旨在帮助读者读懂原汁原味的莎士比亚。注释部分对一些词汇（尤其是莎士比亚时期的英语词汇）、短语、古英语形式、典故、地名等进行了注释，对一些修辞手法和写作风格进行了说明，对一些优美的句子和难懂的句子进行了分析，并提供相应的中译文（大多来自朱生豪和梁实秋的译本）。词语的解释部分基本参照了德国人亚历山大·施米特（Alexander Schmidt）编写的《莎士比亚词典》和我国文学界学者刘炳善编写的《英汉双解莎士比亚大辞典》。导读部分对相应的戏剧故事情节、人物、语言、主题思想等进行了分析，以帮助读者更好地把握作品的全貌。

　　需要特别指出的是，为莎士比亚戏剧提供导读和注释并非轻松容易之事，因为莎士比亚的英语毕竟不是现代英语，它要求注释者本人具有深厚的文学功底和素养以及熟练的英语基本功，还需要静下心来细细地咀嚼和玩味，因此，注释者要耗费大量的时间和精力。在今天这样一个浮躁的时代，几位注释者能够选择接受这样一份工作实属难能可贵，在此深表感谢和敬意。也感谢中国宇航出版社为我们提供了一个向广大读者展示原汁原味莎士比亚戏剧并向莎翁逝世四百周年纪念献礼的机会。当然，由于时间仓促，莎士比亚的语言与我们又有着如此遥远的时空距离，导读和注释难免存在一定的纰漏和不足，恳请广大读者给予谅解，并不吝赐教。

彭萍

2016 年阳春三月

于北京海淀世纪城平心斋

导　读

　　《麦克白》是威廉·莎士比亚（William Shakespeare）的四大悲剧之一。该剧以阴郁神秘的氛围和对剧中人物细腻的心理刻画而著称。故事发生于 11 世纪的苏格兰，主人公麦克白是 11 世纪苏格兰的一位大将，以骁勇善战闻名。在平叛内乱和击退外敌入侵凯旋的路上，麦克白遇到三个女巫。受到女巫预言的蛊惑，麦克白个人野心急剧膨胀；在麦克白夫人的怂恿下，谋杀了他的表兄国王邓肯。篡位登上国王宝座之后，麦克白并未获得九五之尊的快感和满足，相反失眠和疑虑如影随形，内心深受恐惧和悔恨的折磨。为了保住王位，他在收买好友班柯失败后派人将其在路上截杀，接着派人血洗了贵族麦克达夫住宅，对其妻儿痛下毒手。而麦克白夫人也没能逃脱内心的谴责和折磨，发疯而死。在麦克白统治之下，国家陷入混乱，人民生活于水深火热之中，起义此起彼伏。最后众叛亲离的麦克白被邓肯之子马尔科姆率领的讨伐大军杀死。《麦克白》是莎士比亚根据英格兰史学家拉斐尔·霍林献特的《苏格兰编年史》中的古老故事改编而成的。在莎士比亚笔下，原著中正值壮年的邓肯变成一位年老善良的君主，在睡梦中被杀；共犯班柯则变身为天性仁慈、忠心耿耿的大将。

　　麦克白本是邓肯国王的表弟，他自信、执著、勇猛、刚毅，因而也是国王最得力的良将。但他也野心勃勃，面对女巫预言的蛊惑和妻子的竭力怂恿，麦克白的理性（他清醒地知道自己在犯罪，也终将受到惩罚）终究被"想要做非分的攫夺"的欲望取代。为了实现自己成为一个伟大人物的欲望，他抛却君臣之道、血缘亲情、朋友之谊，实施了一系列杀戮。甚至对于朝夕相处、休戚与共的妻子的发疯和自杀也视若无睹。为了一己之私，曾经屡建奇勋、受人敬重的一代战神一步步堕落成一位冷血无情、残忍暴虐的恶魔，众叛亲离之后，不仅自己落得一个身首异处的悲惨结局，也陷整个社会于动乱之中。

麦克白夫人是麦克白走上罪恶之路的最直接的煽动者。她用激将法促使麦克白下定决心杀掉邓肯国王，又冷静地对麦克白刺杀国王之后的现场做了及时的善后处理。她阴冷狠毒、沉着果断，似乎比麦克白还要强大。但身为女人，她摆脱不了天性中的柔弱和善良。她自己也饱受刺杀邓肯国王带来的心理折磨，却还要故作坚强地在麦克白深受幻觉折磨时去宽慰麦克白，分担其忧虑。她也需要安慰和宣泄，梦游和疯癫是她内心极度煎熬的外露。为了成全丈夫她不择手段，而她的丈夫在她自杀后却没有一丝伤感，她失去了女性的柔弱善良，失去了赖以依靠的爱情，直至失去自己宝贵的生命。

班柯是莎士比亚刻画的成功抵制权力诱惑的一个形象。虽然班柯也渴求权力，但理性和道德的力量使他能够从容面对各种诱惑，因而命运对他予以厚报，让他的子孙成为国王。邓肯国王本是麦克白的表兄。他仁慈善良，但作为国王他太过软弱，因而才会有国内的叛乱和外敌的入侵。对麦克白赞誉过度说明他自信不足，临时起意到访麦克白家又说明他缺乏谋略，在麦克白家中的畅饮和烂醉不仅有失君王之威，更说明他没有防人之心。他的"君不君"，直接导致麦克白的"臣不臣"，因而他的命运是偶然，也是必然。

《麦克白》这部悲剧反映的是有关人性的一个永恒主题：善恶的较量，以及道德与欲望的抗争。通过麦克白的个人悲剧，莎士比亚揭示出，不加节制的欲望只会导致个人的毁灭，肯定并呼唤人文主义精神中的"仁爱"和"良知"。世人皆有欲望，欲望会随个人社会地位的提高和外界诱惑的不断刺激逐渐膨胀，如果没有道德和理性的约束而任由其发展下去，人性的善会被恶蒙蔽，悲剧在所难免。因而如何平衡自己内心的欲望和外界诱惑是每个人必须面对的难题。《麦克白》的悲剧再次警示我们，只有恪守内心的善良底线，遵从社会的伦理道德，学会淡然面对各种诱惑，才能做到泰然处之，避免悲剧的发生。这也是《麦克白》悲剧具有的普遍意义。

从《麦克白》中我们可以一睹莎士比亚的语言魅力。他不仅用语精练，精于遣词造句，还善于借助各种修辞手法使人物刻画更加形象生动。他将古英语得以很好地传承，还创造发明了很多新词、短语和习语。他能将一个词信手拈来、灵活应用于各种上下文，还能在本族语和外来语中自如切换。他将英语变成具有诗性的语言，他的语言把英语推向了新高度。

英语向世界的传播也将《麦克白》带给各国观众。19 世纪早期，英国之外已有一些《麦克白》的精品。到 20 世纪，莎士比亚作品在文学作品、歌剧、音乐剧、芭蕾剧、电视及电影中大量涌现。在戏剧方面最受称赞的莫过于劳伦斯·奥利弗（Laurence Olivier，1955年）、伊恩·麦克莱恩（Ian McKellen，1976 年）和安东尼·谢尔（Antony Sher，1999 年）的演出。而在电影领域，《麦克白》更是被改编最多的莎剧之一。从 1905 年，美国最早将《麦克白》搬上银幕开始，意大利（1909 年）、法国（1910 年）、德国（1913 年）、美国（1916 年，1948 年）、日本（1957 年）、波兰（1971 年）、英国（1979 年，1997 年，2010 年）、匈牙利（1982 年）、印度（2003年）、澳大利亚（2006 年，2015 年）都先后将《麦克白》搬上银幕。其中，1948 年美国导演奥逊·威尔斯（Orson Welles）、1957 年日本导演黑泽明（Akira Kurosawa）、1971 年波兰导演罗曼·波兰斯基（Roman Polanski）以及 2015 年澳大利亚导演贾斯汀·库泽尔（Justin Kurzel）的改编被认为是最成功的尝试。此外，《麦克白》还是英国广播公司（BBC）电视台播出最多的莎士比亚戏剧之一。

自莎士比亚作品传入中国后，中国学者也开始了对《麦克白》的翻译，现存的译本主要有以下几种：1904 年林纾以文言文形式翻译的《蛊征》是中国最早的《麦克白》译本；1930 年戴望舒以话剧形式翻译的《麦克倍斯》，由上海金马书堂首发，后于 2012 年安徽人民出版社出版。1936 年梁实秋用散文体翻译了包括《麦克白》在内的四大悲剧和四大喜剧，由商务印书馆发行。1947 年，朱生豪翻译的《麦克佩斯》，收于《莎士比亚戏剧全集》中，由上海世界书局出版；1979 年，曹未风翻译的《马白斯》，由上海译文出版社出版；1984 年杨烈发表了诗体译本《麦克白斯》，收于《莎士比亚精华》中，由复旦大学出版社出版。1988 年卞之琳翻译的散文体《麦克白斯》，由人民文学出版社出版；1994 孙大雨用诗体翻译的《麦克白斯》由上海译文出版社出版。1999 年，曾胡翻译的《麦克白——英汉对照》，由外文出版社出版；2014 年方平以诗体翻译的《麦克白》，收于《莎士比亚全集》中，由上海译文出版社出版。2015 年辜正坤翻译的《麦克白》，由外语教学与研究出版社出版。

在众多译本中，梁实秋、朱生豪以及方平的译本比较受推崇。其中梁、朱都是以散文体翻译，而方平以诗歌体翻译；梁实秋的译本强调"存真"，被认为最符合翻译"信达雅"之中的"雅"；朱生豪追求翻译的"神韵"和"意趣"，他翻译的《麦克白》被公认为是最能再现莎士比亚神韵的译本。许国璋先生认为他的译文"行云流水"，翻译"高于他人"；而台湾学者虞尔昌认为"朱所译信达雅三者都已做到。到目前为止，尚无出其右者"。因而朱生豪翻译的《麦克白》也是市场上最受欢迎、再版最多的译本。

除了译本，《麦克白》也以戏剧的方式进入中国。1916年为了抨击袁世凯称帝而演出的《窃国贼》是《麦克白》在中国最早的戏剧演出。五四运动前夕，《麦克白》还以《巫祸》和《新南北和》为名搬上话剧舞台。1945年，李建吾将《麦克白》改编为古装剧《王德明》，后又更名为《乱世英雄》。之后，《麦克白》又被改编为话剧（1980年）、昆剧《血手记》（1986年）、京剧《欲望城国》和《乱世王》（1987年）、粤剧《英雄叛国》（1996年）、川剧《马克白夫人》（1999年）、越剧《马龙将军》（2001年）。直至今天，《麦克白》不仅活跃于专业剧团，也是大学校园常备剧目。

胡钰翎

参考文献

[1] 张勇先. 英语发展史 [M]. 北京：外语教学与研究出版社，2014.

[2] 李伟民. 中国莎士比亚翻译研究五十年 [J]. 中国翻译，2004（9）：46–53.

[3] 李伟民. 莎士比亚悲剧《麦克白》在中国的传播和影响 [J]. 西北民族大学学报（哲学社会科学版），2006（1）：75–84.

[4] 李伟昉. 接受与流变：莎士比亚在近现代中国 [J]. 中国社会科学，2011（9）：150–166.

Contents 目录

Act III

Act IV

Act V

DRAMATIS PERSONAE①

DUNCAN	King of Scotland②
MALCOLM & DONALBAIN	his sons③
MACBETH & BANQUO	generals of the king's army ④
MACDUFF	
LENNOX	
ROSS	
MENTEITH	noblemen of Scotland
ANGUS	
CAITHNESS	
FLEANCE	son to Banquo
SIWARD	Earl of Northumberland⑤, general of the English forces
YOUNG SIWARD	his son
SEYTON	an officer attending⑥ on Macbeth
Boy	son to Macduff
An English Doctor	
A Scotch Doctor	
A Sergeant	
A Porter	
An Old Man	
LADY MACBETH	

① DRAMATIS PERSONAE:（源自拉丁语）剧中主人公，剧中人物

② King of Scotland：历史上，苏格兰有过国王邓肯一世（1001 年—1040 年），1034 年—1040 年在位，在他统治的最后几年里，苏格兰与境内外数个地方势力发生过冲突，最开始没有反对邓肯一世继承权的麦克白逐渐产生不满。1040 年，邓肯一世率领军队进入莫瑞，双方交战，邓肯一世被杀。在本剧中，邓肯一世被塑造成一位年老的国王。但事实上，邓肯死时才 39 岁。

③ 马尔科姆是邓肯一世的长子，在苏格兰君主列表中被称为马尔科姆三世，1058 年—1093年的苏格兰国王。

④ 麦克白是苏格兰莫瑞地区贵族，身份相当于公爵，其母亲多纳达（Donada）为苏格兰国王马尔科姆二世之女。1020 年，麦克白的父亲在战争中丧生，麦克白接管了莫瑞地区的势力。麦克白战胜邓肯一世后以王室后裔身份继任苏格兰国王，他的统治持续了 17 年。1057 年被为父报仇的马尔科姆在战场上杀死或者重伤。在本剧中，麦克白是谋权篡位的反面角色。

⑤ Earl of Northumberland：英国贵族分为五等，公爵、侯爵、伯爵、子爵、男爵。Earl 为伯爵。Northumberland：诺森伯兰郡，英国英格兰最北部一郡。

⑥ attend：照顾

LADY MACDUFF

Gentlewoman attending on Lady Macbeth

HECATE[1] & Three Witches

Apparitions[2], Lords, Gentlemen, Officers, Soldiers, Murtherers, Attendants, and Messengers[3]

SCENE

Scotland and England

Act I

SCENE I.
A Desert Place.

[Thunder and lightning. Enter three Witches.]

First Witch. When shall we three meet again
    In thunder, lightning, or in rain?

Second Witch. When the hurly-burly's^① done,
    When the battle's lost and won.

Third Witch. That will be ere^② the set of sun.

First Witch. Where the place?

Second Witch. Upon the heath^③.

Third Witch. There to meet with Macbeth.

First Witch. I come, Graymalkin^④!

Second Witch. Paddock^⑤ calls.

Third Witch. Anon^⑥.

ALL. Fair is foul, and foul is fair:
   Hover through the fog and filthy air.^⑦

  [Exeunt^⑧.]

---

① hurly-burly's：hurly-burly，喧嚣；'s 是 is 的缩写
② ere：在……之前
③ heath：长满石楠属灌木（heather）的荒原，在苏格兰很常见
④ Graymalkin：grey cat，女巫化身或常使用的妖怪。三个女巫都有可供自己使用的妖怪。
第一个女巫的是狸猫精，第二个女巫的是癞蛤蟆，第三个女巫的是怪鸟。
⑤ paddock：癞蛤蟆
⑥ anon：立刻，马上，相当于 in a moment
⑦ 这句揭示了该剧很重要的一个主题：价值的颠倒和变化。参考译文：美即丑恶丑恶即美，
翱翔毒雾妖云里。（朱生豪译）（fair：指皮肤白皙的，美丽的；foul：邪恶的，丑恶的；hover：盘
旋，徘徊；filthy：肮脏的，污秽的）
⑧ exeunt：（拉丁语，剧本中的说明，两个以上演员）退场，下场

SCENE II.
A Camp near Forres[①].

[Alarum[②] within. Enter DUNCAN, MALCOLM, DONALBAIN,
LENNOX, with Attendants, meeting a bleeding Sergeant.]

DUNCAN. What bloody man is that[③]? He can report,
As seemeth by his plight, of the revolt
The newest state.[④]

MALCOLM. This is the sergeant
Who, like a good and hardy soldier, fought
'Gainst my captivity.[⑤] Hail[⑥], brave friend!
Say to the king the knowledge of the broil
As thou didst leave it[⑦].

Sergeant. Doubtful it stood;
As two spent swimmers, that do cling together
And choke their art.[⑧] The merciless Macdonwald—
Worthy to be a rebel, for to that
The multiplying villainies of nature
Do swarm upon him—from the western isles

---

① Forres：福累斯，苏格兰国王王宫所在地，在 Moray Firth 海边，驻军在不远处的南边
② alarum：alarm，惊慌，警报
③ 从这节开始，莎士比亚开始用素体诗，也称无韵诗（blank verse）。无韵诗是英语格律诗的一种。每行由五个长短格音步——十个音节组成，每首行数不拘，不押韵。多用在戏剧和叙事诗中。
④ 正常语序应为：As seemeth by his plight, he can report the newest state of the revolt. 参考译文：看他的样子，也许可以向我们报告关于乱事的最近的消息。（朱生豪译）（seemeth：古英语，相当于现在的 seems；plight：境况，困境；revolt：叛乱）
⑤ 参考译文：这就是那个奋勇苦战帮助我冲出敌人重围的军曹。（朱生豪译）（hardy：强壮的，勇敢的；'Gainst：等于 against，抵抗；captivity：被俘，囚禁）
⑥ hail：相当于 hi 或 hello，打招呼用语
⑦ say：这里相当于 tell，告诉；broil：冲突，战争；thou，古英语，相当于现在的 you；didst leave：即 left，thou 后跟的动词一般多加 st 或 est，过去式用 did，是为了多加一个音节，一种修辞用法，下文的 do cling 也是这样的用法；it 指的是刚才提到的 broil
⑧ 正常语序应为：It stood doubtful, as two spent swimmers that do cling together and choke their art. 参考译文：双方还在胜负未决之中；正像两个精疲力竭的游泳者，彼此扭成一团，显不出他们的本领来。（朱生豪译）（spent：相当于 exhausted，精疲力竭的；choke：使……窒息；art 相当于 skill）

4

Of kerns and gallowglasses is supplied;①

And fortune, on his damned quarrel smiling,

Show'd like a rebel's whore:② but all's too weak:

For brave Macbeth——well he deserves that name——

Disdaining fortune, with his brandish'd steel,

Which smoked with bloody execution,

Like valour's minion carved out his passage

Till he faced the slave;

Which ne'er shook hands, nor bade farewell to him,

Till he unseam'd him from the nave to the chaps,

And fix'd his head upon our battlements.③

DUNCAN. O valiant④ cousin⑤! worthy gentleman!

Sergeant. As whence the sun 'gins his reflection

Shipwrecking storms and direful thunders break,

So from that spring, whence comfort seem'd to come,

---

① 这句话的主干是：Macdonwald is supplied of kerns and gallowglasses from the western isles. Macdonwald 是叛军首领；Worthy to be a rebel, for to that the multiplying villanies of nature do swarm upon him 是插入语。参考译文：那残暴的麦克唐华德不愧为一个叛徒，因为无数奸恶的天性都丛集于他的一身；他已经征调了西方各岛上的轻重步兵。（朱生豪译）（kern：轻武器步兵；gallowglass：武装侍从；the western isles：西方各岛，这里指的是 Ireland and the Hebrides；multiplying：倍数的；villainy：奸恶；swarm：蜂拥而来，这里指邪恶集于 Macdonwald 一身）

② 正常语序应为：And fortune show'd like a rebel's whore on his damned quarrel smiling. 参考译文：命运也好像一个娼妓一样，有意向叛徒卖弄风情，助长他的罪恶的气焰。（朱生豪译）（fortune：西方文化中命运女神常被比作朝三暮四的妓女；whore：妓女；show'd 相当于 showed）

③ 这句话对麦克白这一人物的刻画非常成功，形象地描述了麦克白的英勇气质和大义凛然：上文描述了叛军不可一世的嚣张气焰，命运之神对其似乎都无能为力，更何况其他人；而麦克白的出现改变了这一切，麦克白的骁勇善战和王者风范也为后面女巫的预言埋下了伏笔。该句的句子主干是：For brave Macbeth carved out his passage till...; well he deserves that name 是插入语，赞扬麦克白是名副其实的勇士；Disdaining fortune 分词短语作伴随状语，说明麦克白对命运不屑一顾的态度；with his brandish'd steel 介词结构作伴随状语，指明麦克白手拿宝剑；Which smoked with bloody execution 是定语从句，修饰 steel，这里指宝剑；Like valour's minion 比喻用法；两个 till 从句在整个句子中作时间状语，描述麦克白一路所向披靡、勇敢无畏诛杀叛军首领 Macdonwald；Which ne'er shook hands, nor bade farewell to him 是定语从句修饰麦克白；第二个 till 从句中，主干是 he unseam'd him...and fix'd his head...，其中 unseam'd 相当于现在的 unseamed，fix'd 相当于 fixed，下文 'd 结尾的词也是如此。（disdain：蔑视，不屑一顾；brandish'd 相当于 brandished，是 brandish 的过去式，炫耀，挥舞；execution：处决，处死；valour：勇猛，英勇，这里拟人化了；minion：宠儿；carve：切，切开；passage：通道；unseam：拆解，拆开；nave：这里应为 navel，肚脐，中央；chaps：嘴周围的地方；battlement：城楼，城堡）

④ valiant：勇敢的，英勇的

⑤ cousin：一般的亲戚都可叫 cousin，但邓肯和麦克白确实是表兄弟，都是苏格兰国王马尔科姆二世（1005 年—1034 年在位）的外孙

Discomfort swells.[①] Mark, king of Scotland, mark:

No sooner justice had, with valour arm'd,

Compell'd these skipping kerns to trust their heels,

But the Norweyan lord, surveying vantage,

With furbish'd arms and new supplies of men,

Began a fresh assault.[②]

DUNCAN. Dismay'd[③] not this

Our captains, Macbeth and Banquo?

Sergeant. Yes;

As sparrows eagles, or the hare the lion.[④]

If I say sooth, I must report they were

As cannons overcharged with double cracks, so they

Doubly redoubled strokes upon the foe.

Except they meant to bathe in reeking wounds,

Or memorize another Golgotha,

I cannot tell.[⑤]

But I am faint, my gashes[⑥] cry for help.

DUNCAN. So well thy[⑦] words become thee [⑧]as thy wounds;

---

① 参考译文：天有不测风云，从那透露曙光的东方偏卷来了无情的风暴、可怕的雷雨；我们正在兴高采烈的时候，却又遭遇了重大的打击。（朱生豪译）（whence：从何处，从哪里；'gins：begins；reflection：反射，映像；shipwrecking：毁灭性的；direful：可怕的，悲惨的；swell：增强，膨胀）

② 句 子 主 干 是：No sooner justice had compell'd these skipping kerns to trust their heels, but the Norweyan lord began a fresh assault. 其中 surveying vantage 是现在分词短语表原因；with furbish'd arms and new supplies of men 是介词短语表示有或伴随。参考译文：当正义凭着勇气的威力正在驱逐敌军向后溃退的时候，挪威国君看见有机可乘，调了一批甲械精良的生力部队又向我们开始一次新的猛攻。（朱生豪译）（compel：强迫，使不得不；skipping：悄悄溜走的，逃跑的；trust one's heels：逃跑，离开；Norweyan：挪威人的，现在多用 Norwegian；Norweyan lord，指的是 Sweno；vantage：优势，有利地位；furbish'd：改进的，精良的；assault：攻击；袭击）

③ dismay：使……气馁，使……焦虑（例如：The thought that her mother was crying dismayed her much. 想到她母亲正在流泪，她伤心不已。）

④ 省略句，省掉了动词 not dismay。参考译文：要是麻雀能使怒鹰退却，兔子能把雄狮吓走的话。（朱生豪译）

⑤ 参考译文：实实在在地说，他们就像两尊巨炮，满装着双倍火力的炮弹，愈发愈猛地向敌人射击；瞧他们的神气，好像拼着浴血负创，非让尸骸铺满了原野，决不罢手似的。（朱生豪译）这句话中 double, doubly, redouble 是单词重复，有了强调。（overcharge：过度装弹药；crack：重击；redouble：进一步加强，再加倍；stroke：一击；foe：敌人；reeking：发出……的气息；Golgotha：各各他，位于 Jerusalem 附近，是圣经中耶稣被钉死的地方，后指受难场所）

⑥ gash：深而长的伤口

⑦ thy：古英语，相当于 your

⑧ thee：古英语，"你"的宾格

6

They smack of[1] honour both. Go get him surgeons.

[Exit Sergeant, attended.]

Who comes here?

[Enter ROSS.]

MALCOLM. The worthy thane[2] of Ross.

LENNOX. What a haste looks through his eyes! So should he look
That seems to speak things strange.

ROSS. God save the king!

DUNCAN. Whence camest thou, worthy thane?

ROSS. From Fife[3], great king;
Where the Norweyan banners flout[4] the sky
And fan our people cold.

Norway himself,

With terrible numbers,

Assisted by that most disloyal traitor,

The thane of Cawdor, began a dismal[5] conflict;

Till that Bellona's bridegroom, lapp'd in proof,

Confronted him with self-comparisons,

Point against point rebellious, arm 'gainst arm,

Curbing his lavish spirit: and, to conclude,

The victory fell on us.[6]

DUNCAN. Great happiness!

ROSS. That now

---

① smack of：带有……味道，有点像（例如：There is a smack of truth in his joke. 他的玩笑中有一点真理。）

② thane：（苏格兰）爵士，乡绅

③ Fife：法夫郡，英国苏格兰东部旧郡

④ flout：藐视，愚弄（例如：No one can flout the rules and get away with it. 谁也不能违反这些规则而不被处分。）

⑤ dismal：阴沉的，惨淡的

⑥ 这一句将麦克白比作罗马女战神的新郎，是为了说明麦克白的英勇作战。句子主干是 Till that Bellona's bridegroom...confronted him with self-comparisons...and, to conclude, the victory fell on us. 参考译文：直到麦克白擐甲而前，和他奋勇交锋，方才挫折了他的傲气；胜利终于属我们所有。（朱生豪译）（Bellona：罗马神话中的女战神，法国雕塑家罗丹还以其为原型创作了《女战神贝娄娜》；lapp'd=lapped，包裹着；self-comparison：（与别人对比时表现出来的）优势、勇气或技能；lavish：无礼的）

Sweno, the Norways[①]' king, craves[②] composition[③];
Nor would we deign him burial of his men
Till he disbursed, at Saint Colme's inch,
Ten thousand dollars to our general use.[④]

DUNCAN. No more that thane of Cawdor shall deceive
Our bosom[⑤] interest. Go pronounce his present death,
And with his former title greet[⑥] Macbeth.

ROSS. I'll see it done.

DUNCAN. What he hath lost, noble Macbeth hath won.[⑦]

[Exeunt.]

---

① the Norways：这里挪威用了复数形式，是因为当时挪威还处于分裂时期，有几个不同部分

② crave：渴望，恳求（例如：Many young children crave attention. 许多小孩子渴望得到关心。）

③ composition：和解

④ 参考译文：我们责令他在圣戈姆小岛上缴纳一万块钱充入我们的国库，否则不让他把战死的将士埋葬。（朱生豪译）（deign：允许；disburse：付款）

⑤ bosom：亲密的（例如：They were bosom friends. 他们是知心好友。）

⑥ greet：本意是"迎接；致意"，这里指的是将爵位移赠给麦克白

⑦ 参考译文：他所失去的，也就是尊贵的麦克白所得到的。（朱生豪译）

SCENE III.
A Barren Heath.

[Thunder. Enter the three Witches.]

First Witch. Where hast thou been, sister?

Second Witch. Killing swine[1].

Third Witch. Sister, where thou?

First Witch. A sailor's wife had chestnuts in her lap,

And munch'd[2], and munch'd, and munch'd.

'Give me,' quoth[3] I.

'Aroint[4] thee, witch!' the rump-fed[5] ronyon[6] cries.

Her husband's to Aleppo gone, master o' the Tiger:

But in a sieve I'll thither sail,

And, like a rat without a tail,

I'll do, I'll do, and I'll do.[7]

Second Witch. I'll give thee a wind.

First Witch. Thou'rt kind.

Third Witch. And I another[8].

First Witch. I myself have all the other,

And the very ports they blow,

All the quarters that they know

I' the shipman's card.

I will drain him dry as hay:

Sleep shall neither night nor day,

Hang upon his penthouse lid;

---

① swine：猪
② munch：用力咀嚼（某物），大声咀嚼
③ quoth：用在第一与第三人称的过去式，相当于 said
④ aroint：去，走开
⑤ rump-fed：吃别人剩下食物的
⑥ ronyon：古英语中对女人的蔑称，贱人
⑦ 参考译文：她的丈夫是"猛虎号"的船长，到阿勒坡去了；可是我要坐在一张筛子里追上他去，像一头没有尾巴的老鼠，我要去，我要去，我要去。（朱生豪译）（sieve：筛子；thither：到那边，向那方）
⑧ I another：完整结构应为：I give you another wind.

He shall live a man forbid.

Weary se'n nights nine times nine

Shall he dwindle, peak and pine;

Though his bark cannot be lost,

Yet it shall be tempest-toss'd.①

Look what I have.

Second Witch. Show me, show me.

First Witch. Here I have a pilot's thumb,

Wreck'd② as homeward he did come.

[Drum within.]

Third Witch. A drum, a drum!

Macbeth doth come.

ALL. The weird sisters, hand in hand,

Posters③ of the sea and land,

Thus do go about④, about,

Thrice⑤ to thine⑥ and thrice to mine,

And thrice again, to make up nine.

 Peace! the charm's wound up⑦.

[Enter MACBETH and BANQUO.]

MACBETH. So foul⑧ and fair a day I have not seen.

BANQUO. How far is't call'd⑨ to Forres? What are these

---

① 由于船长妻子没有给女巫吃东西，女巫决意报复她出海的丈夫。这段就是描写女巫如何报复船长的。参考译文：到处狂风吹海立，浪打行船无休息；终朝终夜不得安，骨瘦如柴血色干；年年辛苦月月劳，气断神疲精力销；波涛汹涌鱼龙怒，一叶漂流无定处。（朱生豪译）（drain：使耗尽；forbid：这里相当于 forbidden，被禁止的；penthouse lid：眼睑，眼皮；se'n：等于 seven；dwindle：衰落，退化；peak：变憔悴；pine：憔悴，痛苦；bark：船；tempest：暴风雨；toss'd：等于 tossed，摇荡）

② wreck'd：等于 wrecked，毁坏的，（船舶）失事的（例如：The ship was wrecked by an explosion. 这艘船被炸毁了。）

③ posters：古英语，急行的人，匆忙赶路的人

④ go about：四处走

⑤ thrice：三次，三倍

⑥ thine：古英语，等于现在的 yours，你的东西

⑦ wound up：原形是 wind up，收尾，结束

⑧ foul：邪恶的，阴郁的

⑨ is't call'd to：苏格兰语，距离是

So wither'd[①] and so wild[②] in their attire[③],

That look not like the inhabitants o' the earth,

And yet are on't? Live you? or are you aught[④]

That man may question? You seem to understand me,

By each at once her chappy finger laying

Upon her skinny lips: you should be women,

And yet your beards forbid me to interpret

That you are so.[⑤]

MACBETH. Speak, if you can: what are you?

First Witch. All hail[⑥], Macbeth, hail to thee, thane of Glamis!

Second Witch. All hail, Macbeth, hail to thee, thane of Cawdor!

Third Witch. All hail, Macbeth, thou shalt[⑦] be king hereafter[⑧]!

BANQUO. Good sir, why do you start[⑨], and seem to fear

Things that do sound so fair? I' the name of truth[⑩],

Are ye[⑪] fantastical[⑫], or that indeed

Which outwardly ye show? My noble partner

You greet with present grace and great prediction

Of noble having and of royal hope,

That he seems rapt withal;[⑬] to me you speak not.

If you can look into the seeds of time,

---

① wither'd：等于 withered，凋谢的，憔悴的

② wild：发狂的，野蛮的

③ attire：衣服

④ aught：任何事物，零

⑤ 参考译文：每一个人都同时把她满是皱纹的手指按在她的干枯的嘴唇上。你们应当是女人，可是你们的胡须却使我不敢相信你们是女人。（朱生豪译）（chappy：满是皱纹的；interpret：解读）

⑥ all hail：万福

⑦ shalt：古英语用法，等于现在的 shall

⑧ hereafter：今后，从此以后

⑨ start：吃惊

⑩ I' the name of truth：in the name of truth，以真理的名义

⑪ ye：you 的古英语用法

⑫ fantastical：空想的，捕风捉影的

⑬ 正常语序应为：You greet my noble partner with present grace and great prediction. 参考译文：你们向我的高贵的同伴致敬，并且预言他未来的尊荣和远大的希望，使他听得出了神。（朱生豪译）（present grace：现有的荣耀，指麦克白现在有的 thane of Glamis 的衔位；having：拥有，所有，这里指 thane of Cawdor 的新封号；royal hope：指女巫们对麦克白会成为国王的预言。rapt：全神贯注的，入迷的；withal：依然）

And say which grain① will grow and which will not,
Speak then to me, who neither beg nor fear
Your favours nor your hate②.

First Witch. Hail!

Second Witch. Hail!

Third Witch. Hail!

First Witch. Lesser than Macbeth, and greater.③

Second Witch. Not so happy, yet much happier.④

Third Witch. Thou shalt get kings, though thou be none:⑤

So all hail, Macbeth and Banquo!

First Witch. Banquo and Macbeth, all hail!

MACBETH. Stay, you imperfect speakers, tell me more:

By Sinel⑥'s death I know I am thane of Glamis;

But how of Cawdor? The thane of Cawdor lives,

A prosperous gentleman; and to be king

Stands not within the prospect of belief,

No more than to be Cawdor.⑦ Say from whence

You owe this strange intelligence? or why

Upon this blasted⑧ heath you stop our way

With such prophetic⑨ greeting? Speak, I charge⑩ you.

[The witches vanish⑪.]

BANQUO. The earth hath bubbles, as the water has,

---

① grain：颗粒

② hate：这里相当于 hatred

③ 参考译文：比麦克白低微，可是你的地位在他之上。（朱生豪译）

④ 参考译文：不像麦克白那样幸运，可是比他更有福。（朱生豪译）

⑤ 参考译文：你虽然不是君王，你的子孙将要君临一国。（朱生豪译）

⑥ Sinel：麦克白的父亲

⑦ 参考译文：考特爵士现在还活着，他的势力非常煊赫；至于说我是未来的君王，那正像说我是考特爵士一样难以置信。（朱生豪译）（prosperous：繁荣的，兴旺的；prospect：前景，景象）

⑧ blasted：被害的，被诅咒的

⑨ prophetic：预言的，先兆的（例如：Many of his warnings proved prophetic. 他的许多警告都证明是有先见之明的。）

⑩ charge：命令（例如：He charged me to arrange everything. 他要我去安排一切事务。）

⑪ vanish：消失；突然不见（例如：The aircraft vanished without trace. 飞机消失得无影无踪。）

12

And these are of them. Whither① are they vanish'd?

MACBETH. Into the air, and what seem'd corporal② melted

As breath into the wind. Would they had stay'd!

BANQUO. Were such things here as we do speak about?

Or have we eaten on the insane root

That takes the reason prisoner?③

MACBETH. Your children shall be kings.

BANQUO. You shall be king.

MACBETH. And thane of Cawdor too. Went it not so?

BANQUO. To④ the selfsame⑤ tune⑥ and words. Who's here?

[Enter ROSS and ANGUS.]

ROSS. The king hath happily received, Macbeth,

The news of thy success; and when he reads

Thy personal venture⑦ in the rebels' fight,

His wonders and his praises do contend

Which should be thine or his: silenced with that,⑧

In viewing o'er the rest o' the selfsame day,

He finds thee in the stout Norweyan ranks,

Nothing afeard of what thyself didst make,

Strange images of death.⑨ As thick as hail

Came post with post, and every one did bear

---

① whither：到哪里，什么（例如：Who are you and whither are you bound? 你是谁？要去哪里？）

② corporal：人体的

③ 参考译文：还是因为我们误食了令人疯狂的草根，已经丧失了我们的理智？（朱生豪译）（eat on：等于 eat，吃；insane：疯狂的）

④ to：according to

⑤ selfsame：完全一样的，相同的（例如：He won two gold medals on the selfsame day. 他在同一天获得两块金牌。）

⑥ tune：曲调

⑦ venture：冒险，冒险行动

⑧ 参考译文：他简直不知道应当惊异还是应当赞叹，在这两种心理的交相冲突之下，他快乐得说不出话来。（朱生豪译）心理冲突指的是邓肯国王对战绩的赞叹和对麦克白的称赞，以及哪些荣誉给麦克白，哪些给自己。

⑨ 参考译文：他又知道你在同一天之内，又在雄壮的挪威大军的阵地上出现，不因为你自己亲手造成的死亡的惨象而感到些微的恐惧。（朱生豪译）strange images of death 是同位语，解释说明 what thyself didst make，即麦克白造成的死亡惨象。（stout：强壮的，勇敢的；ranks：军队）

13

Thy praises in his kingdom's great defence,

And pour'd them down before him.[①]

ANGUS. We are sent

To give thee, from our royal master[②], thanks;

Only to herald[③] thee into his sight,

Not pay thee.

ROSS. And for an earnest[④] of a greater honour,

He bade[⑤] me, from him, call thee thane of Cawdor.

In which addition, hail, most worthy thane!

For it is thine.

BANQUO. What, can the devil speak true?

MACBETH. The thane of Cawdor lives. Why do you dress me

In borrow'd robes?

ANGUS. Who was the thane lives yet,

But under heavy judgment bears that life

Which he deserves to lose.[⑥] Whether he was combined

With those of Norway, or did line[⑦] the rebel

With hidden help and vantage, or that with both

He labour'd in his country's wreck[⑧], I know not;

But treasons capital[⑨], confess'd and proved,

Have overthrown[⑩] him.

MACBETH. [Aside①.] Glamis, and thane of Cawdor!

The greatest is behind.

[To ROSS and ANGUS.] Thanks for your pains.

[To BANQUO.] Do you not hope your children shall be kings,

When those that gave the thane of Cawdor to me

Promised no less to them?②

BANQUO. That trusted home,

Might yet enkindle you unto the crown,

Besides the thane of Cawdor.③ But 'tis strange;

And oftentimes, to win us to our harm,

The instruments of darkness tell us truths,

Win us with honest trifles, to betray's

In deepest consequence.④

Cousins, a word, I pray you.

MACBETH. [Aside.] Two truths are told,

As happy prologues to the swelling act

Of the imperial theme.⑤ —I thank you, gentlemen.

[Aside.] This supernatural⑥ soliciting⑦

Cannot be ill, cannot be good. If ill,

Why hath it given me earnest of success,

Commencing in a truth? I am thane of Cawdor.

If good, why do I yield to that suggestion

Whose horrid image doth unfix my hair

And make my seated heart knock at my ribs,

---

① aside：旁白

② 参考译文：她们叫我考特爵士，果然被她们说中了；您不希望您的子孙将来做君王吗？（朱生豪译）(those：指三个女巫；them，指班柯的子孙们)

③ 参考译文：您要是果然相信了她们的话，也许做了考特爵士以后，还想把王冠攫到手里。（朱生豪译）(that：that prediction，指女巫的预言；home：彻底地；enkindle：激发，煽起)

④ 参考译文：魔鬼为了要陷害我们起见，往往故意向我们说真话，在小事情上取得我们的信任，然后在重要的关头我们便会坠入他的圈套。（朱生豪译）(the instruments of darkness：女巫；trifle：小事；betray's：betray us；deepest：非常严重的)

⑤ 参考译文：这是我有一天将会跻登王座的幸运的预告。（朱生豪译）(prologues：序言，开场白；swelling：膨胀的，强大的；act：实施；imperial：皇帝的，帝王的)

⑥ supernatural：超自然的，神的

⑦ soliciting：劝说

Against the use of nature?① Present fears

Are less than horrible imaginings:

My thought, whose murther yet is but fantastical,

Shakes so my single state of man that function

Is smother'd in surmise, and nothing is

But what is not.②

BANQUO. Look, how our partner's rapt.

MACBETH. [Aside.] If chance will have me king, why,

chance may crown me, without my stir.③

BANQUO. New honours come upon him,

Like our strange garments④, cleave⑤ not to their mould⑥

But with the aid of use.

MACBETH. [Aside.] Come what come may,

Time and the hour runs through the roughest day.

BANQUO. Worthy Macbeth, we stay upon⑦ your leisure.

MACBETH. Give me your favour; my dull brain was wrought⑧

With things forgotten. Kind gentlemen, your pains

Are register'd where every day I turn

The leaf to read them.⑨ Let us toward⑩ the king.

---

① 参考译文：假如它是吉兆，为什么那句话会在我脑中引起可怖的印象，使我毛发森然，使我的心全然失去常态，怦怦地跳个不住呢？（朱生豪译）（yield to：屈从于，让步于；horrid：可怕的，恐怖的；unfix：使……不稳定，使……不安神；seated：冷静的；use of nature：平常心态）

② 这一段对麦克白的描写其实为日后麦克白杀邓肯做了铺垫。参考译文：想象中的恐怖远过于实际上的恐怖；我的思想中不过偶然浮起了杀人的妄念，就已经使我全身震撼，心灵在疑似的猜测之中丧失了作用，把虚无的幻影认为真实了。（朱生豪译）（horrible：恐怖的，可怕的；imagining：想象之物，想象的东西；shake：使心绪不宁，使发抖；smother'd：使窒息；surmise：臆测，揣测，两个 is 用法需注意，第一个 is 指存在于脑海中的；第二个 is 指存在于现实中的）

③ 参考译文：要是命运将会使我成为君王，那么也许命运会替我加上王冠，用不着我自己费力。（朱生豪译）（chance：命运；crown：加皇冠；stir：行动）

④ garment：衣服（例如：Many of the garments have the customers' name tags sewn into the linings. 这些衣服有很多内衬上缝有顾客的姓名签。）

⑤ cleave：裁剪，剪开

⑥ mould：模式，类型（例如：At first sight, he is not exactly cast in the leading man mould. 第一眼看上去，他并不是当领导的料。）

⑦ stay upon：等待

⑧ wrought：引起的，造成的

⑨ 参考译文：你们的辛苦已经铭刻在我的心版上，我每天都要把它翻开来诵读。（朱生豪译）

⑩ toward：这里相当于 go to，去

Think upon what hath chanced①, and at more time,
The interim② having weigh'd it, let us speak
Our free hearts each to other.

BANQUO. Very gladly.

MACBETH. Till then, enough. Come, friends.

[Exeunt.]

---

① chanced：happened，发生的
② interim：过渡期间

SCENE IV.
Forres. A Room in the Palace.

[Flourish①. Enter DUNCAN, MALCOLM, DONALBAIN, LENNOX, and Attendants.]

DUNCAN. Is execution② done on Cawdor? Are not

Those in commission③ yet return'd?

MALCOLM. My liege④,

They are not yet come back. But I have spoke

With one that saw him die: who did report

That very frankly he confess'd his treasons,

Implored⑤ your highness⑥' pardon and set forth⑦

A deep repentance⑧. Nothing in his life

Became him like the leaving it; he died

As one that had been studied in his death

To throw away the dearest thing he owed,

As 'twere a careless trifle.⑨

DUNCAN. There's no art

To find the mind's construction in the face:⑩

He was a gentleman on whom I built

An absolute trust.

[Enter MACBETH, BANQUO, ROSS, and ANGUS.]

O worthiest cousin!

---

① flourish：花式吹奏，意在宣告国王的到来

② execution：死刑

③ in commission：执行任务的

④ liege：国王，君主

⑤ implore：恳请，恳求（例如：He implored forgiveness for what he had done. 他乞求宽恕他过去所做的事。）

⑥ your highness：对国王的称呼，陛下

⑦ set forth：详尽解释，陈述（例如：Dr. Wang set forth the basis of his teaching method. 王博士阐述了他教学方法的基础。）

⑧ repentance：悔悟，忏悔

⑨ 参考译文：他的一生行事，从来不曾像他临终的时候那样值得钦佩；他抱着视死如归的态度，抛弃了他的最宝贵的生命，就像它是不足介意的琐屑一样。（朱生豪译）（the dearest thing：指生命；as 'twere：as it were）

⑩ 参考译文：世上还没有一种方法，可以从一个人的脸上探察他的居心。（朱生豪译）（art：方法；the mind's construction：一个人的想法）

The sin of my ingratitude even now
Was heavy on me. Thou art① so far before,
That swiftest wing of recompense is slow
To overtake thee.② Would thou hadst less deserved,
That the proportion both of thanks and payment
Might have been mine!③ only I have left to say,
More is thy due than more than all can pay.④

MACBETH. The service and the loyalty I owe,
In doing it, pays itself. Your highness' part
Is to receive our duties, and our duties
Are to your throne and state children and servants,
Which do but what they should, by doing every thing
Safe toward your love and honour.⑤

DUNCAN. Welcome hither⑥.
I have begun to plant⑦ thee, and will labour
To make thee full of growing. Noble Banquo,
That hast no less deserved, nor must be known
No less to have done so, let me enfold thee
And hold thee to my heart.⑧

BANQUO. There if I grow,
The harvest is your own.

DUNCAN. My plenteous joys,
Wanton in fulness, seek to hide themselves

---

① art：古英语，等于现在的 are
② 参考译文：我的忘恩负义的罪恶，刚才还重压在我的心头。你的功劳太超乎寻常了，飞得最快的报酬都追不上你。（朱生豪译）（sin：罪恶；ingratitude：不感激，忘恩负义；swift：迅速的；recompense：酬谢；overtake：追上，赶上）
③ 参考译文：要是它再微小一点，那么也许我可以按照适当的名分，给你应得的感谢和酬劳。（朱生豪译）（hadst：古英语，have 的第二人称单数过去式；proportion：比例，比率）
④ 参考译文：现在我只能这样说，一切的报酬都不能抵偿你的伟大的勋绩。（朱生豪译）
⑤ 参考译文：我们对于陛下和王国的责任，正像子女和奴仆一样，为了尽我们的敬爱之忱，无论做什么事都是应该的。（朱生豪译）
⑥ hither：古英语，到此处，向此处
⑦ plant：栽培，培养
⑧ 参考译文：尊贵的班柯，你的功劳也不在他之下，让我把你拥抱在我的心头。（朱生豪译）（enfold：拥抱，抱紧）

In drops of sorrow.① Sons, kinsmen, thanes,
And you whose places are the nearest, know
We will establish our estate upon
Our eldest, Malcolm, whom we name hereafter
The Prince of Cumberland;② which honour must
Not unaccompanied invest him only,
But signs of nobleness, like stars, shall shine
On all deservers.③ —From hence to Inverness④,
And bind us further to you.

MACBETH. The rest is labour, which is not used for you.

I'll be myself the harbinger and make joyful
The hearing of my wife with your approach;⑤
So humbly⑥ take my leave.

DUNCAN. My worthy Cawdor!

MACBETH. [Aside.] The Prince of Cumberland! that is a step
On which I must fall down, or else o'erleap,
For in my way it lies.⑦ Stars, hide your fires;
Let not light see my black and deep desires.
The eye wink at the hand; yet let that be,

---

① 参考译文：我的洋溢在心头的盛大的喜乐，想要在悲哀的泪滴里隐藏它自己。（朱生豪译）（plenteous：许多的，富足的；wanton：挥霍，放肆；drops of sorrow：眼泪）

② 参考译文：吾儿，各位国戚，各位爵士，以及一切最亲近的人，我现在向你们宣布封我的长子马科姆为肯勃兰亲王，他将来要继承我的王位。（朱生豪译）（establish our estate：将王位传给；the Prince of Cumberland：肯勃兰亲王，苏格兰王储）

③ 参考译文：不仅仅是他一个人受到这样的光荣，广大的恩宠将要像繁星一样，照耀在每一个有功者的身上。（朱生豪译）（not unaccompanied：双重否定表示肯定，意思是陪伴；signs of nobleness：恩宠；deserver：应得者）

④ Inverness：因弗内斯，麦克白城堡所在地

⑤ I'll be myself the harbinger 正常语序应为 I'll be the harbinger myself；make joyful the hearing of my wife with your approach 正常语序应为 make the hearing of my wife joyful with your approach。参考译文：让我做一个前驱者，把陛下光临的喜讯先去报告我的妻子知道。（朱生豪译）（harbinger：先驱）

⑥ humbly：谦逊地，恭顺地

⑦ 正常语序应为：The Prince of Cumberland! that is a step on which I must fall down, or else o'erleap, for it lies in my way. 其中，that 指代前面的 the Prince of Cumberland；for in my way it lies 中，in my way 是状语提前，为了强调。参考译文：这是一块横在我的前途的阶石，我必须跳过这块阶石，否则就要颠仆在它的上面。（朱生豪译）

Which the eye fears, when it is done, to see.[①]

[Exit.]

DUNCAN. True, worthy Banquo: he is full so valiant,

And in his commendations[②] I am fed;

It is a banquet[③] to me. Let's after[④] him,

Whose care is gone before to bid us welcome.

It is a peerless[⑤] kinsman[⑥].

[Flourish. Exeunt.]

---

① 正常语序应为：The eye wink at the hand；yet let that be, which the eye fears to see when it is done. 参考译文：眼睛啊，看着这双手吧；可是我仍要下手，就算干下的事会吓得眼睛不敢卒睹。（朱生豪译）（be：等于 be done；wink at：使眼色，眨眼）

② commendation：表扬；嘉奖

③ banquet：宴会，盛宴（例如：Last night the Prime Minister attended a state banquet at White House. 昨晚总理出席了在白宫举行的国宴。）

④ after：紧随其后，这里 after 是动词用法

⑤ peerless：无与伦比的，盖世无双的（例如：Guilin's scenery is peerless in the world. 桂林山水甲天下。）

⑥ kinsman：亲戚

SCENE V.
Inverness. MACBETH's Castle.

[Enter LADY MACBETH, reading a letter.]

LADY MACBETH. 'They① met me in the day of success, and I have learned by the perfectest② report, they have more in them than mortal③ knowledge. When I burned in desire to question them further, <u>they made themselves air, into which they vanished④.</u> Whiles⑤ I stood rapt in the wonder of it, came missives⑥ from the king, who all-hailed me "Thane of Cawdor;" by which title, before, these weird sisters⑦ saluted me, and referred me to the coming on of time, with "Hail, king that shalt be!" <u>This have I thought good to deliver thee, my dearest partner of greatness, that thou mightst not lose the dues of rejoicing, by being ignorant of what greatness is promised thee.⑧</u> Lay it to thy heart, and farewell.'

Glamis thou art, and Cawdor; and shalt be

What thou art promised. <u>Yet do I fear thy nature;</u>

<u>It is too full o' the milk of human kindness</u>

<u>To catch the nearest way.⑨</u> Thou wouldst be great;

Art not without ambition, but without

---

① they：the three witches
② perfectest：最完美的，最可靠的
③ mortal：凡人的，世间的（例如：It's beyond mortal power to bring a dead person back to life. 让死去的人复活是凡人做不到的。）
④ 参考译文：她们已经化为一阵风不见了。（朱生豪译）
⑤ whiles：等于while，当……的时候
⑥ missive：相当于messenger
⑦ weird sisters：指the three witches. 注意，这里麦克白对三个女巫的称呼发生了变化，也折射出他内心蠢蠢欲动要夺权的想法。
⑧ 参考译文：我想我应该把这样的消息告诉你，我的最亲爱的有福同享的伴侣，好让你不至于因为对于你所将要得到的富贵一无所知，而失去你所应该享有的欢欣。（朱生豪译）（deliver：deliver to，告诉；mightst：等于现在的might；dues：应有的权利，应得到的东西；rejoicing：欣喜，喜悦；ignorant：无知的）
⑨ 参考译文：可是我却为你的天性忧虑：它充满了太多的人情的乳臭，使你不敢采取最近的捷径。（朱生豪译）（too...to...：太……以至于不能做……）

The illness should attend it.[①] What thou wouldst highly,

That wouldst thou holily; wouldst not play false,

And yet wouldst wrongly win.[②] Thou'ldst have, great Glamis,

That which cries 'Thus thou must do, if thou have it';

And that which rather thou dost fear to do

Than wishest should be undone.[③] Hie[④] thee hither,

That[⑤] I may pour my spirits in thine ear,

And chastise with the valour of my tongue

All that impedes thee from the golden round,

Which fate and metaphysical aid doth seem

To have thee crown'd withal.[⑥]

[Enter a Messenger.]

What is your tidings[⑦]?

Messenger. The king comes here to-night.

LADY MACBETH. Thou'rt mad to say it!

Is not thy master with him, who, were't so[⑧],

Would have inform'd[⑨] for preparation?

Messenger. So please you, it is true; our thane is coming.

One of my fellows had the speed of[⑩] him,

Who, almost dead for breath, had scarcely more[⑪]

---

① 参考译文：你希望做一个伟大的人物，你不是没有野心，可是你却缺少和那种野心相联属的奸恶。（朱生豪译）（wouldst：古英语，will 的第二人称单数过去式；illness：这里相当于 wickedness，邪恶，后省略了 that；attend：办理，处理）

② 参考译文：你的欲望很大，但又希望用正直的手段，一方面不愿玩弄机诈，一方面却又要作非分的攫夺。（朱生豪译）（holily：神圣地；play false：弄虚作假）

③ 参考译文：伟大的爵士，你想要的那东西正在喊："你要到手，就得这样干！"你也不是不肯这样干，而是怕干。（朱生豪译）（句子里有两个 that，第一个 that 指的是 the crown，皇冠；第二个 that 指的是谋杀国王；it：这里指皇冠；dost：古英语，do 的第二人称单数现在式；wishest，古英语，相当于 wish）

④ hie：快走

⑤ that：so that

⑥ 正常语序应为：And with the valour of my tongue, chastise all that impedes thee from the golden round... 参考译文：命运和玄奇的力量分明已经准备把黄金的宝冠罩在你的头上，让我用舌尖的勇气，把那阻止你得到那顶王冠的一切障碍驱扫一空吧。（朱生豪译）（chastise：赶走；impede：阻碍，阻止；the golden round：皇冠；which 引导的是定语从句，修饰 the golden round；metaphysical：超自然的；withal：相当于 with that）

⑦ tidings：信息

⑧ were't so：if it were so，果真如此

⑨ inform'd：等于 informed，告知

⑩ had the speed of：比……速度快

⑪ more：more breath

Than would make up his message.

LADY MACBETH. Give him tending[①];

He brings great news.

[Exit Messenger.]

The raven himself is hoarse

That croaks the fatal entrance of Duncan

Under my battlements.[②] Come, you spirits

That tend on mortal thoughts, unsex me here,

And fill me, from the crown to the toe, top-full

Of direst cruelty![③] make thick my blood,

Stop up the access and passage to remorse,

That no compunctious visitings of nature

Shake my fell purpose nor keep peace between

The effect and it![④] Come to my woman's breasts,

And take my milk for gall[⑤], you murthering ministers[⑥],

Wherever in your sightless[⑦] substances

You wait on[⑧] nature's mischief[⑨]! Come, thick night,

And pall thee in the dunnest smoke of hell,

That my keen knife see not the wound it makes,

Nor heaven peep through the blanket of the dark

---

① tending: 照顾，招待

② 正常语序应为：The raven that croaks the fatal entrance of Duncan under my battlements himself is hoarse. 参考译文：报告邓肯走进我这堡门来送死的乌鸦，它的叫声是嘶哑的。(朱生豪译)(raven: 乌鸦；croak: 呱呱地叫；fatal: 致命的；hoarse: 嘶哑的)

③ 句子主干是：you spirits...unsex me here, and fill me...cruelty。That tend on mortal thoughts 为定语从句，修饰 spirits；from the crown to the toe 是方式状语，从头到脚。参考译文：注视着人类恶念的魔鬼们！解除我的女性的柔弱，用最凶恶的残忍自顶至踵贯注在我的全身。(spirit: 魔鬼；tend on: 注视；unsex: 使失去女性特征；direst: 可怕的)

④ 参考译文：凝结我的血液，不要让悔恨通过我的心头，不要让天性中的恻隐摇动我的狠毒的决意！(朱生豪译)其中 make thick my blood, thick 提前为了强调，应为 make my blood thick (thick: 凝固；access: 进入；passage: 通过；remorse: 懊悔，悔恨；that: 等于 so that；compunctious: 懊悔的，良心不安的；compunctious visitings of nature: 天性中的恻隐；shake: 动摇；fell: 残忍的，凶恶的；it: 指 the fell purpose)

⑤ gall: 胆汁，怨恨

⑥ minister: 使者，助手

⑦ sightless: 看不见的，无形的

⑧ wait on: 等待(某事发生)(例如：Since then I've been waiting on him to make changes. 自那以后，我就一直在等他发生改变。)

⑨ mischief: 损害，危害

24

To cry 'Hold, hold!'①

[Enter MACBETH.]

Great Glamis! worthy Cawdor!

Greater than both, by the all-hail hereafter!

Thy letters have transported me beyond

This ignorant present, and I feel now

The future in the instant.②

MACBETH. My dearest love,

Duncan comes here to-night.

LADY MACBETH. And when goes hence③?

MACBETH. To-morrow, as he purposes.

LADY MACBETH. O, never

Shall sun that morrow see!

Your face, my thane, is as a book where men

May read strange matters.④ To beguile the time,

Look like the time;⑤ bear welcome in your eye,

Your hand, your tongue; look like the innocent flower,

But be the serpent⑥ under't⑦. He that's coming

Must be provided for⑧; and you shall put

This night's great business into my dispatch,

Which shall to all our nights and days to come

Give solely sovereign sway and masterdom.⑨

---

① 参考译文：阴沉的黑夜，用最昏暗的地狱中的浓烟罩住你自己，让我的锐利的刀瞧不见它自己切开的伤口，让青天不能从黑暗的重衾里探出头来，高喊"住手，住手！"（朱生豪译）（pall：遮盖，给……蒙上阴影；dun：黑暗的；keen：锋利的；peep：偷窥，窥视）

② 参考译文：你的信使我飞越蒙昧的现在，我已经感觉到未来的搏动了。（朱生豪译）（transported：运输，运送；beyond：超过，越过；in the instant：现在，立刻）

③ hence：从此，从此处

④ 参考译文：您的脸，我的爵爷，正像一本书，人们可以从那上面读到奇怪的事情。（朱生豪译）

⑤ 参考译文：您要欺骗世人，必须装出和世人同样的神气。（朱生豪译）（beguile：欺骗）

⑥ serpent：毒蛇，蛇

⑦ under't：即 under it

⑧ be provided for：被宴请，被招待

⑨ 正常语序应为：Which shall give solely sovereign sway and masterdom to all our nights and days to come. 参考译文：您可以把今晚的大事交给我去办；凭此一举，我们今后就可以永远掌握君临万民的无上权威。（朱生豪译）（great business：指谋杀邓肯国王；dispatch：处理，了结；sovereign sway：皇权；masterdom：支配，掌控）

MACBETH. We will speak further.

LADY MACBETH. Only look up clear^①;

To alter favour ever is to fear.^②

Leave all the rest to me.

[Exeunt.]

---

① clear：明亮的，坦荡的
② 参考译文：脸上变色最易引起猜疑。(朱生豪译)(alter：改变；favour：关切，欢心，这里可理解为面部表情)

SCENE VI.
Before MACBETH's Castle①.

[Hautboys② and torches. Enter DUNCAN, MALCOLM, DONALBAIN, BANQUO, LENNOX, MACDUFF, ROSS, ANGUS, and Attendants.]

DUNCAN. This castle hath a pleasant seat; the air
Nimbly③ and sweetly recommends itself
Unto our gentle senses.

BANQUO. This guest of summer,
The temple-haunting④ martlet⑤, does approve
By his loved mansionry⑥ that the heaven's breath
Smells wooingly⑦ here. No jutty⑧, frieze⑨,
Buttress⑩, nor coign⑪ of vantage, but this bird
Hath made his pendent⑫ bed and procreant⑬ cradle⑭;
Where they most breed⑮ and haunt, I have observed
The air is delicate⑯.

[Enter LADY MACBETH.]

DUNCAN. See, see, our honour'd hostess!
The love that follows us sometime is our trouble,
Which still we thank as love. <u>Herein I teach you</u>

---

① castle：城堡
② hautboy：高音双簧箫，双簧管
③ nimbly：灵活地，灵敏地
④ haunting：常去的
⑤ martlet：圣马丁鸟，学名岩燕，居住在山岩峭壁之上，人们看不到它们休息，只见到圣马丁鸟无休无止地在空中飞翔，因此又称无足之鸟。
⑥ mansionry：大厦，宅第
⑦ wooingly：吸引人地，迷人地
⑧ jutty：突出部分
⑨ frieze：（墙壁高处或屋顶下方的）檐壁
⑩ buttress：撑墙，扶垛
⑪ coign：突出之角，隅石
⑫ pendent：吊着的，下垂的
⑬ procreant：生殖的，多产的
⑭ cradle：摇篮
⑮ breed：产仔，繁殖
⑯ delicate：芬芳的

27

How you shall bid God 'ield us for your pains,

And thank us for your trouble.①

LADY MACBETH. All our service

In every point twice done and then done double,

Were poor and single business to contend

Against those honours deep and broad wherewith

Your majesty loads our house. For those of old,

And the late dignities heap'd up to them,

We rest your hermits.②

DUNCAN. Where's the thane of Cawdor?

We coursed③ him at the heels and had a purpose

To be his purveyor④; but he rides well,

And his great love, sharp as his spur⑤, hath holp⑥ him

To his home before us. Fair and noble hostess,

We are your guest to-night.

LADY MACBETH. Your servants ever

Have theirs, themselves, and what is theirs, in compt,

To make their audit at your highness' pleasure,

Still to return your own.⑦

DUNCAN. Give me your hand;

Conduct me to mine host. We love him highly,

And shall continue our graces towards him.

By your leave, hostess.

[Exeunt.]

---

① 参考译文：所以根据这个道理，我们给你带来了麻烦，你还应该感谢我们，祷告上帝保佑我们。（朱生豪译）herein：于此；bid：祈祷；'ield：相当于 yield，这里为奖励，奖赏；pain：麻烦

② 参考译文：我们的犬马微劳，即使加倍报效，比起陛下赐给我们的深恩广泽来，也还是不足挂齿的；我们只有燃起一瓣心香，为陛下祷祝上苍，报答陛下过去和新近加于我们的荣宠。（朱生豪译）（single：单薄的；contend：竞争，抗衡；wherewith：with which，以其；load：装满；dignity：尊贵，显要；heap'd up：等于 heaped up，堆积；them：指代上文中的 honours，荣誉；hermit：隐修者，向上帝祈祷者）

③ course：追赶，追逐

④ purveyor：供应者，提供者，这里国王的意思是想早到一步为麦克白设宴。

⑤ spur：马刺

⑥ hath holp：相当于 has helped

⑦ 参考译文：只要陛下吩咐，您的仆人们随时准备把他们自己和他们所有的一切开列清单，向陛下报账，把原来属于陛下的依旧呈献给陛下。（朱生豪译）（compt：意同 account，账户；audit：审计，查账）

SCENE VII.
MACBETH's Castle.

[Hautboys and torches. Enter a Sewer, and divers Servants
with dishes and service, who pass over the stage. Then enter
MACBETH.]

MACBETH. <u>If it were done when 'tis done, then 'twere well
It were done quickly.</u>① If the assassination②
Could trammel up③ the consequence, and catch,
With his surcease④ success; <u>that but this blow
Might be the be-all and the end-all:</u>⑤ here,
But here, upon this bank and shoal⑥ of time,
We'd jump the life to come⑦. But in these cases
We still have judgment here, that <u>we but teach
Bloody instructions, which, being taught, return
To plague the inventor: this even-handed justice
Commends the ingredients of our poison'd chalice
To our own lips.</u>⑧ He's here in double trust:
First, as I am his kinsman and his subject,
Strong both against the deed⑨; then, as his host,
Who should against his murderer shut the door,
Not bear the knife myself. Besides, this Duncan

---

① 参考译文：要是干了以后就完了，那么还是快一点干。（朱生豪译）（第一个 done 的意思是结束了，第二个 done 表示做，即谋杀邓肯国王）
② assassination：暗杀
③ trammel up：束缚，妨碍
④ surcease：中止，停止
⑤ 参考译文：要是这一刀砍下去，就可以完成一切、终结一切。（朱生豪译）（that but：if only，要是……就好了）
⑥ shoal：浅滩
⑦ the life to come：来生
⑧ 参考译文：教唆杀人的人，结果自己反而被人所杀；把毒药投入酒杯里的人，结果也会自己饮鸩而死。（朱生豪译）（plague：折磨，使痛苦；even-handed：公平的，不偏不倚；commend：推荐，举荐；chalice：金杯毒酒）
⑨ the deed：指谋杀行为

29

Hath borne[①] his faculties[②] so meek[③], hath been
So clear[④] in his great office, that his virtues
Will plead like angels, trumpet-tongued, against
The deep damnation of his taking-off;[⑤]
And pity, like a naked new-born babe,
Striding the blast, or heaven's cherubim, horsed
Upon the sightless couriers of the air,
Shall blow the horrid deed in every eye,
That tears shall drown the wind.[⑥] I have no spur
To prick[⑦] the sides of my intent, but only
Vaulting ambition, which o'erleaps itself
And falls on the other.

[Enter LADY MACBETH.]

How now! what news?

LADY MACBETH. He has almost supp'd[⑧]. Why have you left the
chamber?

MACBETH. Hath he ask'd for me?

LADY MACBETH. Know you not he has?[⑨]

MACBETH. We will proceed[⑩] no further in this business:
He hath honour'd[⑪] me of late,[⑫] and I have bought

---

① hath borne：即 had borne，具有（borne 是 bear 的过去分词）
② faculty：能力
③ meek：仁慈的，温顺的
④ clear：清白的，没有过错的
⑤ 句子主干：his virtues will plead against the deep damnation of his taking-off. 参考译文：他的生前的美德，将要像天使一般发出喇叭一样清澈的声音，向世人昭告我的弑君重罪。（朱生豪译）（plead：申诉；trumpet-tongued：大声昭告；damnation：罚人地狱，遭天谴；taking-off：谋杀）
⑥ 参考译文："怜悯"像一个赤裸身体在狂风中飘荡的婴儿，又像一个御气而行的天婴，将要把这可憎的行为揭露在每一个人的眼中，使眼泪淹没了叹息。（朱生豪译）（pity：怜悯；babe：等于 baby，婴儿；striding：大步走，阔步走；blast：疾风；cherubim：小天使；horse：像骑马一样，策马前行；sightless：看不见的；couriers：信使；horrid：可怕的，恐怖的；that：as a result，结果是）
⑦ prick：刺激（良心），触动
⑧ supp'd：suppered，动词，吃晚饭
⑨ 正常语序应为：You not know he has？
⑩ proceed：前进，进展
⑪ honour'd：honoured，这里是动词，给予荣誉
⑫ of late：最近

Golden opinions from all sorts of people,

Which would be worn now in their newest gloss,

Not cast aside so soon.①

LADY MACBETH. Was the hope drunk

Wherein you dress'd yourself?② hath it ③slept since?

And wakes it now, to look so green④ and pale

At what it did so freely? From this time

Such⑤ I account thy love. Art thou afeard

To be the same in thine own act and valour

As thou art in desire?⑥ Wouldst thou have that

Which thou esteem'st the ornament of life,

And live a coward in thine own esteem,

Letting 'I dare not' wait upon 'I would,'

Like the poor cat i' the adage?⑦

MACBETH. Prithee⑧, peace:

I dare do all that may become a man;

Who dares do more is none.⑨

LADY MACBETH. What beast was't⑩, then,

That made you break this enterprise⑪ to me?

When you durst⑫ do it, then you were a man,

---

① 参考译文：我也好不容易从各种人的嘴里博到了无上的美誉，我的名声现在正在发射最灿烂的光彩，不能这么快就把它丢弃了。（朱生豪译）（bought：赢得，获得；golden opinions：美誉；worn：wear 的过去分词，穿戴，gloss：光彩，光泽；cast：抛开，抛掉）

② 参考译文：难道你把自己沉浸在里面的那种希望，只是醉后的妄想吗？（朱生豪译）（wherein：在其中）

③ it：指希望

④ green：不成熟的

⑤ such：结合上文麦克白妻子说他出尔反尔，这里理解为"不可靠的"

⑥ 参考译文：你不敢让你在自己的行为和勇气上赶你的欲望一致吗？（朱生豪译）

⑦ 参考译文：你宁愿像一只畏首畏尾的猫儿，顾全你所认为生命的装饰品的名誉，不惜让你在自己眼中成为一个懦夫，让"我不敢"永远跟随在"我想要"的后面吗？（朱生豪译）（esteem'st：等于 esteemed；the ornament of life：荣誉；wait upon：伺候，服侍；i'：等于 in；adage：谚语，格言）

⑧ prithee：求求你

⑨ 参考译文：只要是男子汉做的事，我都敢做；没有人比我有更大的胆量。（朱生豪译）

⑩ was't：等于 was it，是什么

⑪ enterprise：事业心，进取心（例如：The boss of the company lacks enterprise. 这个公司老板缺乏事业心。）

⑫ durst：dare 的过去式

And, to be more than what you were, you would
Be so much more the man^①. Nor time nor place
Did then adhere^②, and yet you would make both.
They have made themselves, and that their fitness now
Does unmake you.^③ I have given suck^④, and know
How tender 'tis to love the babe that milks^⑤ me:
I would, while it was smiling in my face,
Have pluck'd^⑥ my nipple from his boneless gums^⑦,
And dash'd^⑧ the brains out, had I so sworn as you
Have done to this^⑨.

MACBETH. If we should fail?

LADY MACBETH. We fail!

But screw^⑩ your courage to the sticking-place^⑪,
And we'll not fail. When Duncan is asleep—
Whereto the rather shall his day's hard journey
Soundly invite him^⑫—his two chamberlains
Will I with wine and wassail so convince
That memory, the warder of the brain,
Shall be a fume, and the receipt of reason

---

① 参考译文：要是你敢做做你本不能做的事情，那才更是一个男子汉。（朱生豪译）
② adhere：适合
③ 参考译文：现在你有了大好的机会，你又失去勇气了。（朱生豪译）（they：指上文提到的时间和地点，即时机；fitness：合适；unmake：使消失）
④ give suck：给孩子哺乳
⑤ milk：吃奶，吸奶
⑥ pluck'd：等于plucked，拔掉，拔出
⑦ gum：嘴巴
⑧ dash'd：等于dashed，猛摔（例如：She seized the doll and dashed it against the stone wall with tremendous force. 她抓起玩具娃娃，用力往石墙上扔去。）
⑨ 该句用了与过去相反的虚拟语气。参考译文：要是我也像你一样，曾经发誓下这样的毒手的话。（朱生豪译）（to this：指的是谋杀邓肯国王）
⑩ screw：旋紧，拧紧
⑪ the sticking-place：顶点，极限，这里是比喻的用法，意思让麦克白将他的勇气发挥到最大，就如拧螺丝一样，拧到极限
⑫ 正常语序应为：his day's hard journey shall soundly invite him to the sleep. 参考译文：邓肯赶了这一天辛苦的路程，一定睡得很熟。（朱生豪译）（whereto：to which sleep，熟睡中）

A limbeck only.① When in swinish② sleep
Their drenched③ natures lie as in a death,
What cannot you and I perform④ upon
The unguarded Duncan? What not put upon
His spongy officers, who shall bear the guilt
Of our great quell?⑤

MACBETH. Bring forth⑥ men-children only,
For thy undaunted⑦ mettle⑧ should compose⑨
Nothing but males. Will it not be received,
When we have mark'd with blood those sleepy two
Of his own chamber and used their very daggers,
That they have done't?⑩

LADY MACBETH. Who dares receive it other⑪,
As we shall make our griefs and clamour⑫ roar⑬
Upon his death?

---

① 正常语序应为：I will wine and wassail with his two chamberlains so convince that memory shall be a fume, and the receipt of reason a limbeck only. the warder of the brain 是 memory 的同位语。参考译文：我再去陪他那两个侍卫饮酒作乐，灌得他们头脑模糊，记忆化成一阵烟雾。（朱生豪译）（chamberlain：内勤侍卫；wassail：痛饮，为……干杯；warder：看守，守卫；fume：烟气，烟雾；receipt：接收，接收物；limbeck：蒸馏器，里面空无一物，这里指侍卫脑海里什么都不记得）
② swinish：像猪一般的
③ drench：在某人（某物）上大量使用（某液体），这里指将两个侍卫灌得烂醉如泥
④ perform：执行，动手
⑤ 参考译文：我们不是可以把这一件重大的谋杀罪案，推在他的酒醉的侍卫身上吗？（spongy：海绵似的，这里指烂醉如泥的；what not：相当于 why not，为什么；put upon：使成为牺牲品；bear the guilt：承担罪名；quell：古英语，杀戮）
⑥ bring forth：生孩子
⑦ undaunted：不惧怕的，无畏的
⑧ mettle：精神，勇气
⑨ compose：组成，构成（例如：These nine men are believed to compose the committee. 人们认为委员会是由这九人组成的。）
⑩ 正常语序应为：Will it not be received that they have done't, when we have mark'd those sleepy two of his own chamber with blood and used their very daggers? 参考译文：要是我们在那睡在他寝室里的两个人身上涂抹一些血迹，而且就用他们的刀子，人家会不会相信真是他们干下的事？（朱生豪译）（received：accepted as true，认为如此；done't：等于 done it，指谋杀邓肯国王这件事；dagger：短剑，匕首）
⑪ other：otherwise，其他的看法
⑫ clamour：吵闹，喧哗（例如：He raised a hand to still the clamour. 他举手示意大家安静。）
⑬ roar：大哭，咆哮（例如：He began to roar when I took the chocolate away. 当我把巧克力拿走时，他大哭起来。）

MACBETH. I am settled[1] and bend up[2]

Each corporal agent[3] to this terrible feat[4].

Away, and mock[5] the time with fairest[6] show:

False face must hide what the false heart doth know.[7]

[Exeunt.]

---

① settled：决心已定
② bend up：弯曲，这里指调动
③ corporal agent：corporal 相当于 corporeal，身体的各个器官，即用尽全身力量
④ feat：丰功伟绩，壮举
⑤ mock：愚弄，嘲弄（例如：She mocked him as a coward. 她嘲笑他是个懦夫。）
⑥ fair：合理的，说得过去的
⑦ 参考译文：奸诈的心必须罩上虚伪的笑脸。（朱生豪译）

Act II

SCENE I.
Inverness. The Courtyard of MACBETH's Castle.

[Enter BANQUO, and FLEANCE bearing a torch before him.]

BANQUO. How goes the night, boy?

FLEANCE. The moon is down; I have not heard the clock.

BANQUO. And she goes down at twelve.

FLEANCE. I take't, 'tis later, sir.

BANQUO. Hold, take my sword. There's husbandry[1] in heaven,

Their candles[2] are all out. Take thee that too.

A heavy summons[3] lies like lead[4] upon me,

And yet I would not sleep. Merciful[5] powers,

Restrain in me the cursed thoughts that nature

Gives way to in repose![6]

[Enter MACBETH, and a Servant with a torch.]

Give me my sword.

Who's there?

MACBETH. A friend.

BANQUO. What, sir, not yet at rest? The king's a-bed[7].

He hath been in unusual pleasure, and

Sent forth[8] great largess[9] to your offices[10].

This diamond he greets your wife withal[11],

---

① husbandry：节俭

② their candles：指星星

③ summons：召唤，这里指睡眠的召唤

④ lead：铅

⑤ merciful：仁慈的

⑥ 参考译文：抑制那些罪恶的思想，不要让它们潜入我的睡梦之中。（朱生豪译）（restrain：抑制；cursed：罪恶的；give way to：让路，让步；repose：休息，安眠）

⑦ a-bed：in bed，上床了

⑧ send forth：放出，散发，这里指打赏

⑨ largess：慷慨赠予的钱或礼物

⑩ office：这里指仆从

⑪ withal：此外，而且

By the name of most kind hostess, and shut up[①]

In measureless content.

MACBETH. Being unprepared,

Our will became the servant to defect,

Which else should free have wrought.[②]

BANQUO. All's well.

I dreamt last night of the three weird sisters:

To you they have show'd some truth.

MACBETH. I think not of them;

Yet, when we can entreat[③] an hour to serve,

We would spend it in some words upon that business[④],

If you would grant[⑤] the time.

BANQUO. At your kind'st leisure[⑥].

MACBETH. If you shall cleave to[⑦] my consent, when 'tis[⑧],

It shall make honour for you.

BANQUO. So I lose none

In seeking to augment it, but still keep

My bosom franchised and allegiance clear,

I shall be counsell'd.[⑨]

MACBETH. Good repose the while.

BANQUO. Thanks, sir, the like to you.

[Exeunt BANQUO and FLEANCE.]

MACBETH. Go bid[⑩] thy mistress, when my drink is ready,

She strike upon the bell. Get thee to bed.

---

① shut up：结束

② 参考译文：我们因为事先没有准备，恐怕有许多招待不周的地方。（朱生豪译）（will：招待的愿望；wrought：work 的过去式和过去分词，运作，运转）

③ entreat：恳求，乞求（例如：The boy entreated his parents to come back early. 男孩恳求父母早点回来。）

④ that business：指女巫的预言

⑤ grant：给予（例如：He refused to grant them loans. 他拒绝给他们贷款。）

⑥ at your kind'st leisure：悉如遵命

⑦ cleave to：坚持

⑧ when 'tis：when it is，到时候

⑨ 参考译文：为了觊觎富贵而丧失荣誉的事，我是不干的；要是您有什么见教，只要不毁坏我的清白的忠诚，我都愿意接受。（朱生豪译）（augment：增强，增加；it：指荣誉；bosom：胸怀，内心；franchised：给……以特许权，这里指远离罪恶；allegiance：忠诚，忠节；counsell'd：等于 counselled，建议）

⑩ bid：说，要求

[Exit Servant.]

Is this a dagger which I see before me,

The handle toward my hand? Come, let me clutch thee.

I have thee not, and yet I see thee still.

<u>Art thou not, fatal vision, sensible</u>

<u>To feeling as to sight?</u>[①] or art thou but

A dagger of the mind, a false creation,

Proceeding from the heat-oppressed[②] brain?

I see thee yet, in form as palpable[③]

As this which now I draw.

Thou marshall'st[④] me the way that I was going,

And such an instrument I was to use.

<u>Mine eyes are made the fools o' the other senses,</u>

<u>Or else worth all the rest.</u>[⑤] I see thee still,

And on thy blade and dudgeon[⑥], gouts[⑦] of blood,

Which was not so before. There's no such thing:

It is the bloody business which informs

Thus to mine eyes. Now, o'er the one half-world,

Nature seems dead, and wicked dreams abuse

The curtain'd sleep; witchcraft[⑧] celebrates

Pale Hecate's offerings[⑨]; and wither'd murder,

Alarum'd[⑩] by his sentinel[⑪], the wolf,

Whose howl's his watch, thus with his stealthy[⑫] pace,

---

① 主干是：Art thou not sensible to feeling as to sight. 参考译文：不祥的幻象，你只是一件可视不可触的东西吗？（朱生豪译）

② heat-oppressed：狂热的

③ palpable：明显的，可感知的（例如：There is a palpable difference in their characteristics. 他们的性格有着明显的差别。）

④ marshall'st：等于 marshalled，引导，领着

⑤ 参考译文：我的眼睛倘不是受了其他知觉的嘲弄，就是兼领了一切感官的机能。（朱生豪译）

⑥ dudgeon：刀柄

⑦ gout：一滴，一团

⑧ witchcraft：巫术

⑨ offering：供奉物，祭品

⑩ alarum'd：被唤醒的

⑪ sentinel：岗哨，哨兵

⑫ stealthy：悄无声息的，鬼鬼祟祟的

With Tarquin①'s ravishing strides②, towards his design
Moves like a ghost. Thou sure and firm-set earth,
Hear not my steps, which way they walk, for fear
Thy very stones prate of my whereabout,
And take the present horror from the time,
Which now suits with it.③ Whiles I threat, he lives;
Words to the heat of deeds too cold breath gives.④
[A bell rings.]
I go, and it is done; the bell invites me.
Hear it not, Duncan, for it is a knell⑤
That summons thee to heaven, or to hell⑥.
[Exit.]

---

① Tarquin：即 Sextus Tarquinius，他是罗马最后一个国王路修斯·塔昆纽斯（Lucius Tarquinius Superbus）的幼子。其父谋杀岳父、篡夺王位后，暴虐无道，民怨沸腾；他自己则因为强奸鲁克丽丝激起公愤，因而他的家族被放逐，王朝被推翻，罗马共和国成立。

② stride：大步，大踏步

③ 参考译文：坚固结实的大地啊，不要听见我的脚步声音是向什么地方去的，我怕路上的砖石会泄露了我的行踪，打破这一片森然的死寂。（朱生豪译）（prate：古英语，唠叨，啰唆；whereabout：行踪）

④ 正常语序应为：Words gives too cold breath to the heat of deeds. 参考译文：在紧张的行动中间，言语是多么软弱无力。（朱生豪译）（to：according to，根据）

⑤ knell：丧钟声，某事物结束的象征

⑥ hell：地狱，阴间

SCENE II.
The Same.

[Enter LADY MACBETH.]

LADY MACBETH. That which hath made them drunk hath made me bold;

What hath quench'd them hath given me fire.[①] Hark! Peace!

It was the owl that shriek'd[②], the fatal bellman[③],

Which gives the stern'st[④] good-night. He is about it:

The doors are open, and the surfeited[⑤] grooms

Do mock their charge[⑥] with snores. I have drugg'd[⑦] their possets[⑧],

That[⑨] death and nature do contend about them,

Whether they live or die.

MACBETH. [Within.] Who's there? What, ho!

LADY MACBETH. Alack[⑩], I am afraid they have awaked,

And 'tis not done. The attempt and not the deed,

Confounds[⑪] us. Hark! I laid their daggers ready;

He could not miss 'em[⑫]. Had he not resembled

My father as he slept, I had done't.[⑬]

[Enter MACBETH.]

My husband!

MACBETH. I have done the deed. Didst thou not hear a noise?

---

① 参考译文：酒把他们醉倒了，却提起了我的勇气；浇熄了他们的馋焰，却燃起了我心头的烈火。(quench'd: 等于 quenched，解（渴），（用水）扑灭（火焰等）)

② shriek'd: 等于 shrieked，尖叫

③ bellman: 敲钟人

④ stern'st: 等于 sternest，stern 的最高级，苛刻的，严肃的

⑤ surfeited: 吃得过多的 (surfeit 的过去式和过去分词)

⑥ charge: 责任

⑦ drugg'd: drugged，下药

⑧ posset: 牛奶甜酒

⑨ that: so that，以至于

⑩ alack: 呜呼，这里表示"忧伤"

⑪ confound: 使困惑，搞乱，打乱

⑫ miss 'em: miss them，看不见刀子

⑬ 参考译文：倘不是我看他睡着的样子活像我的父亲，我早就自己动手了。(朱生豪译)（he, 指邓肯国王；resembled: 像；done't: done it）

39

LADY MACBETH. I heard the owl scream and the crickets[1] cry.

Did not you speak?

MACBETH. When?

LADY MACBETH. Now.

MACBETH. As I descended[2]?

LADY MACBETH. Ay.

MACBETH. Hark[3]!

Who lies i'[4] the second chamber?

LADY MACBETH. Donalbain.

MACBETH. This is a sorry sight.

[Looking on his hands.]

LADY MACBETH. A foolish thought, to say a sorry sight.

MACBETH. There's one did laugh in's sleep, and one cried 'Murther!'

That they did wake each other. I stood and heard them,

But they did say their prayers[5] and address'd them

Again to sleep.

LADY MACBETH. There are two[6] lodged[7] together.

MACBETH. One cried 'God bless us!' and 'Amen' the other,

As they had seen me with these hangman's hands.

Listening their fear, I could not say 'Amen[8],'

When they did say 'God bless us!'

LADY MACBETH. Consider it not so deeply.[9]

MACBETH. But wherefore[10] could not I pronounce 'Amen'?

I had most need of blessing, and 'Amen'

Stuck in my throat.

---

① cricket：蟋蟀

② descend：下来

③ hark：听，回想

④ lies i'：lies in

⑤ prayer：祈祷文，祈祷

⑥ two：指的是邓肯的两个儿子 Malcolm 和 Donalbain

⑦ lodge：住宿，住（例如：Where we are to lodge is our first problem. 去哪儿住宿是我们的首要问题。）

⑧ Amen："阿门"，希伯来语 [āmēn] 的译音，意为"真诚"，表示"诚心所愿，但愿如此"，基督徒常用在祷告结尾，是"请求上帝垂听我们的祷告"的意思。麦克白说不出"阿门"暗示他内心有愧，不敢再祈求上帝听他的祷告，也已无法再得到上帝的祝福。

⑨ 参考译文：不要把它放在心上。（朱生豪译）（deeply：过多地，严重地）

⑩ wherefore：why，为什么

LADY MACBETH. These deeds must not be thought

After these ways; so, it will make us mad.

MACBETH. Methought① I heard a voice cry 'Sleep no more!

Macbeth does murther sleep,'—the innocent sleep,

Sleep that knits up the ravell'd sleave of care,

The death of each day's life, sore labour's bath,

Balm of hurt minds, great nature's second course,

Chief nourisher in life's feast②,—

LADY MACBETH. What do you mean?

MACBETH. Still it cried 'Sleep no more!' to all the house;

'Glamis hath murther'd sleep, and therefore Cawdor

Shall sleep no more. Macbeth shall sleep no more.'

LADY MACBETH. Who was it that thus cried? Why, worthy thane,

You do unbend③ your noble strength, to think

So brainsickly of things. Go get some water,

And wash this filthy witness from your hand.

Why did you bring these daggers from the place?

They must lie there. Go carry them, and smear

The sleepy grooms with blood.

MACBETH. I'll go no more.

I am afraid to think what I have done;

Look on't again I dare not.

LADY MACBETH. Infirm of purpose!

Give me the daggers. The sleeping and the dead

Are but as pictures; 'tis the eye of childhood

That fears a painted devil.④ If he do bleed,

---

① methought: methink 的过去式，在我看来

② 参考译文：那清白的睡眠，把忧虑的乱丝编织起来的睡眠，那日常的死亡，疲劳者的沐浴，受伤的心灵的油膏，大自然的最丰盛的肴馔，生命的盛筵上主要的营养。（朱生豪译）句中使用了暗喻和类比，说明莎士比亚善用各种修辞手法；而朱生豪的译文也从神韵的角度还原了莎士比亚的原文，可见朱生豪的中英文造诣都很高。（knit up：编织，织补；ravell'd：开了线的；sore：痛处，伤处；balm：香油，香膏；nourisher：滋养，营养；feast：盛宴）

③ unbend：解开，解放

④ 参考译文：意志动摇的人！把刀子给我。睡着的人和死了的人不过和画像一样；只有小儿的眼睛才会害怕画中的魔鬼。（朱生豪译）（infirm：不坚定的；'tis：it is，本句用到了 it is...that... 的强调句型）

I'll gild① the faces of the grooms withal,

For it must seem their guilt②.

[Exit. Knocking within.]

MACBETH. Whence is that knocking?

How is't with me, when every noise appals③ me?

What hands are here? Ha! they pluck out mine eyes.

Will all great Neptune's ocean wash this blood

Clean from my hand? No, this my hand will rather

The multitudinous seas in incarnadine,

Making the green one red.④

[Re-enter LADY MACBETH.]

LADY MACBETH. My hands are of your colour, but I shame

To wear a heart so white⑤. [Knocking within.] I hear a knocking

At the south entry. Retire we to our chamber⑥.

A little water clears us of this deed.

How easy is it, then! Your constancy⑦

Hath left you unattended.

[Knocking within.]

Hark! more knocking.

Get on your nightgown, lest occasion call us,

And show us to be watchers. Be not lost

So poorly in your thoughts.

---

① gild：装饰，修饰（例如：Her beauty gilds her vice. 她的美貌掩盖了她的邪恶。）

② guilt：犯罪行为，罪恶

③ appal：使……惊骇，使……吓坏（例如：We were appalled when we heard that the chairman had been murdered. 听说主席被谋杀，我们都吓坏了。）

④ 参考译文：大洋里所有的水，能够洗净我手上的血迹吗？不，恐怕我这一手的血，倒要把一碧无垠的海水染成一片殷红呢。（朱生豪译）这句话体现出莎士比亚高超的语言技能：在外来语（拉丁语）和本土古英语间随意切换，在句中，the multitudinous seas incarnadine 由较少人使用的拉丁文（外来词）成分构成，而 making the green one red 则用的是简明易懂的盎格鲁－撒克逊词语。（Neptune：罗马神话中的海神尼普顿，海王星以其命名；multitudinous：大量的；incarnadine：染红）

⑤ white：惨白的，这里指害怕的

⑥ chamber：室，卧室

⑦ constancy：坚定不移（例如：The secret of success is constancy of purpose. 成功的秘诀是目标的坚定性。）

MACBETH. To know my deed, 'twere[①] best not know myself.

[Knocking within.]

Wake Duncan with thy knocking! I would thou couldst!

[Exeunt.]

---

① 'twere：it were，这里使用了虚拟语气

SCENE III.
The Same.

[Knocking within. Enter a Porter.]

Porter. Here's a knocking indeed! If a man were porter of hell-gate, he should have old turning the key. [Knocking within.] Knock, knock, knock! Who's there, i' the name of Beelzebub①? Here's a farmer that hanged himself on the expectation of plenty. Come in time! Have napkins enow② about you; here you'll sweat for't.

[Knocking within.] Knock, knock! Who's there, in the other devil's name? <u>Faith, here's an equivocator, that could swear in both the scales against either scale, who committed treason enough for God's sake, yet could not equivocate to heaven.</u>③ O, come in, equivocator. [Knocking within.] Knock, knock, knock! Who's there? Faith, here's an English tailor come hither, for stealing out of a French hose④. Come in, tailor; here you may roast your goose. [Knocking within.] Knock, knock! Never at quiet! What are you? But this place is too cold for hell. I'll devil-porter it no further. I had thought to have let in some of all professions that go the primrose⑤ way to the everlasting bonfire⑥. [Knocking within.] Anon, anon! I pray you, remember the porter.

[Opens the gate.]

[Enter MACDUFF and LENNOX.]

---

① Beelzebub：别西卜，圣经中的恶魔

② enow：足够的，充分的

③ 参考译文：一定是什么讲起话来暧昧含糊的家伙，他会同时站在两方面，一会儿帮着这个骂那个，一会儿帮着那个骂这个；他曾经为了上帝的缘故，干过不少亏心事，可是他那条暧昧含糊的舌头却不能把他送上天堂去。（朱生豪译）（faith：宗教信仰，这里表感叹，可译成"天哪，哼"；scale：程度；treason：背叛；equivocate：含糊其词，说话支吾；equivocator：说模棱话的人，说话支吾的人）

④ hose：男性穿的紧身裤

⑤ primrose：欢乐的（例如：She has led him down the primrose path. 她把他引上了放荡的堕落道路。）

⑥ bonfire：篝火，营火（例如：The camp bonfire flamed away all the evening. 整个晚上野营的篝火都在燃烧。）

44

MACDUFF. Was it so late, friend, ere you went to bed,

That you do lie so late?

Porter. Faith sir, we were carousing① till the second cock; and drink,

sir, is a great provoker② of three things.

MACDUFF. What three things does drink especially provoke?

Porter. Marry, sir, nose-painting③, sleep and urine④. Lechery⑤, sir,

it provokes and unprovokes: it provokes the desire, but it takes

away the performance. Therefore, much drink may be said to be

an equivocator with lechery: it makes him, and it mars him; it

sets him on, and it takes him off; it persuades him, and disheartens

him; makes him stand to, and not stand to; in conclusion,

equivocates him in a sleep, and, giving him the lie, leaves him.⑥

MACDUFF. I believe drink gave thee the lie last night.

Porter. That it did, sir, i' the very throat on me; but I requited him

for his lie; and, I think, being too strong for him, though he took

up my legs sometime, yet I made a shift to cast him.⑦

MACDUFF. Is thy master stirring⑧?

[Enter MACBETH.]

Our knocking has awaked him; here he comes.

LENNOX. Good morrow⑨, noble sir.

MACBETH. Good morrow, both.

MACDUFF. Is the king stirring, worthy thane?

MACBETH. Not yet.

MACDUFF. He did command me to call timely⑩ on him;

---

① carouse：痛饮，闹饮欢宴

② provoker：煽动者，挑事者

③ nose-painting：酒糟鼻

④ urine：尿，小便

⑤ lechery：好色，淫荡

⑥ 参考译文：酒喝多了，对这种事情是两面的：先挑逗它，再打击它；闹得它上了火，又兜头一盆冷水；弄得它挺又挺不起来，趴又趴不下去；到最后让人睡着了，害他做了一场春梦，就溜走了。（朱生豪译）（mar：毁坏，损坏；dishearten：使失去勇气，使失去信心）

⑦ 参考译文：可我也不是好惹的，依我看，我比它强，我虽然不免给它揪住大腿，可我终究把它摔倒了。（朱生豪译）（requite：酬谢，报复；make a shift：设法；cast：把……摔倒）

⑧ stir：起来

⑨ morrow：即 morning

⑩ timely：及时地，适时地

45

I have almost slipp'd[①] the hour.

MACBETH. I'll bring you to him.

MACDUFF. I know this is a joyful trouble to you,

But yet 'tis one.

MACBETH. The labour we delight[②] in physics pain.

This is the door.

MACDUFF. I'll make so bold to call,

For 'tis my limited service.

[Exit.]

LENNOX. Goes the king hence[③] to-day?

MACBETH. He does; he did appoint so.

LENNOX. The night has been unruly[④]. Where we lay,

Our chimneys were blown down[⑤], and as they say,

Lamentings heard i' the air; strange screams of death,

And prophesying with accents terrible

Of dire combustion and confused events

New hatch'd to the woeful time.[⑥] The obscure bird

Clamour'd[⑦] the livelong[⑧] night. Some say the earth

Was feverous[⑨] and did shake.

MACBETH. 'Twas a rough[⑩] night.

LENNOX. My young remembrance cannot parallel

A fellow to it.[⑪]

[Re-enter MACDUFF.]

---

① slipp'd: slipped，（时间）不知不觉过去
② delight：感到高兴
③ hence：从此，因此
④ unruly：不守规矩的，难驾驭的
⑤ blow down：吹倒
⑥ 参考译文：他们还说空中有哀哭的声音，有人听见奇怪的死亡的惨叫，还有人听见一个可怕的声音，预言着将要有一场绝大的纷争和混乱，降临在这不幸的时代。（朱生豪译）（lamenting：痛哭，哀伤；prophesy：预告，预言；combustion：燃烧，烧毁；hatch'd：等于hatched，孵化出，出现；woeful：悲惨的，不幸的）
⑦ clamour'd：clamoured，喧闹的，吵闹的
⑧ livelong：整个的，漫长的（例如：He likes reading all the livelong day. 他喜欢整天看书。）
⑨ feverous：发烧的，热病的
⑩ rough：可怕的，狂暴的
⑪ 参考译文：在我的年轻的经验里唤不起一个同样的回忆。（朱生豪译）（remembrance：记忆，回忆；fellow：同伴，类似的情况）

MACDUFF. O horror, horror, horror! Tongue nor heart
Cannot conceive nor name thee!①

MACBETH & LENNOX. What's the matter.

MACDUFF. Confusion now hath made his masterpiece!
Most sacrilegious murther hath broke ope
The Lord's anointed temple, and stole thence
The life o' the building!②

MACBETH. What is 't you say? the life?

LENNOX. Mean you His Majesty?

MACDUFF. Approach the chamber, and destroy your sight
With a new Gorgon③. Do not bid me speak;
See, and then speak yourselves.
[Exeunt MACBETH and LENNOX.]
Awake, awake!
Ring the alarum-bell. Murther and treason!
Banquo and Donalbain! Malcolm! awake!
Shake off this downy sleep, death's counterfeit,
And look on death itself!④ Up, up, and see
The great doom⑤'s image! Malcolm! Banquo!
As from your graves rise up, and walk like sprites⑥,
To countenance⑦ this horror! Ring the bell!
[Bell rings.]
[Enter LADY MACBETH.]

LADY MACBETH. What's the business,
That such a hideous trumpet calls to parley

---

① 参考译文：不可言说、不可想象的恐怖！（朱生豪译）（conceive：想象出）

② 参考译文：混乱已经完成了他的杰作！大逆不道的凶手打开了王上的圣殿，把它的生命偷走了！（朱生豪译）（sacrilegious：犯渎圣罪的，该受天谴的；ope：等于 open；anointed：抹油膏的，意为接受上帝祝福的）

③ Gorgon：（希腊神话中）三个蛇发女怪之一，看到她眼睛的人会化为石头

④ 参考译文：不要贪恋温柔的睡眠，那只是死亡的假装，瞧一瞧死亡的本身吧！（朱生豪译）（shake off：甩掉，逃脱；downy：柔和的；counterfeit：仿制品，伪造物）

⑤ doom：世界末日

⑥ sprite：幽灵

⑦ countenance：看，面对

The sleepers of the house?[①] Speak, speak!

MACDUFF. O gentle lady,

'Tis not for you to hear what I can speak:

The repetition, in a woman's ear,

Would murther as it fell.[②]

[Enter BANQUO.]

O Banquo, Banquo!

Our royal master 's murder'd!

LADY MACBETH. Woe, alas!

What, in our house?

BANQUO. Too cruel anywhere.

Dear Duff, I prithee[③], contradict[④] thyself,

And say it is not so.

[Re-enter MACBETH and LENNOX, with ROSS.]

MACBETH. Had I but died an hour before this chance,

I had lived a blessed time, for from this instant,

There's nothing serious in mortality.[⑤]

All is but toys; renown and grace is dead,

The wine of life is drawn, and the mere lees

Is left this vault to brag of.[⑥]

[Enter MALCOLM and DONALBAIN.]

DONALBAIN. What is amiss[⑦]?

MACBETH. You are, and do not know't[⑧]:

The spring, the head, the fountain[⑨] of your blood

---

① 参考译文：为什么要吹起这样凄厉的号角，把全屋子睡着的人唤醒？（朱生豪译）
（hideous：令人惊骇的，讨厌的；sleeper：睡觉的人）

② 参考译文：它一进到妇女的耳朵里，是比利剑还要难受的。（朱生豪译）

③ prithee：请，求求你

④ contradict：反驳，驳斥

⑤ 参考译文：要是我在这件变故发生以前一小时死去，我就可以说是活过了一段幸福的时间；因为从这一刻起，人生已经失去它的严肃的意义。（朱生豪译）该句用了与过去相反的虚拟语气。

⑥ 参考译文：一切都不过是儿戏；荣名和美德已经死了，生命的美酒已经喝完，剩下来的只是一些无味的渣滓当做酒窖里的珍宝。（朱生豪译）（renown：名望，声誉；lees：（酒等中的）沉淀物，渣滓；vault：地下储藏室，酒窖）

⑦ amiss：出了差错的，有缺陷的

⑧ know't：等于 know it

⑨ fountain：喷泉，源头

48

Is stopp'd[①]; the very source of it is stopp'd.

MACDUFF. Your royal father's murther'd.

MALCOLM. O, by whom?

LENNOX. Those of his chamber, as it seem'd, had done 't.

Their hands and faces were all badged[②] with blood;

So were their daggers, which unwiped[③] we found

Upon their pillows[④].

They stared and were distracted; no man's life

Was to be trusted with them.

MACBETH. O, yet I do repent[⑤] me of my fury,

That I did kill them.

MACDUFF. Wherefore did you so?

MACBETH. Who can be wise, amazed, temperate and furious,

Loyal and neutral, in a moment?[⑥] No man.

The expedition my violent love

Outrun the pauser, reason.[⑦] Here lay Duncan,

His silver skin laced with his golden blood,

And his gash'd stabs look'd like a breach in nature

For ruin's wasteful entrance; there, the murtherers,

Steep'd in the colours of their trade, their daggers

Unmannerly breech'd with gore.[⑧] Who could refrain[⑨],

That had a heart to love, and in that heart

Courage to make's love known?

LADY MACBETH. Help me hence, ho!

---

① stopp'd: 等于 stopped

② badged: 有标记的

③ unwiped: 没有擦去的

④ pillow: 枕头

⑤ repent: 对（自己的所为）感到懊悔或忏悔

⑥ 参考译文：谁能够在惊愕之中保持冷静，在盛怒之中保持镇定，在激于忠愤的时候，保持他的不偏不倚的精神？（朱生豪译）（temperate: 有节制的，温和的；furious: 狂怒的，暴怒的）

⑦ 参考译文：我的理智来不及控制我的愤激的忠诚。（朱生豪译）（expedition: 迅速（办理）；outrun: 超出，跑得比……快；pauser: 中止者）

⑧ 参考译文：那边站着这两个凶手，身上浸润着他们罪恶的颜色，他们的刀上凝结着刺目的血块。（朱生豪译）（steep'd: 等于 steeped，浸泡的，渗透的；trade: 行业，买卖；unmannerly: 粗鲁地；gore: 流出的血，血块）

⑨ refrain: 抑制，克制（例如：I refrained from making any comment. 我忍住不作任何评论。）

MACDUFF. Look to① the lady.

MALCOLM. [Aside to DONALBAIN.] Why do we hold our tongues②,

That most may claim this argument for ours?

DONALBAIN. [Aside to MALCOLM.] What should be spoken here, where our fate,

Hid in an auger hole, may rush and seize us?③

Let's away④. Our tears are not yet brew'd⑤.

MALCOLM. [Aside to DONALBAIN.] Nor our strong sorrow

Upon the foot of motion.⑥

BANQUO. Look to the lady.

[Exit LADY MACBETH, aided.]

And when we have our naked frailties hid,

That suffer in exposure, let us meet,

And question this most bloody piece of work,

To know it further.⑦ Fears and scruples shake us:

In the great hand of God I stand, and thence

Against the undivulged pretence I fight

Of treasonous malice.⑧

MACDUFF. And so do I.

ALL. So all.

MACBETH. Let's briefly put on⑨ manly readiness

And meet i' the hall together.

ALL. Well contented.

---

① look to：照看，照顾

② hold our tongues：一言不发

③ 参考译文：我们身陷危境，不可测的命运随时都会吞噬我们，还有什么话好说呢？（朱生豪译）（auger：螺旋钻；rush：突袭）

④ away：等于 go away，消失，离开

⑤ brew'd：等于 brewed，酝酿，这里指流泪

⑥ 参考译文：也不是大放悲声的场合。（朱生豪译）（motion：运动，手势）

⑦ 参考译文：等我们把自然流露出来的无遮饰的弱点收藏起来以后，让我们举行一次会议，详细彻查这一件最残酷的血案的真相。（朱生豪译）（frailty：缺点，弱点；question：质问，询问）

⑧ 参考译文：恐惧和疑虑使我们惊惶失措，站在上帝的伟大的指导之下，我一定要从尚未揭发的假面具下面，探出叛逆的阴谋，和它作殊死的奋斗。（朱生豪译）（scruple：良心上的不安，顾虑，顾忌；undivulged：未经透露的；treasonous：叛逆的，不忠的；malice：恶意，怨恨）

⑨ put on：穿上，表现出

[Exeunt all but Malcolm and Donalbain.]

MALCOLM. What will you do? Let's not consort with[①] them.

To show an unfelt sorrow is an office
Which the false man does easy.[②] I'll to England.

DONALBAIN. To Ireland, I; our separated fortune
Shall keep us both the safer. Where we are,
There's daggers in men's smiles; the near in blood,
The nearer bloody.[③]

MALCOLM. This murtherous shaft that's shot
Hath not yet lighted, and our safest way
Is to avoid the aim.[④] Therefore to horse;
And let us not be dainty of leave-taking,
But shift away.[⑤] There's warrant in that theft
Which steals itself when there's no mercy left.[⑥]

[Exeunt.]

---

① consort with：陪伴；与（某人）来往
② 参考译文：假装一副悲哀的脸，是每一个奸人的拿手好戏。（朱生豪译）（unfelt：无感情的，不感动的；office：举动，行为；easy：easily，容易地）
③ 参考译文：我们现在所在的地方，人们的笑脸里都暗藏着利刃；越是跟我们血统相近的人，越是想喝我们的血。（朱生豪译）（blood：血缘关系；bloody：血腥的，残忍的）
④ 参考译文：杀人的利箭已经射出，可是还没有落下，避过它的目标是我们唯一的活路。（朱生豪译）（murtherous：蓄意谋杀的，残忍的；shaft：矛，箭；light：点火，发亮；aim：目标）
⑤ 参考译文：让我们不要拘于告别的礼貌，趁着有便就溜出去。（朱生豪译）（dainty：讲究的，挑剔的；shift away：离开）
⑥ 参考译文：明知没有网开一面的希望，就该及早逃避弋人的罗网。（朱生豪译）（warrant：正当理由，依据；theft：偷窃，失窃案例）

51

SCENE IV.
The Same. Outside MACBETH's Castle.

[Enter ROSS and an Old Man.]

Old Man. <u>Threescore and ten I can remember well,</u>
<u>Within the volume of which time I have seen</u>
<u>Hours dreadful and things strange, but this sore night</u>
<u>Hath trifled former knowings.</u>①

ROSS. Ha, good father,
<u>Thou seest, the heavens, as troubled with man's act,</u>
<u>Threaten his bloody stage. By the clock, 'tis day,</u>
<u>And yet dark night strangles the travelling lamp.</u>②
<u>Is't night's predominance, or the day's shame,</u>
<u>That darkness does the face of earth entomb,</u>
<u>When living light should kiss it?</u>③

Old Man. 'Tis unnatural,
Even like the deed that's done. On Tuesday last,
<u>A falcon, towering in her pride of place,</u>
<u>Was by a mousing owl hawk'd at and kill'd.</u>④

ROSS. And Duncan's horses, a thing most strange and certain,
Beauteous⑤ and swift⑥, the minions⑦ of their race,

---

① 参考译文：我已经活了七十个年头，惊心动魄的日子也经过得不少，稀奇古怪的事情也看到过不少，可是像这样可怕的夜晚，却还是第一次遇见。（朱生豪译）（threescore：六十，六十岁；sore：疼痛的，使人伤心的；trifle：轻视，小看）

② 参考译文：你看上天好像恼怒人类的行为，在向这流血的舞台发出恐吓。照钟上现在应该是白天了，可是黑夜的魔手却把那盏在天空中运行的明灯遮蔽得不露一丝光亮。（朱生豪译）（strangle：扼死，使窒息）

③ 参考译文：难道黑夜已经统治一切，还是因为白昼不好意思抬起头来，所以在这应该有阳光遍吻大地的时候，地面上却被无边的黑暗所笼罩？（朱生豪译）（predominance：主导或支配的地位，运星主宰；entomb：埋葬）

④ 正常语序应为：A falcon, towering in her pride of place, was hawk'd at and kill'd by a mousing owl. 参考译文：有一头雄踞在高岩上的猛鹰，被一只吃田鼠的鸱鸮飞来啄死了。（朱生豪译）（falcon：猎鹰；mousing：捕鼠的；hawk'd：等于 hawked，袭击）

⑤ beauteous：美丽的

⑥ swift：迅速的，敏捷的

⑦ minions：宠儿

Turn'd wild in nature, broke their stalls[1], flung out[2],

Contending[3] 'gainst obedience, as they would

Make war with mankind.

Old Man. 'Tis said they eat each other.

ROSS. They did so, to the amazement of mine eyes,

That look'd upon't.

Here comes the good Macduff.

[Enter MACDUFF.]

How goes the world, sir, now?

MACDUFF. Why, see you not?

ROSS. Is't known who did this more than bloody deed?

MACDUFF. Those that Macbeth hath slain[4].

ROSS. Alas, the day!

What good could they pretend?

MACDUFF. They were suborn'd[5]:

Malcolm and Donalbain, the King's two sons,

Are stol'n[6] away and fled; which puts upon them

Suspicion of the deed.[7]

ROSS. 'Gainst nature still!

Thriftless ambition, that wilt ravin up

Thine own life's means![8] Then 'tis most like

The sovereignty will fall upon Macbeth.

MACDUFF. He is already named[9], and gone to Scone[10]

To be invested[11].

---

① stall：畜栏

② fling out：（尤指生气地）扔出，冲出

③ contend：争夺，搏斗

④ slain：slay 的过去分词，杀死，宰杀

⑤ suborn'd：suborned，教唆，收买

⑥ stol'n：stolen，悄悄地走

⑦ 正常语序应为：which puts suspicion of the deed upon them。参考译文：这使他们也蒙上了嫌疑。（朱生豪译）（suspicion：怀疑，嫌疑；the deed：这件事，指邓肯被杀）

⑧ 参考译文：反噬自己的命根，这样的野心会有什么好结果呢？（朱生豪译）（thriftless：浪费的；wilt：凋谢，（使）枯萎；ravin：猎食，掠夺）

⑨ named：指定的

⑩ Scone：斯贡（苏格兰王加冕的地方）

⑪ invest：使就职，给……穿衣，这里指给麦克白穿皇袍，加冕

ROSS. Where is Duncan's body?

MACDUFF. Carried to Colmekill,

The sacred storehouse① of his predecessors②,

And guardian of their bones.

ROSS. Will you to Scone?

MACDUFF. No, cousin, I'll to Fife.

ROSS. Well, I will thither.

MACDUFF. Well, may you see things well done there.

Adieu③!

Lest our old robes sit easier than our new!④

ROSS. Farewell⑤, father.

Old Man. God's benison go with you; and with those

That would make good of bad, and friends of foes!⑥

[Exeunt.]

---

① storehouse：仓库，存放东西的地方
② predecessor：祖先
③ adieu：再见
④ 参考译文：怕只怕我们的新衣服不及旧衣服舒服哩！（朱生豪译）(lest：唯恐，生怕)
⑤ farewell：告别，再见
⑥ 参考译文：上帝祝福您，也祝福那些把恶事化成善事，把仇敌化为朋友的人们！（朱生豪译）(benison：祝福；of：out of；foe：敌人)

Act III

SCENE I.
Forres. The Palace.

[Enter BANQUO.]

BANQUO. Thou hast it now: King, Cawdor, Glamis, all,

As the weird women promised, and, I fear

Thou play'dst① most foully for't②; yet it was said

It should not stand in thy posterity③,

But that myself should be the root and father

Of many kings. If there come truth from them—

As upon thee, Macbeth, their speeches shine—

Why, by the verities on thee made good,

May they not be my oracles as well,

And set me up in hope?④ But hush! No more.

[Sennet⑤ sounded. Enter MACBETH as King, LADY MACBETH

as Queen, LENNOX, ROSS, Lords, Ladies, and Attendants.]

MACBETH. Here's our chief guest.

LADY MACBETH. If he had been forgotten,

It had been as a gap in our great feast,

And all-thing unbecoming.

MACBETH. To-night we hold a solemn⑥ supper sir,

And I'll request your presence.

BANQUO. Let Your Highness

Command upon me, to the which my duties

Are with a most indissoluble⑦ tie

---

① play'dst：played，耍（花招）

② for't：for it，指麦克白当上国王

③ posterity：后代，子孙

④ 参考译文：她们的话既然已经在你麦克白身上应验，那么难道不也会成为对我的启示，使我对未来发生希望吗？（朱生豪译）（verity：真理，事实；oracle：神谕，神示）

⑤ sennet：喇叭号声

⑥ solemn：庄严的，隆重的

⑦ indissoluble：牢固持久的

For ever knit.

MACBETH. Ride you this afternoon?

BANQUO. Ay, my good lord.

MACBETH. We should have else desired your good advice,

Which still hath been both grave and prosperous①

In this day's council; but we'll take to-morrow.

Is't far you ride?

BANQUO. As far, my lord, as will fill up the time

'Twixt② this and supper. Go not my horse the better,

I must become a borrower of the night

For a dark hour or twain.③

MACBETH. Fail not our feast.

BANQUO. My lord, I will not.

MACBETH. We hear our bloody cousins are bestow'd④

In England and in Ireland, not confessing

Their cruel parricide, filling their hearers

With strange invention. But of that to-morrow,

When therewithal we shall have cause of state

Craving us jointly⑤. Hie you to horse; adieu,

Till you return at night. Goes Fleance with you?

BANQUO. Ay, my good lord. Our time does call upon 's.

MACBETH. I wish your horses swift and sure of foot,

And so I do commend you to their backs.

Farewell.

[Exit BANQUO.]

Let every man be master of his time

Till seven at night; to make society

The sweeter welcome, we will keep ourself

---

① prosperous：繁荣的，兴旺的
② 'twixt：古英语，两者之间
③ 参考译文：要是我的马不跑得快一些，也许要到天黑以后一两小时才能回来。（朱生豪译）
④ bestow'd：等于 bestowed，给……提供住宿，让……留宿
⑤ 参考译文：他们不承认他们的残酷的弑父重罪，却到处向人传播离奇荒谬的谣言；可是我们明天再谈吧，有许多重要的国事要等候我们两人共同处理呢。（朱生豪译）（parricide：杀父母（罪）；therewithal：于是，随其；crave：要求，需要）

Till suppertime alone. While then, God be with you!

[Exeunt all but MACBETH, and an Attendant.]

Sirrah, a word with you. Attend those men

Our pleasure? [①]

ATTENDANT. They are, my lord, without the palace gate.

MACBETH. Bring them before us.

[Exit Attendant.]

To be thus is nothing,

But to be safely thus. Our fears in Banquo.

Stick deep, and in his royalty of nature

Reigns that which would be fear'd. [②] 'Tis much he dares,

And, to that dauntless temper of his mind,

He hath a wisdom that doth guide his valour

To act in safety. [③] There is none but he

Whose being I do fear; and under him

My Genius is rebuked [④]; as, it is said,

Mark Antony [⑤]'s was by Caesar [⑥]. He chid the sisters

When first they put the name of king upon me,

And bade them speak to him; then prophet-like

They hail'd him father to a line of kings. [⑦]

Upon my head they placed a fruitless crown,

And put a barren sceptre [⑧] in my gripe [⑨],

---

① 正常语序应为：Those men attend our pleasure? 参考译文：那两个人是不是在外面等候着我的旨意？（朱生豪译）

② 参考译文：我对于班柯怀着深切的恐惧，他的高贵的天性中有一种使我生畏的东西。（朱生豪译）（royalty：皇室，贵族；reign：当政，统治）这也是双关语，royalty 和 reign 除了指班柯天性中的皇室风范，也指女巫预言中班柯后人会成为苏格兰国王。

③ 参考译文：他是个敢作敢为的人，在他的无畏的精神上，又加上深沉的智虑，指导他的胆勇在确有把握的时机行动。（朱生豪译）（dauntless：无所畏惧的）

④ rebuke：使相形见绌（例如：Her carefulness rebukes me. 她的仔细认真让我相形见绌。）

⑤ Mark Antony：马克·安东尼（公元前 83 年 – 公元前 30 年）是一位古罗马政治家和军事统帅、政治家。他是恺撒最重要的军队指挥官和管理人员之一。

⑥ Caesar：盖乌斯·尤利乌斯·恺撒（公元前 102 年 – 公元前 44 年），罗马共和国末期的军事统帅、政治家。公元前 49 年，他率军占领罗马，打败庞培，集大权于一身，实行独裁统治。公元前 44 年，恺撒遭暗杀身亡。

⑦ 参考译文：当那些女巫们最初称我为王的时候，他呵斥她们，叫她们对他说话；她们就像先知似的说他的子孙将相继为王。（朱生豪译）（chid：责备；bade，是 bid 的过去式，吩咐）

⑧ barren sceptre：光秃秃的皇权，指女巫预言的麦克白自己会成为苏格兰国王，但子孙不会成为国王

⑨ gripe：控制，紧握

Thence to be wrench'd with an unlineal hand,

No son of mine succeeding.① If 't be so,

For Banquo's issue have I filed my mind,

For them the gracious Duncan have I murther'd;

Put rancors in the vessel of my peace

Only for them, and mine eternal jewel

Given to the common enemy of man,

To make them Kings, the seed of Banquo Kings!②

Rather than so, come fate into the list,

And champion③ me to the utterance④! Who's there?

[Re-enter Attendant, with two Murtherers.]

Now go to the door, and stay there till we call.

[Exit Attendant.]

Was it not yesterday we spoke together?

First Murtherer. It was, so please Your Highness.

MACBETH. Well then, now

Have you consider'd of my speeches? Know

That it was he in the times past which held you

So under fortune, which you thought had been

Our innocent self.⑤ This I made good to you

In our last conference, pass'd in probation⑥ with you:

How you were borne in hand, how cross'd, the instruments,

Who wrought with them, and all things else that might

To half a soul and to a notion crazed

---

① 参考译文：然后再从我的手里夺去，我的子孙得不到继承。（朱生豪译）（unlineal：非直系的）

② 参考译文：那么我玷污了我的手，只是为了班柯后裔的好处；我为了他们暗杀了仁慈的邓肯；为了他们良心上负着重大的罪疚和不安；我把我的永生的灵魂给了人类的公敌，只是为了使他们可以登上王座，使班柯的种子登上王座！（朱生豪译）（rancor：深仇，怨恨；eternal：永久的）

③ champion：为……而斗争，捍卫（例如：He passionately championed his country. 他满腔热情地捍卫他的国家。）

④ utterance：言语，言论（例如：the president's public utterances 总统的公开讲话）

⑤ 参考译文：你们知道从前都是因为他的缘故，使你们屈身微贱，虽然你们却错怪到我的身上。（朱生豪译）

⑥ probation：查验，察看

Say 'Thus did Banquo.' [1]

First Murtherer. You made it known to us.

MACBETH. I did so, and went further, which is now
　　Our point of second meeting. Do you find
　　Your patience so predominant[2] in your nature,
　　That you can let this go? Are you so gospell'd[3]
　　To pray for this good man and for his issue,
　　Whose heavy hand hath bow'd you to the grave
　　And beggar'd yours for ever?

First Murtherer. We are men, my liege.

MACBETH. Ay, in the catalogue ye go for men,
　　As hounds and greyhounds, mongrels, spaniels, curs,
　　Shoughs, waterrugs and demi-wolves, are clept
　　All by the name of dogs.[4] The valued file
　　Distinguishes the swift, the slow, the subtle,
　　The housekeeper, the hunter, every one
　　According to the gift which bounteous[5] nature
　　Hath in him closed, whereby he does receive
　　Particular addition, from the bill
　　That writes them all alike; and so of men.
　　Now if you have a station in the file,
　　Not i' the worst rank of manhood, say't,
　　And I will put that business in your bosoms,
　　Whose execution takes your enemy off,
　　Grapples you to the heart and love of us,
　　Who wear our health but sickly in his life,

---

① 参考译文：指出你们怎么被人操纵愚弄、怎样首任牵制压抑、人家对你们是用怎样的手段、这种手段的主动者是谁，以及一切其他的种种，都可以使一个半痴的疯癫的人恍然大悟地说："这些都是班柯干的事。"（朱生豪译）（instrument：手段）

② predominant：主要的，占主导地位的（例如：The predominant feature of his character was pride. 他的性格中主要的特点是骄傲。）

③ gospell'd：等于 gospelled，传播福音的，这里指被说服

④ 参考译文：正像家狗、野狗、猎狗、巴儿狗、狮子狗、杂种狗、癞皮狗，统称为狗一样。（朱生豪译）（mongrel：杂种狗；spaniel：西班牙狗；cur：野狗；shough：卷毛小巴儿狗；clept：clepe 的过去式和过去分词，命名为）

⑤ bounteous：慷慨的，丰富的

59

Which in his death were perfect.[1]

Second Murtherer. I am one, my liege,

Whom the vile blows and buffets of the world

Have so incensed that I am reckless what

I do to spite the world.[2]

First Murtherer. And I another

So weary with disasters, tugg'd with fortune,

That I would set my lie on any chance,

To mend it, or be rid on't.[3]

MACBETH. Both of you

Know Banquo was your enemy.

Both Murtherers. True, my lord.

MACBETH. So is he mine, and in such bloody distance

That every minute of his being thrusts

Against my near'st of life[4]; and though I could

With barefaced[5] power sweep him from my sight

And bid my will avouch[6] it, yet I must not,

For certain friends that are both his and mine,

Whose loves I may not drop, but wail his fall

Who I myself struck down; and thence it is

That I to your assistance do make love,

Masking the business from the common eye,

For sundry weighty reasons.[7]

---

① 参考译文：要是你们在人类的行列之中，并不属于最卑劣的一级，那么说吧，我就可以把一件事情信托你们，你们照我的话干了以后，不但可以除去你们的仇人，而且还可以永远受我的眷宠；他一天活在世上，我的心病一天不能痊愈。（朱生豪译）（rank：等级，级别；grapple：抓住，抓牢；wear：磨损，消耗）

② 参考译文：陛下，我久受世间无情的打击和虐待，为了向这世界发泄我的怨恨起见，我什么事都愿意干。（朱生豪译）（vile：无情的；buffet：反复拍打，猛击；spite：向……泄愤）

③ 参考译文：我也是这样，一次次的灾祸逆运使我厌倦于人世，我愿意拿我的生命去赌博，或者从此交上好运，或者了结我的一生。（朱生豪译）（tugg'd：等于tugged，抗争，斗争；rid：了结）

④ 参考译文：而且他是我的肘腋之患，他的存在每一分钟都威胁着我生命的安全。（朱生豪译）（thrust：刺）

⑤ barefaced：公然的，毫不客气的

⑥ avouch：做出保证

⑦ 参考译文：即使我亲手把他打倒，也必须假意为他的死亡悲泣；所以我只好借重你们两人的助力，为了许多重要的理由，把这件事情遮过一般人的眼睛。（朱生豪译）（wail：哭泣）

Second Murtherer. We shall, my lord,

Perform what you command us.

First Murtherer. Though our lives—

MACBETH. Your spirits shine through you. <u>Within this hour at</u>

<u>most,</u>

<u>I will advise you where to plant yourselves,</u>

<u>Acquaint you with the perfect spy o' the time,</u>

<u>The moment on't; for't must be done to-night,</u>

<u>And something from the palace; always thought</u>

<u>That I require a clearness:</u>① and with him—

<u>To leave no rubs② nor botches③ in the work—</u>

<u>Fleance his son, that keeps him company,</u>

<u>Whose absence is no less material to me</u>

<u>Than is his father's, must embrace the fate</u>

<u>Of that dark hour.</u>④ Resolve yourselves apart;

I'll come to you anon⑤.

Both Murtherers. We are resolved, my lord.

MACBETH. I'll call upon you straight. Abide⑥ within.

[Exeunt Murtherers.]

It is concluded: Banquo, thy soul's flight,

If it find heaven, must find it out to-night.

[Exit.]

---

① 参考译文：最迟在这一小时之内，我就可以告诉你们在什么地方埋伏，在什么时间动手；因为这件事情一定要在今晚干好，而且要离开王宫远一些，你们必须记住不能把我牵涉在内。（plant：安插；something：相当于 somewhere，某个地方；clearness：干净，清白）

② rub：擦伤，摩擦

③ botch：笨拙的工作

④ 参考译文：你们还要把跟在他身边的他的儿子弗里恩斯也一起杀了，他们父子两人的死，对于我是同样重要的，必须让他们同时接受黑暗的命运。（朱生豪译）

⑤ anon：立刻

⑥ abide：停留

SCENE II.

Inside the Palace at Forres.

[Enter LADY MACBETH and a Servant.]

LADY MACBETH. Is Banquo gone from court?

Servant. Ay, madam, but returns again to-night.

LADY MACBETH. Say to the King, I would attend his leisure

For a few words.

Servant. Madam, I will.

[Exit.]

LADY MACBETH. Nought①'s had, all's spent,

Where our desire is got without content.②

'Tis safer to be that which we destroy,

Than by destruction dwell in doubtful joy.③

[Enter MACBETH.]

How now, my lord? Why do you keep alone,

Of sorriest fancies your companions making,

Using those thoughts which should indeed have died

With them they think on?④ Things without all remedy⑤

Should be without regard. What's done is done.

MACBETH. We have scotch'd⑥ the snake, not kill'd it.

She'll close⑦ and be herself, whilst⑧ our poor malice

Remains in danger of her former tooth.

But let the frame of things disjoint, both the worlds suffer,

Ere we will eat our meal in fear and sleep

---

① nought: 零；无

② 参考译文：费尽了一切，结果还是一无所得，我们的目的虽然达到，却一点不感觉满足。（朱生豪译）

③ 参考译文：要是用毁灭他人的手段，使自己置身在充满忧疑的欢娱里，那么还不如那被我们所害的人，倒落得无忧无虑。（朱生豪译）（dwell：存在于）

④ 参考译文：让最悲哀的幻想做您的伴侣，把您的思想念念不忘地集中在一个已死者的身上？（朱生豪译）

⑤ remedy: 补救

⑥ scotch'd: 等于 scotched，为 scotch 的过去式（scotch：使受伤，弄伤）

⑦ close: 复原，恢复

⑧ whilst: 与此同时

In the affliction of these terrible dreams

That shake us nightly: better be with the dead,

Whom we, to gain our peace, have sent to peace,

Than on the torture of the mind to lie

In restless ecstasy.① Duncan is in his grave;

After life's fitful fever he sleeps well;

Treason has done his worst; nor steel, nor poison,

Malice domestic, foreign levy, nothing,

Can touch him further.②

LADY MACBETH. Come on,

Gentle my lord, sleek o'er③ your rugged④ looks;

Be bright and jovial⑤ among your guests to-night.

MACBETH. So shall I, love, and so, I pray, be you.

Let your remembrance apply to Banquo;

Present him eminence⑥, both with eye and tongue:

Unsafe the while, that we

Must lave our honours in these flattering streams,

And make our faces vizards to our hearts,

Disguising what they are.⑦

LADY MACBETH. You must leave this.

MACBETH. O, full of scorpions⑧ is my mind, dear wife!

Thou know'st that Banquo, and his Fleance, lives.

---

① 句子主干是：But let the frame of things disjoint...ere we will eat our meal in fear and sleep. That shake us nightly 作定语，修饰 dreams；better be with the dead...than on the torture of the mind to lie in restless ecstasy 这一对比说明麦克白夫妇都深受恐惧和良心的折磨；Whom we...have sent to peace 作定语，修饰 the dead。参考译文：让活人死人都去受罪吧，为什么我们要在忧虑中进餐，在每夜使我们惊恐的噩梦的虐弄中睡眠呢？我们为了希求自身的平安，把别人送下坟墓里去享受永久的平安，可是我们的心灵却把我们折磨得没有一刻平静的安息，使我们觉得还是跟已死的人在一起，倒要幸福得多了。（朱生豪译）（disjoint：解体；affliction：苦难，折磨；torture：折磨）

② 参考译文：经过一场人生的热病，他现在睡得好好的，叛逆已经对他施过最狠毒的伤害，再没有刀剑、毒药、内乱、外患，可以加害于他了。（朱生豪译）

③ sleek o'er: sleek over，掩饰，使整洁

④ rugged: 凹凸不平的，这里指烦恼的，皱着眉的

⑤ jovial: 快乐的，好交际的

⑥ eminence: 显赫，卓越

⑦ 参考译文：我们的地位现在还没有巩固，必须把我们的尊严濡染在这种谄媚的流水里，用我们的外貌遮掩着我们的内心，不要给人家窥破。（朱生豪译）（lave：洗涤，沐浴；flattering：奉承的，谄媚的；vizard：面颊，面具）

⑧ scorpion: 蝎子，恶毒的人

63

LADY MACBETH. But in them nature's copy's not eterne①.

MACBETH. There's comfort yet; they are assailable.

Then be thou jocund.② Ere the bat hath flown

His cloister'd flight, ere to black Hecate's summons

The shard-borne beetle with his drowsy hums

Hath rung night's yawning peal, there shall be done

A deed of dreadful note.③

LADY MACBETH. What's to be done?

MACBETH. Be innocent of the knowledge, dearest chuck④,

Till thou applaud⑤ the deed. Come, seeling night,

Scarf up the tender eye of pitiful day,

And with thy bloody and invisible hand

Cancel and tear to pieces that great bond

Which keeps me pale!⑥ Light thickens, and the crow

Makes wing to the rooky⑦ wood;

Good things of day begin to droop and drowse,

While night's black agents to their preys do rouse.⑧

Thou marvell'st⑨ at my words, but hold thee still:

Things bad begun make strong themselves by ill.

So, prithee, go with me.

[Exeunt.]

---

① eterne：古英语，永久的，长生不老的

② 参考译文：那还可以给我几分安慰，他们是可以侵害的。（朱生豪译）（assailable：受攻击的，有隙可乘的；jocund：快活的，高兴的）

③ 参考译文：所以你快乐起来吧。在蝙蝠完成它黑暗中的飞翔以前，在振翅而飞的甲虫应答着赫卡忒的呼唤，用嗡嗡的声音摇响催眠的晚钟以前，将要有一件可怕的事情干完。（朱生豪译）（shard-borne：展翅的；drowsy：昏昏欲睡的；yawning：催眠的；peal：隆隆声，洪亮的钟声）

④ chuck：亲爱的

⑤ applaud：鼓掌，拍手

⑥ 参考译文：来，使人盲目的黑夜，遮住可怜的白昼的温柔的眼睛，用你的无形的毒手，撕毁那使我畏惧的重大的束缚吧！（朱生豪译）（seeling：闭眼的，盲目的；scarf：遮住）

⑦ rooky：昏暗的

⑧ 参考译文：一天的好事开始沉沉睡去，黑夜的罪恶的使者却在准备攫捕他们的猎物。（朱生豪译）（prey：猎物）

⑨ marvell'st：等于 marvelled，惊讶于

64

SCENE III.
A Park near the Palace.

[Enter three Murtherers.]

First Murtherer. But who did bid thee join with us?

Third Murtherer. Macbeth.

Second Murtherer. He needs not our mistrust, since he delivers

Our offices and what we have to do,

To the direction just.[①]

First Murtherer. Then stand with us.

The west yet glimmers[②] with some streaks[③] of day;

Now spurs the lated traveller apace

To gain the timely inn, and near approaches

The subject of our watch.[④]

Third Murtherer. Hark[⑤]! I hear horses.

BANQUO. [Within.] Give us a light there, ho!

Second Murtherer. Then 'tis he: the rest

That are within the note of expectation

Already are i' the court.[⑥]

First Murtherer. His horses go about[⑦].

Third Murtherer. Almost a mile: but he does usually,

So all men do, from hence to the palace gate

Make it their walk.

---

① 正常语序应为：He needs not our mistrust, since he just delivers the direction and what we have to do to our offices. 参考译文：他不必不信任我们，他已经把我们的任务和怎样动手的方法都指示给我们了。（朱生豪译）(deliver：委托，托付)

② glimmer：闪烁（例如：The moon glimmered faintly through the mists. 月亮透过薄雾洒下微光。）

③ streak：条痕

④ 正常语序应为：Now the lated traveller spurs apace to gain the timely inn, and the subject of our watch approaches near. 参考译文：晚归的行客现在快马加鞭，要来找寻宿处了；我们守候的目标已经在那儿向我们走近。（朱生豪译）(the lated traveller：指班柯，下文的 the subject of our watch 也指班柯；spur：策马前进；apace：急速地，飞快地)

⑤ hark：听

⑥ 参考译文：别的客人们都已经到了宫里了。（朱生豪译）(note：通知；i' the court：等于 in the court，到宫里去)

⑦ go about：指人下马，由马夫牵过马转圈，等马落汗后再牵到马厩

Second Murtherer. A light, a light!

    [Enter BANQUO, and FLEANCE with a torch.]

Third Murtherer. 'Tis he.

First Murtherer. Stand to't^①.

BANQUO. It will be rain to-night.

First Murtherer. Let it come down.

    [They set upon BANQUO.]

BANQUO. O, treachery^②! Fly, good Fleance, fly, fly, fly!

    Thou mayst^③ revenge. O slave!

    [Dies. FLEANCE escapes.]

Third Murtherer. Who did strike out the light?

First Murtherer. Wast not the way?

Third Murtherer. There's but one down; the son is fled.

Second Murtherer. We have lost

    Best half of our affair^④.

First Murtherer. Well, let's away^⑤ and say how much is done.

    [Exeunt.]

---

① stand to't：准备好

② treachery：叛乱，阴谋

③ mayst：等于 might，也许

④ affair：事务，工作（例如：If they want to stay, then I guess that's their affair. 如果他们想留下来，我想那是他们自己的事。）

⑤ away：等于 go away，离开

66

SCENE IV.

The Same. Hall in the Palace.

[A banquet① prepared. Enter MACBETH, LADY MACBETH, ROSS, LENNOX, Lords, and Attendants.]

MACBETH. You know your own degrees; sit down. At first
And last the hearty② welcome.

Lords. Thanks to Your Majesty.

MACBETH. Ourself will mingle with③ society,
And play the humble④ host.
Our hostess keeps her state, but in best time
We will require her welcome.⑤

LADY MACBETH. Pronounce it for me, sir, to all our friends,
For my heart speaks they are welcome.

[Enter first Murtherer to the door.]

MACBETH. See, they encounter thee with their hearts' thanks.
Both sides are even; here I'll sit i' the midst.
Be large in mirth⑥; anon we'll drink a measure⑦
The table round. [Approaches the door.]
There's blood on thy face.

First Murtherer. 'Tis Banquo's then.

MACBETH. 'Tis better thee without than he within⑧.
Is he dispatch'd⑨?

First Murtherer. My lord, his throat is cut; that I did for him.

MACBETH. Thou art the best o' the cut-throats! Yet he's good

---

① banquet：宴会
② hearty：衷心的，热诚的
③ mingle with：加入
④ humble：谦逊的
⑤ 参考译文：我们的主妇现在还坐在她的宝座上，可是我就要请她对你们殷勤招待。（朱生豪译）（require her welcome：请她致欢迎词）
⑥ mirth：欢笑
⑦ measure：每人喝一口大杯传递的酒，作为一种祝酒方式
⑧ 参考译文：我宁愿你站在门外，不愿他置身室内。（朱生豪译）
⑨ dispatch'd：等于 dispatched，了结，杀死

That did the like for Fleance. If thou didst it,

Thou art the nonpareil.①

First Murtherer. Most royal sir,

Fleance is 'scaped.

MACBETH. Then comes my fit② again. I had else been perfect,

Whole as the marble, founded as the rock,

As broad and general as the casing air;

But now I am cabin'd, cribb'd, confin'd, bound in

To saucy doubts and fears.③ But Banquo's safe?

First Murtherer. Ay, my good lord. Safe in a ditch he bides④,

With twenty trenched⑤ gashes on his head,

The least a death to nature.⑥

MACBETH. Thanks for that.

There the grown serpent⑦ lies; the worm that's fled

Hath nature that in time will venom breed,

No teeth for the present.⑧ Get thee gone. To-morrow

We'll hear ourselves again.

[Exit Murtherer.]

LADY MACBETH. My royal lord,

You do not give the cheer. The feast is sold

That is not often vouch'd, while 'tis a-making,

'Tis given with welcome: to feed were best at home;

From thence the sauce to meat is ceremony;

---

① 参考译文：可是谁杀死了弗里恩斯，也一样值得夸奖；要是你也把他杀了，那你才是一个无比的好汉。（朱生豪译）（nonpareil：无敌的，无可比拟的）

② fit：(心病) 发作

③ 参考译文：我本来可以像大理石一样完整，像岩石一样坚固，像空气一样广大自由，现在我却被恼人的疑惑和恐惧所包围拘束。（朱生豪译）（marble：大理石；founded：有基础的；casing：周围的；cabin'd：等于 cabined，拘束的，狭窄的；crib：束缚；confine：限制；saucy：烦人的）

④ bide：居住

⑤ trenched：像沟一般深的

⑥ 参考译文：最轻的一道也可以致他死命。（朱生豪译）（a death to nature：足以致命）

⑦ grown serpent：大蛇，这里指班柯

⑧ 正常语序应为：the worm that's fled hath nature that will breed venom in time, for the present no teeth. 参考译文：那逃走了的小虫，将来会用它的毒液害人，可是现在它的齿牙还没有长成。（朱生豪译）（the worm：小虫，这里指班柯的儿子弗里恩斯；venom：毒液；in time：将来）

Meeting were bare without it.①

MACBETH. Sweet remembrancer②!

Now good digestion③ wait on appetite,

And health on both!

LENNOX. May't please Your Highness sit.④

[The Ghost of BANQUO enters and sits in MACBETH's place.]

MACBETH. Here had we now our country's honour roof'd,

Were the graced person of our Banquo present;⑤

Who may I rather challenge for unkindness

Than pity for mischance.⑥

ROSS. His absence, sir,

Lays blame upon his promise. Please't Your Highness

To grace us with your royal company.

MACBETH. The table's full.

LENNOX. Here is a place reserved, sir.

MACBETH. Where?

LENNOX. Here, my good lord. What is't that moves⑦ Your Highness?

MACBETH. Which of you have done this?

Lords. What, my good lord?

MACBETH. Thou canst⑧ not say I did it; never shake

Thy gory locks at me.⑨

---

① 正常语序应为：The feast that is not often vouch'd is sold, while 'tis a-making, 'tis given with welcome: to feed best were at home; from thence the sauce to meat is ceremony; without it meeting were bare. 参考译文：宴会上倘没有主人的殷勤招待，那就不是在请酒，而是在卖酒了；这倒不如在自己家里吃饭来得舒适呢。既然出来作客，在席面上最让人开胃的就是主人的礼节，缺少了它，那就会使合席失去了兴致的。（朱生豪译）（the feast：宴会；vouch'd：保证，担保；sauce：调味酱；ceremony：礼节，礼仪）

② remembrancer：提醒者

③ digestion：消化

④ 正常语序应为：May't Your Highness sit please. 参考译文：陛下请安坐。（朱生豪译）

⑤ 正常语序应为：Were the graced person of our Banquo present, we had now our country's honour roof'd here. 参考译文：要是班柯在座，那么全国的英俊，真可以说是汇集于一堂了。（朱生豪译）

⑥ 正常语序应为：Who I may rather challenge for unkindness than pity for mischance. 参考译文：我宁愿因为他的疏忽而嗔怪他，不愿因为他遭到什么意外而为他惋惜。（朱生豪译）（unkindness：怠慢；mischance：厄运，不幸）

⑦ move：脸色改变

⑧ canst：古英语用法，can 的第二人称单数现在时陈述语气，与 thou 连用

⑨ 参考译文：别这样对我摇着你的染着血的头发。（朱生豪译）（shake：摇动，摇晃；gory：血淋淋的，沾满血的；locks：头发）

ROSS. Gentlemen, rise; His Highness is not well.

LADY MACBETH. Sit, worthy friends; my lord is often thus,

And hath been from his youth. Pray you, keep seat.

The fit is momentary①; upon a thought

He will again be well. If much you note him,

You shall offend him and extend his passion:

Feed, and regard him not.②

Are you a man?

MACBETH. Ay, and a bold one, that dare look on that

Which might appal③ the devil.

LADY MACBETH. O proper stuff!

This is the very painting④ of your fear;

This is the air-drawn dagger which, you said,

Led you to Duncan. O, these flaws and starts,

Impostors to true fear, would well become

A woman's story at a winter's fire,

Authorized by her grandam.⑤ Shame itself!

Why do you make such faces? When all's done,

You look but on a stool⑥.

MACBETH. Prithee, see there! Behold! Look! Lo! How say you?

Why, what care I? If thou canst nod, speak too.

If charnel houses and our graves must send

Those that we bury back, our monuments

Shall be the maws of kites.⑦

---

① momentary：短暂的，瞬间的

② 正常语序应为：If you note him much, you shall offend him and extend his passion: Feed, and not regard him. 参考译文：要是你们太注意了他，他也许会动怒，发起狂来更加厉害；尽管自己吃喝，不要理他吧。（朱生豪译）（note：注意；regard：理会，注视）

③ appal：惊吓

④ painting：画

⑤ 参考译文：要是在冬天的火炉旁，听一个妇女讲述她的老祖母告诉她的故事的时候，那么这种情绪的冲动、恐惧的伪装，倒是非常合适的。（朱生豪译）（flaw：瑕疵，缺点；start：吃惊；impostor：骗子，这里指伪装）

⑥ stool：凳子

⑦ 参考译文：要是殡舍和坟墓必须把我们埋葬了的人送回世上，那么我们的坟墓都要变成鸷鸟的胃囊了。（朱生豪译）（charnel：停尸房；maw：动物的胃；kite：传说尸体被鸷鸟吃掉后，鬼魂就不会出现）

[Exit Ghost.]

LADY MACBETH. What, quite unmann'd in folly①?

MACBETH. If I stand here, I saw him.

LADY MACBETH. Fie, for shame!

MACBETH. Blood hath been shed ere now, i' the olden time,
Ere human statute purged the gentle weal;②
Ay, and since too, murthers have been perform'd
Too terrible for the ear. The times have been,
That, when the brains were out, the man would die,
And there an end; but now they rise again,
With twenty mortal murthers on their crowns,
And push us from our stools.③ This is more strange
Than such a murther is.

LADY MACBETH. My worthy lord,
Your noble friends do lack you.

MACBETH. I do forget.
Do not muse at④ me, my most worthy friends.
I have a strange infirmity⑤, which is nothing
To those that know me. Come, love and health to all;
Then I'll sit down. Give me some wine; fill full.
I drink to the general joy o' the whole table,
And to our dear friend Banquo, whom we miss.
Would he were here! To all, and him, we thirst,
And all to all!

Lords. Our duties and the pledge.

[Re-enter Ghost.]

MACBETH. Avaunt⑥! And quit my sight! Let the earth hide thee!

---

① folly：蠢笨，愚行
② 参考译文：在人类不曾制定法律保障公众福利以前的古代，杀人流血是不足为奇的事。（朱生豪译）（statute：法令；purge：清除，消除；weal：幸福，福利）
③ 参考译文：可是现在他们却会从坟墓中起来，他们的头上戴着二十件谋杀的重罪，把我们推下座位。（朱生豪译）（mortal：严重的）
④ muse at：（古英语）感到惊讶，感到惊异
⑤ infirmity：虚弱
⑥ avaunt：滚开，走开

Thy bones are marrowless[①], thy blood is cold;

Thou hast no speculation[②] in those eyes

Which thou dost glare with.

LADY MACBETH. Think of this, good peers,

But as a thing of custom. 'Tis no other,

Only it spoils[③] the pleasure of the time.

MACBETH. What man dare, I dare.

Approach thou like the rugged[④] Russian bear,

The arm'd rhinoceros[⑤], or the Hyrcan tiger;

Take any shape but that, and my firm nerves

Shall never tremble: or be alive again,

And dare me to the desert with thy sword;

If trembling I inhabit then, protest me

The baby of a girl.[⑥] Hence, horrible shadow!

Unreal mockery[⑦], hence!

[Exit Ghost.]

Why, so, being gone,

I am a man again. Pray you, sit still.

LADY MACBETH. You have displaced[⑧] the mirth, broke the good

meeting,

With most admired disorder.

MACBETH. Can such things be,

And overcome us like a summer's cloud,

Without our special wonder? You make me strange

Even to the disposition that I owe,

When now I think you can behold such sights,

---

① marrowless：无力的

② speculation：思考，思索

③ spoil：破坏

④ rugged：粗暴的

⑤ rhinoceros：犀牛

⑥ 参考译文：只要不是你现在的样子，我的坚定的神经绝不会起半分战栗；或者你现在死而复活，用你的剑向我挑战，要是我会惊惶胆怯，那么你就可以宣称我是一个少女怀抱中的婴孩。（朱生豪译）

⑦ mockery：嘲弄，模仿

⑧ displace：取代，移走

And keep the natural ruby of your cheeks,

When mine is blanch'd with fear.[①]

ROSS. What sights, my lord?

LADY MACBETH. I pray you, speak not; he grows worse and worse;

Question enrages[②] him. At once, good night.

Stand not upon the order of your going,

But go at once.[③]

LENNOX. Good night; and better health

Attend His Majesty!

LADY MACBETH. A kind good night to all!

[Exeunt all but MACBETH and LADY MACBETH.]

MACBETH. It will have blood; they say blood will have blood.

Stones have been known to move and trees to speak;

Augurs and understood relations have

By magot pies and choughs and rooks brought forth

The secret'st man of blood.[④] What is the night?

LADY MACBETH. Almost at odds with morning, which is which.

MACBETH. How say'st thou, that Macduff denies his person

At our great bidding?

LADY MACBETH. Did you send to him, sir?

MACBETH. I hear it by the way, but I will send.

There's not a one of them but in his house

I keep a servant fee'd[⑤] I will to-morrow,

And betimes I will, to the weird sisters[⑥].

---

① 参考译文：我吓得面无人色，你们眼看着这样的怪象，你们的脸上却仍然保持着天然的红润，这才怪哩。（朱生豪译）（disposition：性情，性格；behold：看到，注视；ruby：红润的；blanch'd：blanched，惨白的）

② enrage：激怒，使暴怒（例如：He was enraged to find his employees had disobeyed his orders. 发现员工违抗了他的命令，老板极为恼火。）

③ 参考译文：大家不必推先让后，请立刻就去。（朱生豪译）

④ 参考译文：他们说，流血是免不了的；流血必须引起流血。据说石块曾经自己转动，树木曾经开口说话；鸦鹊的鸣声里已经预示着阴谋作乱的人。（朱生豪译）（augur：预示，预兆；chough：红嘴乌鸦；rook：秃鼻乌鸦；bring forth：出示，展示；secret'st：隐匿，隐藏）

⑤ 参考译文：他们这一批人家里谁都有一个被我买通的仆人，替我窥探他们的动静。（朱生豪译）

⑥ weird sisters：指三个女巫（weird：超自然的，会巫术的）

More shall they speak; for now I am bent to① know,
By the worst means, the worst. For mine own good,
All causes shall give way. I am in blood
Stepp'd in so far that, should I wade no more,
Returning were as tedious as go o'er.②
Strange things I have in head that will to hand,
Which must be acted ere they may be scann'd.③

LADY MACBETH. You lack the season④ of all natures, sleep.

MACBETH. Come, we'll to sleep. My strange and self-abuse
Is the initiate fear that wants hard use:
We are yet but young in deed.⑤

[Exeunt.]

---

① be bent to：下定决心，专心做某事
② 参考译文：为了我自己的好处，只好把一切置之不顾。我已经两足深陷于血泊之中，要是不再涉血前进，那么回头的路也是同样使人厌倦的。（cause：理由；give way：让路；stepp'd：stepped，前进；wade：跋涉）
③ 参考译文：我想起了一些非常的计谋，必须在不曾被人察觉以前迅速实行。（朱生豪译）（scann'd：scanned，细看，细查）
④ season：（废语）调剂
⑤ 参考译文：我的疑鬼疑神、出乖露丑，都是因为未经历练、心怀恐惧的缘故；我们在行事上太缺少经验了。（朱生豪译）（self-abuse：自责，自虐；initiate：最初的，开始的）

SCENE V.
A Heath.

[Thunder. Enter the three Witches, meeting HECATE.]

First Witch. Why, how now, Hecate! you look angerly.

HECATE. Have I not reason, beldams[①] as you are,

Saucy[②] and overbold[③]? How did you dare

To trade and traffic[④] with Macbeth

In riddles[⑤] and affairs of death;

And I, the mistress of your charms,

The close contriver of all harms,

Was never call'd to bear my part,

Or show the glory of our art?[⑥]

And, which is worse, all you have done

Hath been but for a wayward son,

Spiteful and wrathful, who, as others do,

Loves for his own ends, not for you.[⑦]

But make amends[⑧] now. Get you gone,

And at the pit of Acheron[⑨]

Meet me i' the morning. Thither he

Will come to know his destiny.

Your vessels and your spells provide,

Your charms and every thing beside.[⑩]

---

① beldam：恶婆
② saucy：粗鲁的，莽撞的
③ overbold：过于大胆的，冒失的
④ traffic：非法交易
⑤ riddle：谜语
⑥ 参考译文：我是你们魔法的总管，一切的灾祸都由我主持支配，你们却不通知我一声，让我也来显一显我们的神通？（朱生豪译）(mistress：主人；charm：魔力；contriver：创造者)
⑦ 参考译文：而且你们所干的事，都只是为了一个刚愎自用、残忍狂暴的人；他像所有的世人一样，只知道自己的利益，一点不是对你们存着什么好意。（朱生豪译）(wayward：刚愎自用的；spiteful：恶意的；wrathful：愤怒的)
⑧ amend：改正，改善
⑨ Acheron：希腊神话中的地狱，阴间
⑩ 参考译文：把你们的符咒、魔蛊和一切应用的东西预备齐整，不得有误。（朱生豪译）(vessel：法器；spell：符咒)

I am for the air; this night I'll spend
Unto a dismal and a fatal end.①
Great business must be wrought ere noon:
Upon the corner of the moon
There hangs a vaporous drop profound;
I'll catch it ere it come to ground.

And that distill'd by magic sleights,
Shall raise such artificial sprites
As by the strength of their illusion
Shall draw him on to his confusion.②
He shall spurn fate, scorn death, and bear
He hopes 'bove wisdom, grace, and fear.
And you all know security
Is mortals' chiefest enemy.③
[Music and a song within, 'Come away, come away.']
Hark! I am call'd; my little spirit, see,
Sits in a foggy cloud, and stays for me.
[Exit.]

First Witch. Come, let's make haste④; she'll soon be back again.

[Exeunt.]

---

①　参考译文：我现在乘风而去，今晚我要用整夜的工夫，布置出一场悲惨的结果。（朱生豪译）（dismal：阴沉的；fatal：致命的）

②　参考译文：用魔术提炼以后，就可以凭着它呼灵召鬼，让种种虚妄的幻影迷乱了他的本性。（朱生豪译）（distill：提取，提炼；sleight：手法，法术；illusion：幻觉，错觉）

③　参考译文：他将要藐视命运，唾斥死生，超越一切的情理，排弃一切的疑虑，执著他的不可能的希望，你们都知道自信是人类最大的仇敌。（朱生豪译）（spurn：蔑视；scorn：轻蔑，嘲笑；security：自信；mortal：凡人，人类）

④　haste：赶紧，匆忙

SCENE VI.
Forres. The Palace.

[Enter LENNOX and another Lord.]

LENNOX. My former speeches have but hit your thoughts,

Which can interpret further: only, I say,

Things have been strangely borne. The gracious Duncan

Was pitied[①] of Macbeth; marry, he was dead.

And the right-valiant Banquo walk'd too late,

Whom, you may say, if't please you, Fleance kill'd,

For Fleance fled: men must not walk too late.

Who cannot want the thought, how monstrous

It was for Malcolm and for Donalbain

To kill their gracious father?[②] Damned fact!

How it did grieve Macbeth! Did he not straight,

In pious rage, the two delinquents tear,

That were the slaves of drink and thralls of sleep?[③]

Was not that nobly done? Ay, and wisely too,

For 'twould have anger'd any heart alive

To hear the men deny't.[④] So that, I say,

He has borne all things well; and I do think

That, had he Duncan's sons under his key[⑤]—

As, an't please heaven, he shall not—they should find

What 'twere to kill a father; so should Fleance.[⑥]

---

① pitied：哀悼的，可怜的

② 参考译文：哪一个人不以为马尔科姆和道纳本杀死他们仁慈的父亲，是一件多么惊人的巨变？（朱生豪译）(monstrous：怪异的，惊人的)

③ 正常语序应为：Did he not straight tear the two delinquents, that were the slaves of drink and thralls of sleep in pious rage? 参考译文：他不是乘着一时的忠愤，把那两个酗酒贪睡的溺职卫士杀了吗？（朱生豪译）(pious：十分的；delinquent：渎职的人；thrall：奴隶，奴役)

④ 参考译文：嗯，而且也干得很聪明；因为要是人家听见他们抵赖他们的罪状，谁都会怒从心起的。（朱生豪译）('twould: it would; deny't: deny it, 否认)

⑤ key：拘禁，锁上

⑥ 参考译文：上天保佑他们不会落在他的手里——他们就会知道向自己的父亲行弑，必须受到怎样的报应；弗里恩斯也是一样。（朱生豪译）

But, peace! For from broad[①] words, and 'cause he fail'd

His presence at the tyrant's feast, I hear,

Macduff lives in disgrace. Sir, can you tell

Where he bestows himself?

Lord. The son of Duncan,

From whom this tyrant holds the due of birth,

Lives in the English court, and is received

Of the most pious Edward with such grace

That the malevolence of fortune nothing

Takes from his high respect.[②] Thither[③] Macduff

Is gone to pray the holy king, upon his aid

To wake Northumberland[④] and warlike[⑤] Siward;

That by the help of these, with Him above

To ratify the work, we may again

Give to our tables meat, sleep to our nights,

Free from our feasts and banquets bloody knives,

Do faithful homage, and receive free honours:[⑥]

All which we pine[⑦] for now. And this report

Hath so exasperate[⑧] the king that he

Prepares for some attempt of war.

LENNOX. Sent he to Macduff?

Lord. He did, and with an absolute 'Sir, not I,'

The cloudy[⑨] messenger turns me his back,

And hums, as who should say, 'You'll rue the time

———————

① broad：不敬的

② 参考译文：对他非常优待，一点不因为他处境颠危而减削了敬礼。(朱生豪译)（malevolence：恶劣）

③ thither：向那里；到那里

④ Northumberland：诺森伯兰郡，在英国英格兰

⑤ warlike：好战的

⑥ 参考译文：使他们出兵相援，凭着上帝的意旨帮助我们恢复已失的自由，使我们仍旧能够享受食桌上的盛馔和酣畅的睡眠，不再畏惧宴会中有沾血的刀剑，让我们能够一方面输忠效信，一方面安受爵赏而心无疑虑。(朱生豪译)（ratify：批准；banquet：宴席；homage：效忠，顺从）

⑦ pine：渴望

⑧ exasperate：激怒，使震怒（例如：We were exasperated at his ill behaviour. 我们对他的恶劣行为非常恼怒。）

⑨ cloudy：愤怒的，愁容满面的

That clogs me with this answer.'[①]

LENNOX. And that well might
Advise him to a caution, to hold what distance
His wisdom can provide.[②] Some holy angel
Fly to the court of England and unfold
His message ere he come, that a swift blessing
May soon return to this our suffering country
Under a hand accursed![③]

Lord. I'll send my prayers with him.

[Exeunt.]

---

① 参考译文:"你给我这样的答复,看着吧,你一定会自食其果。"(朱生豪译)(rue:后悔; clog:给予)
② 参考译文:那很可以叫他留心留心远避当前的祸害。(朱生豪译)
③ 参考译文:但愿什么神圣的天使飞到英格兰的宫廷里,预先把他的信息带来给我们,让上天的祝福迅速回到我们这一个在毒手压制下备受苦难的国家!(accursed:被诅咒的)

79

Act IV

SCENE I.
A Cavern. In the Middle, a Boiling Cauldron①.

[Thunder. Enter the three Witches.]

First Witch. Thrice the brinded② cat hath mew'd③.

Second Witch. Thrice and once the hedge-pig④ whined⑤.

Third Witch. Harpier⑥ cries ''Tis time, 'tis time'.

First Witch. Round about the cauldron go;

In the poison'd entrails throw.⑦

Toad, that under cold stone,

Days and nights has thirty-one

Swelter'd venom sleeping got,

Boil thou first i' the charmed pot.⑧

ALL. Double, double toil and trouble;

Fire burn, and cauldron bubble.⑨

Second Witch. Fillet of a fenny⑩ snake,

In the cauldron boil and bake;

Eye of newt and toe of frog,

---

① cauldron：大锅

② brinded：有斑纹的

③ mew：喵喵叫

④ hedge-pig：刺猬

⑤ whined：whine 的过去式和过去分词，哀鸣，哀叫

⑥ Harpier：哈比，是古希腊神话中的一种怪物，它的身体和面孔像人，但翅膀和爪子像鸟，生性残忍

⑦ 参考译文：绕釜环行火融融，毒肝腐脏置其中。（朱生豪译）（entrail：内脏）原文中莎士比亚用了押韵的修辞手法，go 和 throw 都是发 /əu/ 的音。而译文不仅意思准确，形式工整，选择了汉语的七言诗形式来翻译，还从修辞角度与原文一致，选择了押韵的"融"和"中"。下文中的"浆"和"汤"、"烦"和"澜"也是如此。译文从音、形、意的角度完美再现了原文，同时兼顾了翻译中"信、达、雅"的要求。这一场的翻译可以很好地看出朱生豪过人的中文和英文素养，翻译功底实在是无人能及。

⑧ 参考译文：蛤蟆蛰眠寒石底，三十一日夜相继；汗出淋漓化毒浆，投之鼎釜沸为汤。（朱生豪译）（toad：癞蛤蟆；swelter：闷热，使出汗；venom：毒液，毒物；charmed：施了魔法的）

⑨ 参考译文：不惮辛劳不惮烦，釜中沸沫总成澜。（朱生豪译）（toil：辛劳，困苦）

⑩ fenny：沼泽的

Wool of bat and tongue of dog,
Adder's fork and blind-worm's sting,
Lizard's leg and howlet's wing,
For a charm of powerful trouble,
Like a hell-broth boil and bubble.①

ALL. Double, double toil and trouble;
Fire burn and cauldron bubble.

Third Witch. Scale② of dragon, tooth of wolf,
Witches' mummy③, maw④ and gulf⑤
Of the ravin'd salt-sea shark,
Root of hemlock⑥ digg'd i' the dark,
Liver of blaspheming⑦ Jew,
Gall⑧ of goat, and slips of yew⑨
Silver'd in the moon's eclipse⑩,
Nose of Turk and Tartar⑪'s lips,
Finger of birth-strangled⑫ babe
Ditch-deliver'd⑬ by a drab⑭,
Make the gruel⑮ thick⑯ and slab⑰.

---

① 参考译文：沼地蝾蛇取其肉，鬻以为片煮至熟；蝾螈之目青蛙趾，蝙蝠之毛犬之齿，蝮舌如叉蚯蚓刺，蜥蜴之足枭之翅，炼为毒蛊鬼神惊，扰乱人世无安宁。（朱生豪译）（newt：蝾螈；adder：蝮蛇，一种毒蛇；blind-worm：蚯蚓；sting：毒刺，刺毛；howlet：猫头鹰；hell-broth：巫师行邪术调制的羹汤）
② scale：鳞片
③ mummy：木乃伊，干尸
④ maw：（动物的）胃
⑤ gulf：gullet，咽喉，食管
⑥ hemlock：铁杉，一种常绿乔木，为耐阴树种，根系发达，能够抗风、抗雪压，寿命长，但生长较慢。
⑦ blaspheming：受到诅咒的
⑧ gall：胆汁
⑨ yew：紫杉，别名红豆杉，属常绿乔木或灌木，球花小，早春开放。紫杉树较高，可达15米左右，因此花语为"高傲"，其枝叶熬汤可以治疗胃病。但现在80%的中国紫杉资源已经遭到严重破坏。
⑩ eclipse：日食，月食（例如：It was reported that there would be a lunar eclipse tomorrow evening. 据报道说，明天晚上有月食。）
⑪ Tartar：鞑靼人（蒙古人和突厥人），后也指凶悍的人或难对付的人
⑫ birth-strangled：在出生时就窒息而死的（strangle：窒息，扼死）
⑬ ditch-deliver'd：出生于臭水沟的（ditch：沟渠；deliver：出生）
⑭ drab：娼妇
⑮ gruel：粥
⑯ thick：浓稠的
⑰ slab：厚的

Add thereto a tiger's chawdron①,

For the ingredients② of our cauldron.

ALL. Double, double toil and trouble;

Fire burn and cauldron bubble.

Second Witch. Cool it with a baboon③'s blood,

Then the charm is firm and good.

[Enter HECATE to the other three Witches.]

HECATE. O well done! I commend your pains,

And every one shall share i' the gains.

And now about the cauldron sing,

Live elves④ and fairies⑤ in a ring,

Enchanting⑥ all that you put in.

[Music and a song: 'Black spirits'.]

[HECATE retires.]

Second Witch. By the pricking⑦ of my thumbs,

Something wicked this way comes.

Open, locks,

Whoever knocks!

[Enter MACBETH.]

MACBETH. How now, you secret, black⑧, and midnight hags⑨!

What is't you do?

ALL. A deed without a name.

MACBETH. I conjure you, by that which you profess,

Howe'er you come to know it, answer me:⑩

Though you untie the winds and let them fight

---

① chawdron：内脏

② ingredient：材料，作料

③ baboon：狒狒

④ elf：精灵

⑤ fairy：仙女

⑥ enchant：施魔法，迷惑（例如：The witch enchanted the prince. 女巫迷惑了王子。）

⑦ pricking：刺，刺痛

⑧ black：实施黑魔法的

⑨ hag：女巫

⑩ 参考译文：凭着你们的职业，我吩咐你们回答我，不管你们的知识是从哪里得来的。
（朱生豪译）（conjure：召唤，以魔法召唤；profess：声称，公开表明；which you profess：指魔法）

Against the churches; though the yesty waves
Confound and swallow navigation up;
Though bladed corn be lodged and trees blown down;
Though castles topple on their warders' heads;
Though palaces and pyramids do slope
Their heads to their foundations; though the treasure
Of nature's germens tumble altogether,
Even till destruction sicken, answer me
To what I ask you.①

First Witch. Speak.

Second Witch. Demand.

Third Witch. We'll answer.

First Witch. Say, if thou'dst rather hear it from our mouths,
Or from our masters?

MACBETH. Call 'em, let me see 'em.

First Witch. Pour in sow's blood that hath eaten
Her nine farrow; grease that's sweaten
From the murtherer's gibbet, throw
Into the flame.②

ALL. Come, high or low;
Thyself and office deftly③ show!

[Thunder. First Apparition④: an armed Head.]

MACBETH. Tell me, thou unknown power —

First Witch. He knows thy thought:
Hear his speech, but say thou nought⑤.

First Apparition. Macbeth! Macbeth! Macbeth! beware Macduff,

---

① 参考译文：即使你们的嘴里会放出狂风，让它们向教堂猛击；即使汹涌的波涛会把航海的船只颠覆吞噬；即使谷物的叶片会倒折在田亩上，树木会连根拔起；即使城堡会向它们的守卫者的头上倒下；即使宫殿和金字塔都会倾圮；即使大自然所孕育的一切灵奇完全归于毁灭，我也要你们回答我的问题。（朱生豪译）（untie：放出，松开；yesty：汹涌的；confound：挫败；使倾覆；navigation：航行；bladed：有叶片的；lodge：倒伏；castle：城堡；topple：推翻，倾覆；germen：胚，幼芽；tumble：倒塌，跌倒）

② 参考译文：母猪九子食其豚，血浇火上焰生腥；杀人恶犯上刑场，汗脂投火发凶光。（朱生豪译）（sow：母猪；farrow：一窝小猪；gibbet：绞死，吊刑）

③ deftly：熟练地，巧妙地

④ apparition：幽灵，幻影

⑤ nought：即 nothing

Beware the thane of Fife①. Dismiss me. Enough.

[Descends.]

MACBETH. Whate'er thou art, for thy good caution, thanks;

Thou hast harp'd② my fear aright③. But one word more—

First Witch. He will not be commanded: here's another,

More potent④ than the first.

[Thunder. Second Apparition: a bloody Child.]

Second Apparition. Macbeth! Macbeth! Macbeth!

MACBETH. Had I three ears, I'ld hear thee.

Second Apparition. Be bloody, bold, and resolute: laugh to scorn⑤

The power of man, for none of woman born

Shall harm Macbeth.

[Descends.]

MACBETH. Then live, Macduff. What need I fear of thee?

But yet I'll make assurance double sure,

And take a bond of fate: thou shalt not live,

That I may tell pale-hearted fear it lies,

And sleep in spite of thunder.⑥

[Thunder. Third Apparition. a Child crowned, with a tree in his hand.]

What is this,

That rises like the issue of a king,

And wears upon his baby-brow the round

And top of sovereignty⑦?

ALL. Listen, but speak not to't.

Third Apparition. Be lion-mettled⑧, proud, and take no care

---

① thane of Fife：法夫爵士，指麦克达夫

② harp：道破，反复诉说

③ aright：正确地

④ potent：强有力的

⑤ scorn：轻蔑，嘲笑（例如：He were to become a mark of public scorn. 他将成为公众奚落的典型。）

⑥ 参考译文：从命运手里接受切实的保证。我还是要你死，让我可以斥胆怯的恐惧为虚妄，在雷电怒作的夜里也能安心睡觉。（朱生豪译）（shalt：应该，将要，should 的古英语写法）

⑦ sovereignty：主权，统治权

⑧ lion-mettled：像狮子一样勇敢的

Who chafes[1], who frets[2], or where conspirers[3] are.

Macbeth shall never vanquish'd[4] be until

Great Birnam[5] wood to high Dunsinane[6] hill

Shall come against him.

[Descends.]

MACBETH. That will never be.

Who can impress[7] the forest, bid the tree

Unfix his earth-bound root? Sweet bodements[8]! good!

Rebellion's head, rise never till the wood

Of Birnam rise, and our high-placed Macbeth

Shall live the lease of nature, pay his breath

To time and mortal custom.[9] Yet my heart

Throbs[10] to know one thing: tell me, if your art

Can tell so much: shall Banquo's issue ever

Reign[11] in this kingdom?

ALL. Seek to know no more.

MACBETH. I will be satisfied. Deny me this,

And an eternal[12] curse[13] fall on you! Let me know.

Why sinks that cauldron, and what noise is this?

[Hautboys.]

First Witch. Show!

Second Witch. Show!

---

① chafe. 激怒（例如：Young people often chafe under the yoke of parental control. 年轻人常因父母的管束而恼火。）

② fret：焦急，烦恼

③ conspirer：策划阴谋者

④ vanquish：击败，征服

⑤ Great Birnam：勃南，勃南森林距离邓斯纳恩山约 12 公里

⑥ Dunsinane：邓斯纳恩山，苏格兰境内，靠近珀斯郡

⑦ impress：命令，强迫

⑧ bodement：预兆

⑨ 参考译文：勃南的树林不会移动，叛徒的举事也不会成功，我们巍巍高位的麦克白将要尽其天年，在他寿数告终的时候奄然物化。（朱生豪译）(rebellion：叛乱；head：举事，前进；lease：租约) 麦克白的自信使他没有仔细揣摩女巫的话，也导致了他日后的被杀。这个时候的麦克白明显已经听不进任何人的忠告了。

⑩ throb：跳动

⑪ reign：统治，支配

⑫ eternal：永恒的

⑬ curse：诅咒

Third Witch. Show!

ALL. Show his eyes, and grieve his heart;

Come like shadows, so depart①!

[A show of eight Kings②, the last with a glass in his hand; Ghost
of BANQUO following.]

MACBETH. Thou art too like the spirit of Banquo: down!

Thy crown does sear③ mine eyeballs. And thy hair,

Thou other gold-bound brow, is like the first.

A third is like the former. Filthy hags!

Why do you show me this? A fourth! Start, eyes!

What, will the line stretch out to the crack of doom?④

Another yet? A seventh! I'll see no more!

And yet the eighth appears, who bears a glass

Which shows me many more; and some I see

That two-fold balls and treble scepters carry.

Horrible sight! Now, I see 'tis true;

For the blood-bolter'd Banquo smiles upon me,⑤

And points at them for his.

[Apparitions vanish.]

What, is this so?

First Witch. Ay, sir, all this is so. But why

Stands Macbeth thus amazedly⑥?

Come, sisters, cheer we up his sprites,

And show the best of our delights⑦.

---

① depart：离开，去世（例如：He will depart for Shanghai this evening. 他今天晚上动身去上海。）

② eight Kings：指的是八个苏格兰国王：Robert II，Robert III，六个 James，最后一个 James VI 是 1603 年继任英国国王的 James I）

③ sear：刺痛，灼烤（例如：I distinctly felt the heat start to sear my throat. 我分明感觉到嗓子开始烧得难受。）

④ 参考译文：什么！这一连串戴着王冠的，要到世界末日才会完结吗？（朱生豪译）（crack of doom：世界末日）

⑤ 参考译文：有几个还拿着两重的球，三头的御杖。可怕的景象！啊，现在我知道这不是虚妄的幻象，因为血污的班柯在向我微笑。（朱生豪译）（two-fold balls：ball 指的是国王左手所持象征王权的、顶上有十字架的圆球；two-fold balls 是双重加冕，第六个詹姆士国王先是在斯贡加冕为苏格兰国王，后来又在伦敦的威斯敏斯特加冕为英国国王；scepter：国王右手所持的权杖，象征王权）

⑥ amazedly：吃惊地，惊奇地

⑦ delight：高兴

I'll charm the air to give a sound,
While you perform your antic round,
That this great king may kindly say,
Our duties did his welcome pay.①

[Music. The Witches dance and then vanish, with HECATE.]

MACBETH. Where are they? Gone? Let this pernicious② hour
Stand aye③ accursed④ in the calendar!

Come in, without there!

[Enter LENNOX.]

LENNOX. What's Your Grace's will?

MACBETH. Saw you the weird sisters?

LENNOX. No, my lord.

MACBETH. Came they not by you?

LENNOX. No, indeed, my lord.

MACBETH. Infected be the air whereon they ride,
And damn'd all those that trust them!⑤ I did hear
The galloping⑥ of horse. Who was't came by?

LENNOX. 'Tis two or three, my lord, that bring you word
Macduff is fled⑦ to England.

MACBETH. Fled to England!

LENNOX. Ay, my good lord.

MACBETH. Time, thou anticipatest⑧ my dread⑨ exploits⑩.
The flighty purpose never is o'ertook

---

① 参考译文：我先用魔法使空中奏起乐来，你们就搀成一个圈子团团跳舞，让这位伟大的君王知道，我们并没有怠慢了他。（朱生豪译）（antic：滑稽可笑的）

② pernicious：有害的，恶性的（例如：Business may be troublesome, but idleness is pernicious. 事业虽扰人，怠惰害更大．）

③ aye：永远

④ accursed：被诅咒的

⑤ 参考译文：愿她们所驾乘的空气都化为毒雾，愿一切相信她们言语的人都永堕沉沦！（朱生豪译）（whereon：在……上面）

⑥ gallop：疾驰

⑦ is fled：等于 has fled

⑧ anticipatest：等于 anticipate，预料

⑨ dread：可怕的

⑩ exploit：行为

Unless the deed go with it.① From this moment
The very firstlings of my heart shall be
The firstlings of my hand.② And even now,
To crown my thoughts with acts, be it thought and done:
The castle of Macduff I will surprise;
Seize upon Fife, give to the edge o' the sword
His wife, his babes, and all unfortunate souls
That trace him in his line.③ No boasting④ like a fool;
This deed I'll do before this purpose cool.
But no more sights⑤!—Where are these gentlemen?
Come, bring me where they are.
[Exeunt.]

---

① 参考译文：无远弗至的恶念，一旦见之事实，就容易被人所乘。（朱生豪译）（flighty：迅速的，飞快的；o'ertook：等于 overtook，赶上，超过）
② 参考译文：从这一刻起，我心里一想到什么，便要把它立刻实行，没有迟疑的余地。（朱生豪译）（firstling：最初成果，最早的东西）
③ 参考译文：把他的妻子儿女和一切追随他的不幸的人们一起杀死。（朱生豪译）
④ boast：吹嘘（例如：He's always boasting his rich children. 他老吹他的孩子很有钱。）
⑤ sight：幻象，景象

SCENE II.
Fife. MACDUFF's Castle.

[Enter LADY MACDUFF, her Son, and ROSS.]

LADY MACDUFF. What had he done, to make him fly the land?

ROSS. You must have patience, madam.

LADY MACDUFF. He had none;

His flight was madness. When our actions do not,

Our fears do make us traitors^①.

ROSS. You know not

Whether it was his wisdom or his fear.

LADY MACDUFF. Wisdom! To leave his wife, to leave his babes,

His mansion^② and his titles in a place

From whence himself does fly? He loves us not;

He wants the natural touch; for the poor wren^③,

The most diminutive^④ of birds, will fight,

Her young ones in her nest, against the owl.

All is the fear and nothing is the love;

As little is the wisdom, where the flight

So runs against all reason.

ROSS. My dearest coz^⑤,

I pray you, school^⑥ yourself. But for your husband,

He is noble, wise, judicious^⑦, and best knows

The fits o' the season. I dare not speak much further;

But cruel are the times, when we are traitors

And do not know ourselves;^⑧ when we hold rumour

---

① traitor：叛徒
② mansion：宅邸
③ wren：鹪鹩
④ diminutive：小型的，微小的
⑤ coz：嫂子，堂兄弟姐妹
⑥ school：抑制，克制
⑦ judicious：明智的
⑧ 参考译文：现在这种时世太冷酷无情了，我们自己还不知道，就已经背上了叛徒的恶名。（朱生豪译）

89

From what we fear, yet know not what we fear,

But float upon a wild and violent sea

Each way and move.① I take my leave of you;

Shall not be long but I'll be here again.

Things at the worst will cease, or else climb upward

To what they were before. My pretty cousin,

Blessing upon you!

LADY MACDUFF. Father'd he is, and yet he's fatherless.②

ROSS. I am so much a fool, should I stay longer,

It would be my disgrace③ and your discomfort④.

I take my leave at once.

[Exit.]

LADY MACDUFF. Sirrah⑤, your father's dead;

And what will you do now? How will you live?

Son. As birds do, mother.

LADY MACDUFF. What, with worms and flies?

Son. With what I get, I mean; and so do they.

LADY MACDUFF. Poor bird! Thou'ldst never fear the net nor lime,

The pitfall nor the gin.⑥

Son. Why should I, mother? Poor birds they are not set for.

My father is not dead, for all your saying.

LADY MACDUFF. Yes, he is dead. How wilt thou do for a father?

Son. Nay, how will you do for a husband?

LADY MACDUFF. Why, I can buy me twenty at any market.

Son. Then you'll buy 'em to sell again.

LADY MACDUFF. Thou speak'st with all thy wit, and yet, i' faith,

With wit enough for thee.⑦

---

① 参考译文：一方面恐惧流言，一方面却又不知道为何而恐惧，就像在一个风波险恶的海上漂浮，全没有一定的方向。（朱生豪译）（rumour：谣言；violent：猛烈的）

② 参考译文：他虽然有父亲，却和没有父亲一样。（朱生豪译）

③ disgrace：耻辱，难过

④ discomfort：不安，不愉快

⑤ sirrah：小子

⑥ 参考译文：可怜的鸟儿！你从来不怕有人在张起网儿，布下陷阱，捉了你去哩。（朱生豪译）（lime：捉鸟用的胶；pitfall：陷阱，圈套；gin：罗网）

⑦ 参考译文：这刁钻的小油嘴；可也亏你想得出来。（朱生豪译）（wit：聪明，智慧）

Son. Was my father a traitor, mother?

LADY MACDUFF. Ay, that he was.

Son. What is a traitor?

LADY MACDUFF. Why, one that swears and lies.

Son. And be all traitors that do so?

LADY MACDUFF. Every one that does so is a traitor, and must be hanged.

Son. And must they all be hanged that swear and lie?

LADY MACDUFF. Every one.

Son. Who must hang them?

LADY MACDUFF. Why, the honest men.

Son. Then the liars and swearers^① are fools, for there are liars and swearers enow to beat the honest men and hang up them.

LADY MACDUFF. Now, God help thee, poor monkey!
But how wilt^② thou do for a father?

Son. If he were dead, you'ld weep for him; if you would not, it were a good sign that I should quickly have a new father.

LADY MACDUFF. Poor prattler^③, how thou talk'st!

[Enter a Messenger.]

Messenger. Bless you, fair dame! I am not to you known,
Though in your state of honour I am perfect.
I doubt some danger does approach you nearly.
If you will take a homely man's advice,
Be not found here; hence, with your little ones.^④
To fright you thus, methinks, I am too savage;
To do worse to you were fell cruelty,
Which is too nigh your person.^⑤ Heaven preserve you!
I dare abide no longer.

---

① swearer：宣誓者，发誓的人

② wilt：等于 will

③ prattler：空谈者，油嘴滑舌的人

④ 参考译文：我怕夫人目下有极大的危险，要是您愿意接受一个微贱之人的忠告，那么还是离此地，赶快带着您的孩子们避一避的好。（朱生豪译）(homely：卑微的)

⑤ 参考译文：我这样惊吓着您，已经是够残忍的了；要是有人再要加害于您，那真是太没有人道了，可是这没人道的事儿快要落到您头上了。上天保佑您！我不敢多耽搁时间。（朱生豪译）(fright：惊吓；methink：依我看来；savage：残酷的；nigh：靠近的，接近的)

[Exit.]

LADY MACDUFF. Whither[①] should I fly?

I have done no harm. But I remember now

I am in this earthly[②] world, where to do harm

Is often laudable[③], to do good sometime

Accounted dangerous folly[④]. Why then, alas,

Do I put up that womanly defence,

To say I have done no harm?

[Enter Murtherers.]

What are these faces?

First Murtherer. Where is your husband?

LADY MACDUFF. I hope, in no place so unsanctified

Where such as thou mayst find him.[⑤]

First Murtherer. He's a traitor.

Son. Thou liest[⑥], thou shag-hair'd[⑦] villain[⑧]!

First Murtherer. What, you egg!

[Stabbing[⑨] him.]

Young fry[⑩] of treachery[⑪]!

Son. He has kill'd me, mother.

Run away, I pray you!

[Dies.]

[Exit LADY MACDUFF, crying 'Murther!']

[Exeunt Murtherers, following her.]

---

① whither：哪里（例如：Whither should they go? 他们应往何处去？）
② earthly：尘世的
③ laudable：值得赞赏的
④ 参考译文：做了好事反会被人当做危险的傻瓜。（朱生豪译）（accounted：被当做）
⑤ 参考译文：我希望他是在光天化日之下，你们这些鬼东西不敢露脸的地方。（朱生豪译）（unsanctified：不圣洁的）
⑥ liest：等于 lied，胡说
⑦ shag-hair'd：蓬头垢面的
⑧ villain：恶人
⑨ stab：用刀捅
⑩ fry：孽种
⑪ treachery：背叛，背叛行为

92

SCENE III.
England. Before the King's Palace.

[Enter MALCOLM and MACDUFF.]

MALCOLM. Let us seek out some desolate shade, and there
  Weep our sad bosoms empty.[1]

MACDUFF. Let us rather
  Hold fast the mortal sword, and like good men
  Bestride our down-fall'n birthdom.[2] Each new morn
  New widows howl, new orphans cry, new sorrows
  Strike heaven on the face, that it resounds
  As if it felt with Scotland and yell'd out
  Like syllable of dolour.[3]

MALCOLM. What I believe, I'll wail[4];
  What know, believe; and what I can redress[5],
  As I shall find the time to friend, I will.
  What you have spoke[6], it may be so perchance[7].
  This tyrant, whose sole name blisters our tongues,
  Was once thought honest.[8] You have loved him well;
  He hath not touch'd you yet. I am young; but something
  You may deserve of him through me, and wisdom
  To offer up a weak poor innocent lamb,

---

① 参考译文：让我们找一处没有人踪的树荫，在那里把我们胸中的悲哀痛痛快快地哭个干净吧。（朱生豪译）（desolate：荒凉的，无人烟的；shade：树荫）

② 参考译文：我们还是紧握着利剑，像好汉子似的卫护我们被蹂躏的祖国吧。（朱生豪译）（bestride：保卫；birthdom：祖国）

③ 参考译文：每一个新的黎明都听得见新孀的寡妇在哭泣，新失父母的孤儿在号啕，新的悲哀上冲霄汉，发出凄厉的回声，就像哀悼苏格兰的命运，替她奏唱挽歌一样。（朱生豪译）（morn：早晨；orphan：孤儿；resound：回荡着声音；dolour：悲哀，伤心）

④ wail：痛哭

⑤ redress：救济，矫正

⑥ spoke：即 spoken

⑦ perchance：也许，偶然

⑧ 参考文献：一提起这个暴君的名字，就使我们切齿腐舌，可是他曾经有过正直的名声。（朱生豪译）（blister：使起水泡）

93

To appease an angry god.①

MACDUFF. I am not treacherous②.

MALCOLM. But Macbeth is.

A good and virtuous nature may recoil

In an imperial charge.③ But I shall crave④ your pardon;

That which you are, my thoughts cannot transpose⑤.

Angels are bright still, though the brightest fell;⑥

Though all things foul would wear the brows of grace,

Yet grace must still look so.⑦

MACDUFF. I have lost my hopes.

MALCOLM. Perchance even there where I did find my doubts.

Why in that rawness left you wife and child,

Those precious motives, those strong knots of love,

Without leave-taking?⑧ I pray you,

Let not my jealousies be your dishonours⑨,

But mine own safeties. You may be rightly just,

Whatever I shall think.

MACDUFF. Bleed, bleed, poor country!

Great tyranny! Lay thou thy basis sure,

For goodness dare not check thee. Wear thou thy wrongs;

The title is affeer'd⑩! Fare thee well⑪, lord.

I would not be the villain that thou think'st

---

① 参考译文：我虽然年轻识浅，可是您也许可以利用我向他邀功求赏，把一头柔弱无罪的羔羊向一个愤怒的天神献祭，不失为一件聪明的事。（朱生豪译）（innocent：无辜的，无罪的；appease：平息，使满足）

② treacherous：不忠的，不可信的

③ 参考译文：在尊严的王命之下，忠实仁善的人也许不得不背着天良行事。（virtuous：善良的；recoil：畏缩行事；imperial：至高无上的，威严的）

④ crave：渴望（例如：I am craving for some fresh air. 我想呼呼吸吸新鲜空气。）

⑤ transpose：转移，变化

⑥ 参考译文：最光明的天使也许会堕落，可是天使总是光明的。（朱生豪译）

⑦ 参考译文：丑恶的东西总要做出一副美德的表象来，美德自身的样子还是美德。（朱生豪译）（brow：容貌，表情）

⑧ 参考译文：也许正是这一点刚才引起了我的怀疑。您为什么不告而别，丢下您的妻子儿女，那些生活中的宝贵的原动力，爱情的坚强的联系，让她们担惊受险呢？（朱生豪译）（rawness：未准备，没告知；knot：联系）

⑨ dishonour：耻辱，羞辱

⑩ affeer'd：确定的，确认的

⑪ fare thee well：再会，再见

For the whole space that's in the tyrant's grasp,

And the rich East to boot.[①]

MALCOLM. Be not offended[②];

I speak not as in absolute fear of you.

I think our country sinks beneath[③] the yoke[④];

It weeps, it bleeds, and each new day a gash

Is added to her wounds. I think withal

There would be hands uplifted[⑤] in my right;

And here from gracious England have I offer

Of goodly thousands. But for all this,

When I shall tread[⑥] upon the tyrant's head,

Or wear it on my sword, yet my poor country

Shall have more vices than it had before,

More suffer and more sundry[⑦] ways than ever,

By him that shall succeed.

MACDUFF. What should he be?

MALCOLM. It is myself I mean, in whom I know

All the particulars of vice so grafted

That, when they shall be open'd, black Macbeth

Will seem as pure as snow, and the poor state

Esteem him as a lamb, being compared

With my confineless harms.[⑧]

MACDUFF. Not in the legions[⑨]

Of horrid hell can come a devil more damn'd

---

① 参考译文：即使把这暴君掌握下的全部土地一起给我，再加上富庶的东方，我也不愿做一个像你所猜疑我那样的奸人。（朱生豪译）（to boot：此外）

② offended：生气的

③ beneath：在……之下

④ yoke：束缚

⑤ uplift：抬高；抬起

⑥ tread：踩；踏（例如：I'm sorry, I didn't mean to tread on your foot. 对不起，我不是故意踩你脚的。）

⑦ sundry：各种各样的（例如：You could call for food and drink, and sundry services. 你可以打电话订餐和饮料，叫各种服务。）

⑧ 参考译文：我的意思就是说我自己。我知道在我的天性之中，深植着各种的罪恶，要是有一天暴露出来，黑暗的麦克白在相形之下，将会变成白雪一样纯洁。我们的可怜的国家看见了我的无限的暴虐，将会把他当做一头羔羊。（朱生豪译）（esteem：尊敬；confineless：无限制的）

⑨ legion：大军，军团

In evils to top Macbeth.

MALCOLM. I grant him bloody,

Luxurious, avaricious, false, deceitful,

Sudden, malicious, smacking of every sin

That has a name.① But there's no bottom, none,

In my voluptuousness: your wives, your daughters,

Your matrons② and your maids, could not fill up

The cistern③ of my lust④, and my desire

All continent impediments would o'erbear

That did oppose my will. Better Macbeth

Than such an one to reign.⑤

MACDUFF. Boundless intemperance

In nature is a tyranny;⑥ it hath been

The untimely⑦ emptying of the happy throne⑧,

And fall of many kings. But fear not yet

To take upon you what is yours. You may

Convey your pleasures in a spacious plenty,

And yet seem cold, the time you may so hoodwink.

We have willing dames enough; there cannot be

That vulture in you, to devour so many

As will to greatness dedicate themselves,

Finding it so inclined.⑨

MALCOLM. With this there grows

In my most ill-composed affection such

---

① 参考译文：我承认他嗜杀、骄奢、贪婪、虚伪、欺诈、狂暴、凶恶，一切可以指名的罪恶他都有。(朱生豪译)(grant：承认；luxurious：奢侈的，放纵的；deceitful：欺诈的；malicious：恶毒的，凶恶的)

② matron：已婚妇女

③ cistern：蓄水池，容器

④ lust：欲望

⑤ 参考译文：我的猖狂的欲念会冲决一切节制和约束。与其让这样一个人做国王，还是让麦克白统治的好。(朱生豪译)(continent：自制的，克制的；impediment：障碍，束缚)

⑥ 参考译文：人性中无限制的纵欲是一种虐政。(朱生豪译)(intemperance：放纵，不节制)

⑦ untimely：不合时宜的，不长久的

⑧ throne：王位

⑨ 参考译文：可是您还不必担心，谁也不能禁止您满足您的分内的欲望。您可以一方面尽情欢乐，一方面在外表上装出庄重的神气，世人的耳目是很容易遮掩过去的。我们国内尽多自愿献身的女子，无论您怎样贪欢好色，也应付不了这许多求荣献媚的娇娥。(朱生豪译)(convey：偷偷拿走；hoodwink：蒙蔽；dame：夫人，女士；vulture：秃鹫)

A stanchless avarice that, were I king,
I should cut off the nobles for their lands,
Desire his jewels and this other's house,
And my more-having would be as a sauce
To make me hunger more, that I should forge
Quarrels unjust against the good and loyal,
Destroying them for wealth.[①]

MACDUFF. This avarice
Sticks deeper, grows with more pernicious root
Than summer-seeming lust, and it hath been
The sword of our slain kings;[②] yet do not fear;
Scotland hath foisons[③] to fill up your will,
Of your mere own: all these are portable,
With other graces weigh'd.[④]

MALCOLM. But I have none: the king-becoming graces,
As justice, verity, temperance, stableness,
Bounty, perseverance, mercy, lowliness,
Devotion, patience, courage, fortitude,
I have no relish of them, but abound
In the division of each several crime,
Acting it many ways.[⑤] Nay, had I power, I should
Pour the sweet milk of concord[⑥] into hell,

---

① 参考译文：除了这一种弱点以外，在我的邪僻的心中还有一种不顾廉耻的贪婪，要是我做了国王，我一定要诛除贵族，侵夺他们的土地；不是向这个人索取珠宝，就是向那个人索取房屋；我所有的越多，我的贪心越不知道餍足，我一定会为了图谋财富的缘故，向善良忠贞的人无端寻衅，把他们陷于死地。（朱生豪译）（composed：组成的，构成的；stanchless：不顾廉耻的；avarice：贪婪；quarrel：挑衅，争端）

② 参考译文：这一种贪婪比起少年的情欲来，它的根是更深而更有毒的，我们曾经有许多过去的国王死在它的剑下。（朱生豪译）（stick：扎根；slain：杀死的）

③ foison：财富，丰收

④ 参考译文：它都是属于您的；只要有其他的美德，这些缺点都不算什么。（朱生豪译）（portable：无足轻重的）

⑤ 参考译文：什么公平、正直、节俭、镇定、慷慨、坚毅、仁慈、谦恭、诚敬、宽容、勇敢、刚强，我全没有；各种罪恶却应有尽有，在各方面表现出来。（朱生豪译）（verity：真诚；temperance：节制；bounty：慷慨；perseverance：坚毅，坚持不懈；mercy：仁慈，宽容；devotion：奉献，献身；patience：耐心，忍耐；courage：勇气，胆量；fortitude：刚强；abound：充满）

⑥ concord：和谐（例如：living in concord with neighbour 与邻居和睦相处）

Uproar^① the universal peace, confound
All unity on earth.

MACDUFF. O Scotland, Scotland!

MALCOLM. If such a one be fit to govern, speak:
I am as I have spoken.

MACDUFF. Fit to govern!

No, not to live. O nation miserable,
With an untitled tyrant bloody-scepter'd,
When shalt thou see thy wholesome days again,
Since that the truest issue of thy throne
By his own interdiction stands accursed,
And does blaspheme his breed?^② Thy royal father
Was a most sainted^③ king; the queen that bore thee,
Oftener upon her knees than on her feet,
Died every day^④ she lived. Fare thee well!
These evils thou repeat'st upon thyself
Have banish'd me from Scotland.^⑤ O my breast,
Thy hope ends here!

MALCOLM. Macduff, this noble passion,
Child of integrity, hath from my soul
Wiped the black scruples, reconciled my thoughts
To thy good truth and honour.^⑥ Devilish Macbeth,
By many of these trains hath sought to win me
Into his power, and modest^⑦ wisdom plucks^⑧ me

---

① uproar: 扰乱，使骚动
② 参考译文为：不，这样的人是不该让他留在人世的。啊，多难的国家，一个篡位的暴君握着染血的御杖高踞在王座上，你的最合法的嗣君又亲口吐露了他是这样一个可诅咒的人，辱没了他的高贵的血统，那么你几时才能重见天日呢？（朱生豪译）（miserable: 悲惨的；untitled: 篡位的；wholesome: 健全的；interdiction: 透露；blaspheme: 咒骂）
③ sainted: 圣明的
④ died every day: 指基督徒每天忏悔自己的行为，因上帝的恩典而获得重生
⑤ 参考译文：你自己供认的这些罪恶，已经把我从苏格兰放逐。（朱生豪译）（banish: 放逐）
⑥ 正常语序应为：this noble passion, child of integrity, hath wiped the black scruples from my soul, reconciled my thoughts to thy good truth and honour. 参考译文：只有一颗正直的心，才会有这种勃发的忠义之情，它已经把黑暗的疑虑从我的灵魂上一扫而空，使我充分信任你的真诚。（朱生豪译）（scruple: 疑虑，顾虑；reconcile: 和解，调和）
⑦ modest: 谨慎的
⑧ pluck: 拉，拽

From over-credulous① haste. But God above

Deal between thee and me! For even now

I put myself to thy direction, and

Unspeak mine own detraction; here abjure

The taints and blames I laid upon myself,

For strangers to my nature.② I am yet

Unknown to woman, never was forsworn,

Scarcely have coveted what was mine own,

At no time broke my faith, would not betray

The devil to his fellow and delight

No less in truth than life. My first false speaking

Was this upon myself.③ What I am truly

Is thine and my poor country's to command.

Whither indeed, before thy here-approach,

Old Siward, with ten thousand warlike men,

Already at a point, was setting forth.

Now we'll together, and the chance of goodness

Be like our warranted④ quarrel! Why arc you silent?

MACDUFF. Such welcome and unwelcome things at once

'Tis hard to reconcile.

[Enter a Doctor.]

MALCOLM. Well, more anon. Comes the king forth, I pray you?

Doctor. Ay, sir, there are a crew of wretched souls

That stay his cure. Their malady convinces

The great assay of art, but at his touch,

Such sanctity hath heaven given his hand,

They presently amend.⑤

---

① over-credulous：过于轻信的

② 参考译文：从现在起，我委身听从你的指导，并且撤回我刚才对我自己所讲的坏话，我所加在我自己身上的一切污点，都是我的天性中所没有的。（朱生豪译）（unspeak：收回，撤回；detraction：诽谤，坏话；abjure：宣布撤回；taint：污点）

③ 参考译文：我从不曾失信于人，我不愿把魔鬼出卖给他的同伴，我珍爱忠诚不亚于生命；刚才我对自己所作的诽语，是我第一次的说谎。（朱生豪译）

④ warranted：担保的，堂堂正正的

⑤ 参考译文：有一大群不幸的人们在等候他的医治，他们的疾病使最高明的医生束手无策，可是上天给他这样神奇的力量，只要他的手一触，他们就立刻痊愈了。（朱生豪译）（malady：疾病，痛苦；convince：克服；assay：尝试；amend：痊愈）

MALCOLM. I thank you, doctor.

[Exit Doctor.]

MACDUFF. What's the disease he means?

MALCOLM. 'Tis call'd the Evil:

A most miraculous work in this good king,

Which often, since my here-remain in England,

I have seen him do.[①] How he solicits heaven,

Himself best knows; but strangely-visited people,

All swol'n and ulcerous, pitiful to the eye,

The mere despair of surgery, he cures,

Hanging a golden stamp about their necks,

Put on with holy prayers; and 'tis spoken,

To the succeeding royalty he leaves

The healing benediction.[②] With this strange virtue[③]

He hath a heavenly gift of prophecy,

And sundry blessings hang about his throne

That speak him full of grace.[④]

[Enter ROSS.]

MACDUFF. See, who comes here?

MALCOLM. My countryman, but yet I know him not.

MACDUFF. My ever-gentle cousin, welcome hither.

MALCOLM. I know him now. Good God, betimes remove

The means that makes us strangers!

ROSS. Sir, amen.

MACDUFF. Stands Scotland where it did?[⑤]

ROSS. Alas, poor country!

---

① 参考译文：自从我来到英格兰以后，我常常看见这位善良的国王显示他的奇妙无比的本领。（朱生豪译）

② 参考译文：除了他自己以外，谁也不知道他是怎样祈求着上天；可是害着怪病的人，浑身肿烂，惨不忍睹，一切外科手术所无法医治的，他只要嘴里念着祈祷，用一枚金章亲手挂在他们的颈上，他们便会霍然痊愈；据说他这种治病的天能，是世世相传永袭罔替的。（朱生豪译）（solicit：祈求，恳求；strangely-visited：得怪病的；swol'n：膨胀的，肿起的；ulcerous：溃疡性的；succeeding：传承的；benediction：祝福，赐福）

③ virtue：美德，本事

④ 参考译文：除了这种特殊的本领以外，他还是一个天生的预言者，福祥环拱着他的王座，表示他具有各种美德。（朱生豪译）（prophecy：预言）

⑤ 等于 Does Scotland stand where it did? 参考译文：苏格兰还是原来那样子吗？（朱生豪译）

Almost afraid to know itself. It cannot

Be call'd our mother, but our grave; where nothing,

But who knows nothing, is once seen to smile;

Where sighs and groans and shrieks that rend the air

Are made, not mark'd; where violent sorrow seems

A modern ecstasy.① The dead man's knell

Is there scarce ask'd for who, and good men's lives

Expire before the flowers in their caps,

Dying or ere they sicken.②

MACDUFF. O, relation

Too nice, and yet too true!

MALCOLM. What's the newest grief?

ROSS. That of an hour's age doth hiss the speaker;

Each minute teems a new one.③

MACDUFF. How does my wife?

ROSS. Why, well.

MACDUFF. And all my children?

ROSS. Well too.

MACDUFF. The tyrant has not batter'd④ at their peace?

ROSS. No, they were well at peace, when I did leave 'em.

MACDUFF. But not a niggard⑤ of your speech. How goes't?

ROSS. When I came hither to transport the tidings,

Which I have heavily borne, there ran a rumour

Of many worthy fellows that were out,

Which was to my belief witness'd the rather,

---

① 参考译文：它不能再称为我们的母亲，只是我们的坟墓；除了浑浑噩噩、一无所知的人以外，谁的脸上也不曾有过一丝笑容；叹息、呻吟、震撼天空的呼号，都是日常听惯的声音，不能再引起人们的注意；剧烈的悲哀变成一般的风气。（朱生豪译）（sigh：叹息；groan：呻吟；shriek：呼号；ecstasy：无法自控的情绪）

② 参考译文：葬钟敲响的时候，谁也不再关心它是为谁而鸣；善良人的生命往往在他们帽上的花朵还没有枯萎以前就化为朝露。（朱生豪译）（knell：丧钟声；scarce：稀少的；expire：枯萎，死亡）

③ 参考译文：一小时以前的变故，在叙述者的嘴里就已经变成陈迹了；每一分钟都产生新的祸难。（朱生豪译）（hiss：嘘声，嘶嘶声；teem：产生，出现）

④ batter'd：等于battered，batter的过去式，毁损，毁坏

⑤ niggard：吝啬鬼，小气的人

For that I saw the tyrant's power a-foot:[①]
Now is the time of help; your eye in Scotland
Would create soldiers, make our women fight,
To doff[②] their dire distresses.

MALCOLM. Be't their comfort
We are coming thither. Gracious England hath
Lent us good Siward and ten thousand men;
An older and a better soldier none
That Christendom gives out.[③]

ROSS. Would I could answer
This comfort with the like! But I have words
That would be howl'd[④] out in the desert air,
Where hearing should not latch them.

MACDUFF. What concern they?
The general cause? or is it a fee-grief
Due to some single breast?

ROSS. No mind that's honest
But in it shares some woe, though the main part
Pertains to you alone.[⑤]

MACDUFF. If it be mine,
Keep it not from me, quickly let me have it.

ROSS. Let not your ears despise my tongue for ever,
Which shall possess them with the heaviest sound
That ever yet they heard.[⑥]

MACDUFF. Humph! I guess at it.

ROSS. Your castle is surprised; your wife and babes

---

① 参考译文：当我带着沉重的消息、预备到这儿来传报的时候，一路上听见谣传，说是许多有名望的人都已经纷纷起义；这种谣言照我想起来是很可靠的，因为我亲眼看见那暴君的肆虐。（朱生豪译）（hither：这里，这边；transport：传递；a-foot：正在进行的）

② doff：脱掉，丢弃，解脱了

③ 参考译文：友好的英格兰已经借给我们西沃德将军和一万兵士，所有基督教的国家里找不出一个比他更老练、更优秀的军人。（朱生豪译）（Christendom：基督教世界）

④ howl'd：howled，哀号，呼喊

⑤ 参考译文：天良未泯的人，对于这件事谁都要觉得像自己身受一样伤心，虽然你是最感到切身之痛的一个。（朱生豪译）（woe：悲哀，伤痛；pertain：属于，从属）

⑥ 参考译文：但愿你的耳朵不要从此永远憎恨我的舌头，因为它将要让你听见你有生以来所听到的最惨痛的声音。（朱生豪译）（despise：鄙视，憎恨）

Savagely[1] slaughter'd[2]. To relate the manner,
Were, on the quarry of these murther'd deer,
To add the death of you.[3]

MALCOLM. Merciful[4] heaven!

What, man! Ne'er pull your hat upon your brows;
Give sorrow words. The grief that does not speak
Whispers the o'er-fraught heart and bids it break.[5]

MACDUFF. My children too?

ROSS. Wife, children, servants, all
That could be found.

MACDUFF. And I must be from thence!
My wife kill'd too?

ROSS. I have said.

MALCOLM. Be comforted.

Let's make us medicines of our great revenge,
To cure this deadly grief.[6]

MACDUFF. He has no children. All my pretty ones?
Did you say all? O hell-kite[7]! All?
What, all my pretty chickens and their dam[8]
At one fell swoop[9]?

MALCOLM. Dispute[10] it like a man.

MACDUFF. I shall do so;
But I must also feel it as a man.
I cannot but remember such things were,

---

① savagely：野蛮地，残忍地
② slaughter'd：等于 slaughtered，slaughter 的过去分词（slaughter：屠杀）
③ 参考译文：要是我把他们的死状告诉你，那么不但他们已经成为猎场上被杀害的驯鹿，就是你也要痛不欲生的。（朱生豪译）（quarry：猎物）
④ merciful：仁慈的，慈悲的
⑤ 参考译文：不要把你的帽子拉下来遮住你的额角；用言语把你的悲伤倾泻出来吧；无言的哀痛是会向那不堪重压的心低声耳语，叫它裂成片片的。（朱生豪译）（ne'er：never，永远不；o'er-fraught：over-fraught，过分担心的，过分忧虑的）
⑥ 参考译文：让我们用壮烈的复仇做药饵，治疗这一段残酷的悲痛。（朱生豪译）（revenge：报复，复仇）
⑦ hell-kite：地狱的恶鸟
⑧ dam：古英语中有"母亲"的意思
⑨ swoop：猛扑
⑩ dispute：抗争，对……表示异议（例如：He disputed the allegations. 他对指控表示怀疑。）

That were most precious to me.[①] Did heaven look on,

And would not take their part? Sinful Macduff,

They were all struck for thee! Naught that I am,

Not for their own demerits, but for mine,

Fell slaughter on their souls.[②] Heaven rest them now!

MALCOLM. Be this the whetstone of your sword: let grief

Convert to anger; blunt not the heart, enrage it.[③]

MACDUFF. O, I could play the woman with mine eyes

And braggart with my tongue![④] But, gentle heavens,

Cut short all intermission[⑤]; front to front

Bring thou this fiend[⑥] of Scotland and myself;

Within my sword's length set him; if he 'scape,

Heaven forgive him too!

MALCOLM. This tune goes manly.

Come, go we to the king; our power is ready,

Our lack is nothing but our leave. Macbeth

Is ripe for shaking, and the powers above

Put on their instruments. Receive what cheer you may,

The night is long that never finds the day.[⑦]

[Exeunt.]

---

① 参考译文：我怎么能够把我所最珍爱的人置之度外，不去想念他们呢？（朱生豪译）

② 参考译文：我真该死，他们没有一点罪过，只是因为我自己不好，无情的屠戮才会降临到他们的身上。（朱生豪译）（naught：无价值的，一钱不值的；demerit：罪过，过失）

③ 参考译文：把这一桩仇恨作为磨快你的剑锋的砺石；让哀痛变成愤怒；不要让你的心麻木下去，激起它的怒火来吧。（朱生豪译）（whetstone：磨石；enrage：激怒，使暴怒）

④ 参考译文：啊！我可以一方面让我的眼睛里流着妇人之泪，一方面让我的舌头发出豪言壮语。（朱生豪译）

⑤ intermission：间歇，停顿（例如：The violinist resumed playing after the intermission. 幕间休息之后，那小提琴手又重新开始演奏。）

⑥ fiend：恶魔

⑦ 参考译文：麦克白气数将绝，天诛将至；黑夜无论怎样悠长，白昼总会到来。（朱生豪译）（ripe：时机成熟，时候到了；instrument：武器）

Act V

SCENE I.
Dunsinane. Anteroom in the Castle.

[Enter a Doctor of Physic and a Waiting Gentlewoman.]

Doctor. I have two nights watched with you, but can perceive no truth in your report. When was it she last walked?

Gentlewoman. Since His Majesty went into the field[1], I have seen her rise from her bed, throw her nightgown[2] upon her, unlock[3] her closet, take forth paper, fold it, write upon't, read it, afterwards seal[4] it, and again return to bed; yet all this while in a most fast sleep.

Doctor. A great perturbation[5] in nature, to receive at once the benefit of sleep and do the effects of watching. In this slumbery[6] agitation[7], besides her walking and other actual performances, what, at any time, have you heard her say?

Gentlewoman. That, sir, which I will not report after her.

Doctor. You may to me, and 'tis most meet you should.

Gentlewoman. Neither to you nor any one, having no witness to confirm[8] my speech.

[Enter LADY MACBETH, with a taper[9].]

Lo you, here she comes! This is her very guise[10], and, upon my life[11], fast asleep. Observe her; stand close.

---

① field：战场
② nightgown：睡袍
③ unlock：打开
④ seal：封住
⑤ perturbation：不安（例如：This message caused perturbation among the people. 这则消息引起人们的不安。）
⑥ slumbery：催眠的，睡眠的
⑦ agitation：（情绪的）纷乱，激动不安
⑧ confirm：确认，确定
⑨ taper：细蜡烛
⑩ guise：装束，形象
⑪ upon my life：以我的生命起誓

Doctor. How came she by that light?

Gentlewoman. Why, it stood by her. She has light by her continually; 'tis her command.

Doctor. You see, her eyes are open.

Gentlewoman. Ay, but their sense is shut.

Doctor. What is it she does now? Look, how she rubs[①] her hands.

Gentlewoman. It is an accustomed[②] action with her, to seem thus washing her hands. I have known her continue in this a quarter of an hour.

LADY MACBETH. Yet here's a spot[③].

Doctor. Hark! she speaks. I will set down what comes from her, to satisfy my remembrance[④] the more strongly.

LADY MACBETH. Out, damned spot! Out, I say!—One: two: why, then, 'tis time to do't. Hell is murky[⑤]! Fie[⑥], my lord, fie! A soldier, and afeard? What need we fear who knows it, when none can call our power to account? Yet who would have thought the old man to have had so much blood in him?

Doctor. Do you mark that?

LADY MACBETH. The thane of Fife had a wife; where is she now? What, will these hands ne'er be clean? No more o' that, my lord, no more o' that. You mar[⑦] all with this starting.

Doctor. Go to, go to; you have known what you should not.

Gentlewoman. She has spoke what she should not, I am sure of that. Heaven knows what she has known.

LADY MACBETH. Here's the smell of the blood still. All the

---

① rub：擦，搓

② accustomed：习惯的，通常的（例如：My eyes were becoming accustomed to the gloom. 我的眼睛渐渐适应了黑暗。）

③ spot：污点，血迹

④ remembrance：回忆，记忆（例如：happier remembrances of family holidays 关于家庭假日的更愉快的记忆）

⑤ murky：黑暗的，幽暗的（例如：murky light 阴暗的光线）

⑥ fie：（表示嫌恶、震惊等）呸

⑦ mar：摧毁，弄糟（例如：A number of problems marred the smooth running of this event. 许多问题影响了这件事的顺利进行。）

perfumes[①] of Arabia[②] will not sweeten this little hand. Oh, oh, oh!

Doctor. What a sigh is there! The heart is sorely[③] charged[④].

Gentlewoman. I would not have such a heart in my bosom for the dignity of the whole body.[⑤]

Doctor. Well, well, well—

Gentlewoman. Pray God it be, sir.

Doctor. This disease is beyond my practice. Yet I have known those which have walked in their sleep who have died holily[⑥] in their beds.

LADY MACBETH. Wash your hands, put on your nightgown, look not so pale. I tell you yet again, Banquo's buried; he cannot come out on's grave.

Doctor. Even so?

LADY MACBETH. To bed, to bed; there's knocking at the gate. Come, come, come, come, give me your hand. What's done cannot be undone. To bed, to bed, to bed.

[Exit.]

Doctor. Will she go now to bed?

Gentlewoman. Directly.

Doctor. Foul whisperings are abroad. Unnatural deeds
Do breed unnatural troubles; infected minds
To their deaf pillows will discharge their secrets.[⑦]
More needs she the divine than the physician.
God, God, forgive us all! Look after her;
Remove from her the means of all annoyance,

---

① perfume：香水，香料
② Arabia：阿拉伯半岛
③ sorely：痛苦的，悲伤的
④ charged：有负担的，负担重的
⑤ 参考译文：我不愿为了身体上的尊荣，而让我的胸膛里装着这样一颗心。（朱生豪译）（bosom：胸怀，内心）
⑥ holily：神圣地，虔诚地
⑦ 参考译文：外边很多骇人听闻的流言。反常的行为引起了反常的纷扰；良心负疚的人往往会向无言的衾枕泄露他们的秘密。（朱生豪译）（breed：引起）

And still keep eyes upon her.[①] So, good night.

My mind she has mated[②] and amazed my sight.

I think, but dare not speak.

Gentlewoman. Good night, good doctor.

[Exeunt.]

---

① 正常语序应为：Remove the means of all annoyance from her and still keep eyes upon her. 参考译文：避免一切足以使她烦恼的根源，随时看顾着她。（朱生豪译）（means：工具，方法；annoyance：可恶的东西，烦人的事情）

② 正常语序应为：She has mated my mind.（mate：扰乱）

SCENE II.

The Country near Dunsinane.

[Drum[①] and colours. Enter MENTEITH, CAITHNESS, ANGUS, LENNOX, and Soldiers.]

MENTEITH. The English power[②] is near, led on by Malcolm,

His uncle Siward and the good Macduff.

Revenges burn in them, for their dear causes

Would to the bleeding and the grim alarm

Excite the mortified man.[③]

ANGUS. Near Birnam wood

Shall we well meet them; that way are they coming.

CAITHNESS. Who knows if Donalbain be with his brother?

LENNOX. For certain, sir, he is not; I have a file

Of all the gentry[④]: there is Siward's son

And many unrough youths that even now

Protest their first of manhood.[⑤]

MENTEITH. What does the tyrant?

CAITHNESS. Great Dunsinane he strongly fortifies[⑥].

Some say he's mad; others, that lesser hate him,

Do call it valiant fury; but, for certain,

He cannot buckle his distemper'd cause

Within the belt of rule.[⑦]

ANGUS. Now does he feel

---

① drum：鼓声

② power：军队

③ 参考译文：他们的胸头燃起复仇的怒火；即使心如死灰的人，这种痛入骨髓的仇恨也会激起他溅血的决心。（朱生豪译）（dear：高贵的；excite：使兴奋；mortified：受辱的，心如死灰的）

④ gentry：高级将领，贵族

⑤ 参考译文：里面有西沃德的儿子，还有许多初上战场、乳臭未干的少年。（朱生豪译）（unrough：乳臭未干的；protest：申明）

⑥ fortify：筑防御工事，加强

⑦ 参考译文：对他比较没有什么恶感的人，却说那是一个猛士的愤怒；可是他不能自己约束住他的惶乱的心情，却是一件无疑的事实。（朱生豪译）这里buckle his distemper'd cause within the belt of rule 是双关语，其一指苏格兰国内纷乱的现状，其二指他自己内心的不安（buckle：束缚；distemper：狂乱，惶恐）

His secret murthers sticking on his hands,
Now minutely revolts upbraid his faith-breach;①
Those he commands move only in command,
Nothing in love. Now does he feel his title
Hang loose about him, like a giant's robe
Upon a dwarfish thief.②

MENTEITH. Who then shall blame
His pester'd senses to recoil and start,
When all that is within him does condemn
Itself for being there?③

CAITHNESS. Well, march we on,
To give obedience④ where 'tis truly owed.
Meet we the medicine of the sickly weal,
And with him pour we, in our country's purge,
Each drop of us.

LENNOX. Or so much as it needs,
To dew⑤ the sovereign flower and drown the weeds.
Make we our march towards Birnam.

[Exeunt, marching.]

---

① 参考译文：现在他已经感觉到他的暗杀的罪恶紧粘在他的手上；每分钟都有一次叛变，谴责他的不忠不义。（朱生豪译）（minutely：每分钟的，随时的；revolt：反抗，叛变；upbraid：谴责，责难）

② 参考文献：现在他已经感觉到他的尊号罩在他的身上，就像一个矮小的偷儿穿了一件巨人的衣服一样拖手绊脚。（朱生豪译）（dwarfish：矮小的，侏儒似的）

③ 参考译文：他自己的灵魂都在谴责它本身的存在，谁还能怪他的昏乱的知觉怔忡不安呢。（朱生豪译）（pester'd：等于pestered，使烦恼，纠缠；recoil：报应）

④ obedience：顺从，服从

⑤ dew：弄湿，浇灌

SCENE III.
Dunsinane. A Room in the Castle.

[Enter MACBETH, Doctor, and Attendants.]

MACBETH. Bring me no more reports; let them fly all:

Till Birnam wood remove to Dunsinane,

I cannot taint with fear. What's the boy Malcolm?

Was he not born of woman? The spirits that know

All mortal consequences have pronounced me thus:

'Fear not, Macbeth; no man that's born of woman

Shall e'er have power upon thee.'① Then fly, false thanes,

And mingle with the English epicures②:

The mind I sway by and the heart I bear,

Shall never sag with doubt nor shake with fear.③

[Enter a Servant.]

The devil damn thee black, thou cream-faced loon!

Where got'st thou that goose look?④

Servant. There is ten thousand—

MACBETH. Geese, villain?

Servant. Soldiers, sir.

MACBETH. Go prick thy face, and over-red thy fear,

Thou lily-liver'd boy.⑤ What soldiers, patch?

Death of thy soul! Those linen cheeks of thine

Are counsellors to fear.⑥ What soldiers, whey-face?

---

① 参考译文：预知人类死生的精灵曾经这样向我宣告："不要害怕，麦克白；没有一个妇人所生下的人可以加害于你。"（朱生豪译）（consequence：后果）

② epicure：享乐者

③ 参考译文：我的头脑，永远不会被疑虑所困扰，我的心灵永远不会被恐惧所震荡。（朱生豪译）（sway：统治，影响；sag：消沉）

④ 参考译文：魔鬼罚你变成炭团一样黑，你这脸色惨白的狗头！你从哪儿得来这么一副呆鹅的蠢相？（朱生豪译）（damn：惩罚，定罪；cream-faced：脸色苍白的；loon：笨蛋）

⑤ 参考译文：去刺破你自己的脸，把你那吓得毫无血色的两颊染一染红吧，你这鼠胆的小子。（朱生豪译）（over-red：形容词用作动词，变太红；lily-live：胆小的，中世纪认为人的勇气都源自于肝，如果肝白得像百合花，则说明没有勇气）

⑥ 参考译文：瞧你吓得脸像白布一般。（朱生豪译）（linen：亚麻布；counsellor：忠告者，顾问）

111

Servant. The English force, so please you.

MACBETH. Take thy face hence.

 [Exit Servant.]

 Seyton①!—I am sick at heart,

 When I behold—Seyton, I say!—This push

 Will cheer me ever, or disseat② me now.

 I have lived long enough: my way of life

 Is fall'n into the sear③, the yellow leaf;

 And that which should accompany old age,

 As honour, love, obedience, troops of friends,

 I must not look to have;④ but, in their stead,

 Curses, not loud but deep, mouth-honour, breath,

 Which the poor heart would fain deny and dare not.⑤

 Seyton!

 [Enter SEYTON.]

SEYTON. What is your gracious pleasure?

MACBETH. What news more?

SEYTON. All is confirm'd, my lord, which was reported.

MACBETH. I'll fight, till from my bones my flesh be hack'd.⑥

 Give me my armour⑦.

SEYTON. 'Tis not needed yet.

MACBETH. I'll put it on.

 Send out more horses, skirr⑧ the country round,

 Hang those that talk of fear. Give me mine armour.

 How does your patient, doctor?

———————————

 ① Seyton：他家是世代相传的重臣，可以在苏格兰国王面前带盔甲。

 ② disseat：倾覆，取代……地位

 ③ sear：烙印，烧焦痕迹

 ④ 参考译文：凡是老年人所应该享有的尊荣、敬爱、服从和一大群的朋友，我是没有希望再得到的了。（朱生豪译）（look to：期待）

 ⑤ 参考译文：代替这一切的，只有低声而深刻的诅咒，口头上的恭维和一些违心的假话。（朱生豪译）（mouth-honour：口头上的荣誉；fain：古英语，热切地，乐意地，仅与 would 连用，后接动词原形）

 ⑥ 正常语序应为：I'll fight, till my flesh be hack'd from my bones. 参考译文：我要战到我的全身不剩一块好肉。（朱生豪译）

 ⑦ armour：铠甲

 ⑧ skirr：快速越过，飞速掠过（例如：An air plane skirred our heads. 一架飞机嗖地一下从我们的头顶飞掠而过。）

112

Doctor. Not so sick, my lord,

As she is troubled with thick-coming fancies,

That keep her from her rest.①

MACBETH. Cure her of that:

Canst thou not minister to a mind diseased,

Pluck from the memory a rooted sorrow,

Raze out the written troubles of the brain,

And with some sweet oblivious antidote

Cleanse the stuff'd bosom of that perilous stuff

Which weighs upon the heart?②

Doctor. Therein the patient

Must minister to himself.

MACBETH. Throw physic③ to the dogs; I'll none of it.

Come, put mine armour on; give me my staff④.

Seyton, send out. Doctor, the thanes fly from me.

Come, sir, dispatch⑤. If thou couldst, doctor, cast

The water of my land, find her disease,

And purge it to a sound and pristine⑥ health,

I would applaud thee to the very echo,

That should applaud again.⑦—Pull't off, I say.—

What rhubarb⑧, cyme, or what purgative⑨ drug,

Would scour⑩ these English hence? Hear'st thou of them?

Doctor. Ay, my good lord; your royal preparation

Makes us hear something.

---

① 参考译文：只是因为思虑太过，继续不断的幻想扰乱了她的神经，使她不得安息。（朱生豪译）（thick：密集的，浓浓的）

② 参考译文：你难道不能诊治一个病态的心理，从记忆中拔出一桩根深蒂固的忧郁，拭掉那写在脑筋上的烦恼，用一种使人忘却一切的甘美的药剂，把那堆满在胸间、重压在心头的积毒扫除干净吗？（朱生豪译）（minister to：帮助，服侍，这里指治疗，诊治；pluck：拔除；raze：消除，除去；cleanse：清除；oblivious：遗忘的；antidote：解药；perilous：危险的）

③ physic：医药，泻药

④ staff：指挥杖

⑤ dispatch：派遣，迅速完成

⑥ pristine：原本的

⑦ 参考译文：我一定要使太空之中充满着我对你的赞美的回声。（朱生豪译）（echo：回声）

⑧ rhubarb：大黄肉桂

⑨ purgative：泻药

⑩ scour：冲刷，冲走

MACBETH. Bring it after me.

　　I will not be afraid of death and bane,

　　Till Birnam forest come to Dunsinane.

Doctor. [Aside.] Were I from Dunsinane away and clear,

　　Profit again should hardly draw me here.[①]

　　[Exeunt.]

SCENE IV.
Country near Birnam Wood.

[Drum and colours. Enter MALCOLM, SIWARD and YOUNG SIWARD, MACDUFF, MENTEITH, CAITHNESS, ANGUS, LENNOX, ROSS, and Soldiers, marching.]

MALCOLM. Cousins, I hope the days are near at hand
  That chambers will be safe. ①

MENTEITH. We doubt it nothing.

SIWARD. What wood is this before us?

MENTEITH. The wood of Birnam.

MALCOLM. Let every soldier hew him down a bough,
  And bear't before him; thereby shall we shadow
  The numbers of our host, and make discovery
  Err in report of us. ②

Soldiers. It shall be done.

SIWARD. We learn no other but the confident tyrant
  Keeps still in Dunsinane, and will endure
  Our setting down before 't.

MALCOLM. 'Tis his main hope;
  For where there is advantage to be given,
  Both more and less have given him the revolt,
  And none serve with him but constrained things
  Whose hearts are absent too. ③

MACDUFF. Let our just censures ④

---

① 参考译文：我希望大家都能够安枕而寝的日子已经不远了。（朱生豪译）（chamber：卧室）

② 参考译文：每一个兵士都砍下一根树枝来，把它举起在各人的面前；这样我们可以隐匿我们全军的人数，让敌人无从知道我们的实力。（朱生豪译）（hew：砍；bough：大树枝；bear：举起；shadow：这里是动词，隐藏；host：军队；err：错误）

③ 参考译文：因为在他手下的人，不论地位高低，一找到机会都要叛弃他，他们接受他的号令，都只是出于被迫，并不是自己心愿。（朱生豪译）（advantage：优势，这里指机会；both more and less：无论职位高低；constrained：被迫的，强迫的）

④ censure：责难，责备

115

Attend the true event, and put we on
Industrious^① soldiership^②.

SIWARD. The time approaches

That will with due decision make us know

What we shall say we have and what we owe.

Thoughts speculative their unsure hopes relate,

But certain issue strokes must arbitrate.^③

Towards which advance the war.

[Exeunt, marching.]

---

① industrious：勤劳的，勤勉的
② soldiership：士兵精神
③ 正常语序应为：Speculative thoughts relate their unsure hopes, but certain issue strokes must arbitrate. 参考译文：口头的推测不过是一些悬空的希望，实际的行动才能够产生决定的结果。（朱生豪译）（speculative：推测的；unsure：不确定的；stroke：举动，尝试，这里指作战；arbitrate：决断）

SCENE V.
Dunsinane. Within the Castle.

[Enter MACBETH, SEYTON, and Soldiers, with drum and colours.]

MACBETH. Hang out our banners[①] on the outward walls;

The cry is still 'They come!' Our castle's strength

Will laugh a siege to scorn.[②] Here let them lie

Till famine[③] and the ague[④] eat them up.

Were they not forced with those that should be ours,

We might have met them dareful, beard to beard,

And beat them backward home.[⑤]

[A cry of women within.]

What is that noise?

SEYTON. It is the cry of women, my good lord.

[Exit.]

MACBETH. I have almost forgot the taste of fears:

The time has been, my senses would have cool'd

To hear a night-shriek; and my fell of hair

Would at a dismal treatise rouse and stir

As life were in't: I have supp'd full with horrors;

Direness, familiar to my slaughterous thoughts,

Cannot once start me.[⑥]

[Re-enter SEYTON.]

---

① banner：旗帜
② 参考译文：我们这座城堡防御得这样坚强，还怕他们围攻吗？（朱生豪译）（siege：围攻）
③ famine：饥荒
④ ague：疟疾
⑤ 参考译文：我们尽可以挺身出战，把他们赶回老家去。（朱生豪译）（dareful：大胆的）
⑥ 正常语序应为：The time has been, to hear a night-shriek my senses would have cool'd and my fell of hair would rouse and stir at a dismal treatise as life were in't: I have supp'd full with horrors; Direness cannot once start me. 其中 familiar to my slaughterous thoughts 是插入语，解释 direness。参考译文：从前一声晚间的哀叫，可以把我吓出一身冷汗，听着一段可怕的故事，我的头发也会像有了生命似的竖起来。现在我已经饱尝无数的恐怖；我的习惯于杀戮的思想，再也没有什么悲惨的事情可以使它惊悸了。（朱生豪译）（cool'd：等于 cooled，变冷；treatise：（废语）故事；direness：可怕，悲惨；slaughterous：杀戮的；start：使惊恐）

117

Wherefore was that cry?

SEYTON. The queen, my lord, is dead.

MACBETH. She should have died hereafter;

There would have been a time for such a word.

To-morrow, and to-morrow, and to-morrow,

Creeps in this petty pace from day to day,

To the last syllable of recorded time;[①]

And all our yesterdays have lighted fools

The way to dusty death. Out, out, brief candle!

Life's but a walking shadow, a poor player,

That struts and frets his hour upon the stage,

And then is heard no more.[②] It is a tale

Told by an idiot, full of sound and fury,

Signifying[③] nothing.

[Enter a Messenger.]

Thou comest to use thy tongue; thy story quickly.

Messenger. Gracious my lord,

I should report that which I say I saw,

But know not how to do it.

MACBETH. Well, say, sir.

Messenger. As I did stand my watch upon the hill,

I look'd toward Birnam, and anon, methought,

The wood began to move.

MACBETH. Liar and slave!

Messenger. Let me endure your wrath, if't be not so:

Within this three mile may you see it coming;

I say, a moving grove.

MACBETH. If thou speak'st false,

Upon the next tree shalt thou hang alive,

---

① 参考译文：明天，明天，再一个明天，一天接着一天地蹑步前进，直到最后一秒钟的时间。（朱生豪译）（creeps：爬行；syllable：声音）

② 参考译文：人生不过是一个行走的影子，一个在舞台上指手画脚的拙劣的伶人，登场片刻，就在无声无臭中悄然退下。（朱生豪译）（strut：大摇大摆地走；fret：烦躁，苦恼）

③ signify：说明，预示（例如：Do dark clouds signify rain? 乌云是否预示要下雨？）

118

Till famine cling thee;[①] if thy speech be sooth,
I care not if thou dost for me as much.
I pull in resolution, and begin
To doubt the equivocation of the fiend
That lies like truth: 'Fear not, till Birnam wood
Do come to Dunsinane;'[②] and now a wood
Comes toward Dunsinane. Arm, arm, and out!
If this which he avouches does appear,
There is nor flying hence nor tarrying[③] here.
I 'gin to be aweary[④] of the sun,
And wish the estate[⑤] o' the world were now undone.
Ring the alarum bell! Blow, wind! come, wrack[⑥]!
At least we'll die with harness on our back[⑦].
[Exeunt.]

---

① 正常语序应为：If thou speak'st false, thou shalt hang alive upon the next tree till famine cling thee. 参考译文：要是你说了谎话，我要把你活活吊在树上，让你饥饿而死。（朱生豪译）

② 参考译文：要是你的话是真的，我也希望你把我吊死了吧。我的决心已经有些动摇，我开始怀疑起那魔鬼所说的似是而非的暧昧的谎话了："不要害怕，除非勃南森林会到邓斯纳恩来。"（朱生豪译）（sooth：真实的；dost：do 的第二人称单数现在式；equivocation：含糊的话；fiend：恶魔般的人，这里指上文中出现的女巫；that lies like truth：谎言成为现实）

③ tarrying：耽搁，逗留（例如：He tarried for a few days in my house. 他在我家里小住了几天。）

④ aweary：疲倦的，厌倦的，倦怠的

⑤ estate：状态，秩序

⑥ wrack：毁灭（例如：wrack and ruin 毁灭）

⑦ die with harness on our back：战死在沙场；die with harness 是莎士比亚首次在他的作品中使用的新短语，一直流传下来，意思为因公殉职（harness：甲胄，盔甲）

SCENE VI.
Dunsinane. Before the Castle.

[Drum and colours. Enter MALCOLM, SIWARD, MACDUFF, and their Army, with boughs.]

MALCOLM. Now near enough; your leavy screens throw down, And show like those you are.[①] You, worthy uncle, Shall, with my cousin, your right-noble son, Lead our first battle. Worthy Macduff and we Shall take upon 's what else remains to do, According to our order.

SIWARD. Fare you well. Do we but find the tyrant's power to-night, Let us be beaten[②], if we cannot fight.

MACDUFF. Make all our trumpets speak; give them all breath, Those clamorous harbingers of blood and death.[③]

[Exeunt.]

---

① 参考译文：现在已经相去不远；把你们树叶的幕障抛下，现出你们威武的军容来。（朱生豪译）

② beat：打败

③ 参考译文：把我们所有的喇叭一齐吹起来；鼓足了你们的中气，把流血和死亡的消息吹进敌人的耳里。（朱生豪译）（trumpet：喇叭；clamorous：吵闹的；harbinger：预示，预兆）

SCENE VII.
Another Part of the Field.

[Alarums. Enter MACBETH.]

MACBETH. <u>They have tied me to a stake; I cannot fly</u>[①],

But, bear-like, I must fight the course. What's he

That was not born of woman? Such a one

Am I to fear, or none.

[Enter YOUNG SIWARD.]

YOUNG SIWARD. What is thy name?

MACBETH. Thou'lt be afraid to hear it.

YOUNG SIWARD. <u>No, though thou call'st thyself a hotter name</u>

<u>Than any is in hell.</u>[②]

MACBETH. My name's Macbeth.

YOUNG SIWARD. The devil himself could not pronounce a title

More hateful to mine ear.

MACBETH. No, nor more fearful.

YOUNG SIWARD. Thou liest[③], abhorred[④] tyrant; with my sword

I'll prove the lie thou speak'st.

[They fight and YOUNG SIWARD is slain.]

MACBETH. <u>Thou wast born of woman.</u>

<u>But swords I smile at, weapons laugh to scorn,</u>

<u>Brandish'd by man that's of a woman born.</u>[⑤]

[Exit.]

[Alarums. Enter MACDUFF.]

MACDUFF. That way the noise is. Tyrant, show thy face!

If thou be'st slain and with no stroke of mine,

---

① 参考译文：他们已经缚住我的手脚；我不能逃走。（朱生豪译）（stake：桩）

② 参考译文：即使你给自己取了一个比地狱里的魔鬼更炽热的名字，也吓不倒我。（朱生豪译）

③ liest：等于 lied，撒谎

④ abhorred：可恶的

⑤ 正常语序应为：Thou wast born of woman, but I smile at swords, laugh to scorn weapons, brandish'd by man that's of a woman born. 参考译文：你是妇人所生的；我瞧不起一切妇人之子手里的刀剑。（朱生豪译）（brandish'd：等于 brandished，挥，挥舞）

My wife and children's ghosts will haunt me still.

I cannot strike at wretched kerns, whose arms

Are hired to bear their staves.① Either thou, Macbeth,

Or else my sword with an unbatter'd edge,

I sheathe again undeeded.② There thou shouldst be;

By this great clatter, one of greatest note

Seems bruited. Let me find him, Fortune!

And more I beg not.③

[Exit. Alarums.]

[Enter MALCOLM and SIWARD.]

SIWARD. This way, my lord; the castle's gently render'd④:

The tyrant's people on both sides do fight;

The noble thanes do bravely in the war;

The day almost itself professes yours,

And little is to do.⑤

MALCOLM. We have met with foes⑥

That strike beside us.

SIWARD. Enter, sir, the castle.

[Exeunt. Alarums.]

[Re-enter MACBETH.]

MACBETH. Why should I play the Roman fool, and die

On mine own sword? Whiles I see lives, the gashes

Do better upon them.

[Enter MACDUFF.]

MACDUFF. Turn, hell-hound, turn!

MACBETH. Of all men else I have avoided thee.

---

① 参考译文：我不能杀害那些被你雇用的倒霉的士卒。（朱生豪译）（wretched：可怜的，倒霉的）

② 参考译文：我的剑倘不能刺中你，麦克白，我宁愿让它闲置不用，保全它的锋刃，把它重新插回鞘里。（朱生豪译）（sheathe：把……插入鞘）

③ 参考译文：这一阵高声的呐喊，好像是宣布什么重要的人物上阵似的。命运，让我找到他吧！我没有此外的奢求了。（clatter：高声的呐喊；bruit：宣布）

④ render'd：等于 rendered，render 的过去式，投降

⑤ 参考译文：您已经胜算在握，大势就可以决定了。（朱生豪译）（professes：承认，归顺）

⑥ foe：敌人

But get thee back; my soul is too much charged
With blood of thine already.[1]

MACDUFF. I have no words.

My voice is in my sword, thou bloodier[2] villain
Than terms can give thee out!

[They fight.]

MACBETH. Thou losest labour.

As easy mayst thou the intrenchant air
With thy keen sword impress as make me bleed.
Let fall thy blade on vulnerable crests;[3]
I bear a charmed life, which must not yield,
To one of woman born.

MACDUFF. Despair thy charm,

And let the angel whom thou still hast served[4]
Tell thee, Macduff was from his mother's womb[5]
Untimely ripp'd.

MACBETH. Accursed be that tongue that tells me so,
For it hath cow'd my better part of man![6]
And be these juggling fiends no more believed,
That palter with us in a double sense,
That keep the word of promise to our ear,
And break it to our hope.[7] I'll not fight with thee.

MACDUFF. Then yield thee, coward,

And live to be the show and gaze o' the time:
We'll have thee, as our rarer monsters are,

---

① 参考译文：可是你回去吧，我的灵魂里沾着你一家人的血，已经太多了。(朱生豪译)

② bloodier: bloody 的比较级，血腥的，嗜杀的

③ 正常语序应为：Thou mayst impress the intrenchant air with thy keen sword as easy as make me bleed. Let thy blade fall on vulnerable crests. 参考译文：你要使我流血，正像用你锐利的剑锋在空气上划一道痕迹一样困难。让你的刀刃降落别人的头上吧。(朱生豪译)(intrenchant: 不能被砍伤的；blade: 刀刃；vulnerable: 易受伤害的)

④ serve: 服侍

⑤ womb: 子宫

⑥ 参考译文：愿那告诉我这样的话的舌头永受诅咒，因为它使我失去了男子汉的勇气！(朱生豪译)

⑦ 参考译文：愿这些欺人的魔鬼再也不要被人相信，他们用模棱两可的话愚弄我们，听来好像大有希望，结果却完全和我们原来的期望相反。(朱生豪译)(juggling: 欺骗人的)

Painted on a pole, and underwrit,

'Here may you see the tyrant.' ①

MACBETH. I will not yield,

To kiss the ground before young Malcolm's feet,

And to be baited② with the rabble③'s curse.

Though Birnam wood be come to Dunsinane,

And thou opposed, being of no woman born,

Yet I will try the last. Before my body

I throw my warlike shield④. Lay on, Macduff,

And damn'd be him that first cries, 'Hold, enough!'

[Exeunt, fighting. Alarums.]

[Retreat. Flourish. Enter, with drum and colours, MALCOLM,

SIWARD, ROSS, the other Thanes, and Soldiers.]

MALCOLM. I would the friends we miss were safe arrived.⑤

SIWARD. Some must go off⑥. and yet, by these I see,

So great a day as this is cheaply bought.

MALCOLM. Macduff is missing, and your noble son.

ROSS. Your son, my lord, has paid a soldier's debt⑦.

He only lived but till he was a man,

The which no sooner had his prowess⑧ confirm'd

In the unshrinking⑨ station where he fought,

But like a man he died.

SIWARD. Then he is dead?

ROSS. Ay, and brought off the field. Your cause of sorrow

Must not be measured by his worth, for then

---

① 参考译文：我们可以饶你活命，可是要叫你在众人的面前出丑：我们要把你当做一头稀有的怪物一样，把你缚在柱上，涂上花脸，下面写着："请看暴君的原形。"（朱生豪译）（pole：柱子；underwrite：写在……下面）

② bait：欺负，折磨

③ rabble：乌合之众，暴民

④ shield：盾牌

⑤ 参考译文：我希望我们所失去的朋友都能够安然到来。（朱生豪译）

⑥ go off：消失，这里指牺牲

⑦ pay a debt：还清债务，这里指尽职责

⑧ prowess：英勇

⑨ unshrinking：不畏缩的，坚定的（例如：Her glance was perfectly direct and unshrinking. 她的目光非常坦诚坚定。）

It hath no end.①

SIWARD. Had he his hurts② before?

ROSS. Ay, on the front.

SIWARD. Why then, God's soldier be he!

Had I as many sons as I have hairs,

I would not wish them to a fairer death.③

And so, his knell is knoll'd.

MALCOLM. He's worth more sorrow,

And that I'll spend for④ him.

SIWARD. He's worth no more:

They say he parted well, and paid his score,

And so, God be with him! Here comes newer comfort.

[Re-enter MACDUFF, with MACBETH's head.]

MACDUFF. Hail, king! For so thou art. Behold, where stands

The usurper⑤'s cursed head. The time is free.

I see thee compass'd with thy kingdom's pearl,⑥

That speak my salutation in their minds,

Whose voices I desire aloud with mine:⑦

Hail, King of Scotland!

ALL. Hail, King of Scotland!

[Flourish.]

MALCOLM. We shall not spend a large expense of time

Before we reckon with your several loves,

And make us even with you.⑧ My thanes and kinsmen,

---

① 参考译文：他的死是一桩无价的损失，您必须勉抑哀思才好。（朱生豪译）

② hurt：伤口

③ 参考译文：要是我有像头发一样多的儿子，我也不希望他们得到一个更光荣的结局。（朱生豪译）（hairs：与 heirs 是谐音，这里是双关用法；fair：正大光明的）

④ spend for：这里指为……治丧

⑤ usurper：篡位者

⑥ 参考译文：无道的虐政从此推翻了。我看见全国的英俊拥绕在你的周围。（朱生豪译）（compass'd：等于 compassed，包围，包含；pearl：本意为珍珠，这里指贵族们）

⑦ 参考译文：他们心里都在发出跟我同样的敬礼；现在我要请他们陪着我高呼。（朱生豪译）（salutation：致意，致敬）

⑧ 参考译文：多承各位拥戴，论功行赏，在此一朝。（朱生豪译）（reckon：评定，估计；even：公平的）

Henceforth[①] be earls[②], the first that ever Scotland
In such an honour named. What's more to do,
Which would be planted newly with the time,
As calling home our exiled friends abroad
That fled the snares of watchful tyranny,[③]
Producing forth the cruel ministers
Of this dead butcher and his fiend-like queen,
Who, as 'tis thought, by self and violent hands
Took off her life;[④] this, and what needful else
That calls upon us, by the grace of Grace,
We will perform in measure, time and place.
So thanks to all at once and to each one,
Whom we invite to see us crown'd at Scone.[⑤]
[Flourish. Exeunt.]

[①] henceforth：从今以后
[②] earls：伯爵
[③] 正常语序应为：As calling our exiled friends abroad that fled the snares of watchful tyranny home. 参考译文：那些因为逃避暴君的罗网而出亡国外的朋友们，我们必须召唤他们回来。（朱生豪译）（exiled：放逐的；snare：陷阱，罗网；watchful：警惕的，戒备的）
[④] 参考译文：这个屠夫虽然已经死了，他的魔鬼一样的王后，据说也已经亲手杀害了自己的生命，可是帮助他们杀人行凶的党羽，我们必须一一搜捕，处以极刑。（朱生豪译）（produce forth：找出来；fiend-like：魔鬼一样的；take off：取走）
[⑤] 参考译文：现在我要感谢各位的相助，还要请你们陪我到斯贡去，参与加冕大典。（朱生豪译）（at once：现在）

MACBETH

麦克白

[英]威廉·莎士比亚◎著

朱生豪◎译

中国宇航出版社

·北京·

图书在版编目（CIP）数据

麦克白：汉英对照 /（英）威廉·莎士比亚
（William Shakespeare）著；朱生豪译. --北京：中
国宇航出版社，2016.7（2019.8重印）
　　书名原文：Macbeth
　　ISBN 978-7-5159-1131-1

　　Ⅰ. ①麦… Ⅱ. ①威… ②朱… Ⅲ. ①英语—汉语—
对照读物②悲剧—剧本—英国—中世纪 Ⅳ.
①H319.4：I

中国版本图书馆CIP数据核字（2016）第139226号

策划编辑　战　颖　李　莹　　　装帧设计　李彦生
责任编辑　孙冠群　　　　　　　　责任校对　刘　杰

出　版
发　行　中国宇航出版社

社　址　北京市阜成路8号　　　邮　编　100830
　　　　（010）60286808　　　　（010）68768548
网　址　www.caphbook.com
经　销　新华书店
发行部　（010）60286888　　　　（010）68371900
　　　　（010）60286887　　　　（010）60286804（传真）
零售店　读者服务部
　　　　（010）68371105
承　印　北京中科印刷有限公司
版　次　2016年7月第1版　　　2019年8月第7次印刷
规　格　880×1230　　　　　　开　本　1/32
印　张　3　　　　　　　　　　字　数　57千字
书　号　ISBN 978-7-5159-1131-1
定　价　29.80元

本书如有印装质量问题，可与发行部联系调换

目录
Contents

剧中人物

邓肯	苏格兰国王
马尔科姆 道纳本	邓肯之子
麦克白 班柯	苏格兰军中大将
麦克达夫 伦诺克斯 罗斯 门蒂思 安格斯 凯恩尼斯	苏格兰贵族
弗里恩斯	班柯之子
西沃德	诺森伯兰伯爵，英格兰军中大将
小西沃德	西沃德之子
西登	麦克白的侍臣
麦克达夫的幼子	
一英格兰医生	
一苏格兰医生	
一军曹	

一司阍

一老翁

麦克白夫人

麦克达夫夫人

麦克白夫人的侍女

赫卡忒及三女巫

贵族、绅士、将领、兵士、刺客、侍从及使者等

班柯的鬼魂及其他幽灵等

地点

苏格兰　英格兰

第一幕

第一场　荒野

　　　　雷电。三女巫上。

女巫甲　何时姊妹再相逢，

　　　　雷电轰轰雨蒙蒙？

女巫乙　且等烽烟静四陲，

　　　　败军高奏凯歌回。

女巫丙　半山夕照尚含晖。

女巫甲　何处相逢？

女巫乙　荒野遇。

女巫丙　共同去见麦克白。

女巫甲　我来了，狸猫精。

女巫乙　癞蛤蟆在叫我。

女巫丙　来也。①

三女巫　（合）美即丑恶丑即美，

---

① 三女巫各有一精怪听其驱使：侍候女巫甲的是狸猫精，侍候女巫
　乙的是癞蛤蟆，侍候女巫丙的是怪鸟。

3

翱翔毒雾妖云里。（同下）

第二场　福累斯附近的营地

内号角声。邓肯、马尔科姆、道纳本、伦诺克斯及侍从等上，与一流血之军曹相遇。

邓肯　那个流血的人是谁？看他的样子，也许可以向我们报告关于乱事的最近的消息。

马尔科姆　这就是那个奋勇苦战帮助我冲出敌人重围的军曹。祝福，勇敢的朋友！把你离开战场以前的战况报告王上。

军曹　双方还在胜负未决之中；正像两个精疲力竭的游泳者，彼此扭成一团，显不出他们的本领来。那残暴的麦克唐华德不愧为一个叛徒，因为无数奸恶的天性都丛集于他的一身；他已经征调了西方各岛上的轻重步兵，命运也好像一个娼妓一样，有意向叛徒卖弄风情，助长他的罪恶的气焰。可是这一切都无能为力，因为英勇的麦克白——真当得起"英勇"这话——不以命运的喜怒为意，挥舞着他的血腥的宝剑，一路砍杀过去，直到了那奴才的面前，也不打一句话，就挺剑从他的肚脐上刺了进去，把他的胸膛划破，一直划到下巴上；他的头已经割下来挂在我们的城楼上了。

4

邓肯 啊，英勇的表弟！尊贵的壮士！

军曹 天有不测风云，从那透露曙光的东方偏卷来了无情的风暴、可怕的雷雨；我们正在兴高采烈的时候，却又遭遇了重大的打击。听着，陛下，听着：当正义凭着勇气的威力正在驱逐敌军向后溃退的时候，挪威国君看见有机可乘，调了一批甲械精良的生力部队又向我们开始一次新的猛攻。

邓肯 我们的将军们，麦克白和班柯有没有因此而气馁？

军曹 是的，要是麻雀能使怒鹰退却，兔子能把雄狮吓走的话。实实在在地说，他们就像两尊巨炮，满装着双倍火力的炮弹，愈发愈猛地向敌人射击；瞧他们的神气，好像拼着浴血负创，非让尸骸铺满了原野，决不罢手似的。可是我的气力已经不济了，我的伤口需要医治。

邓肯 你的叙述和你的伤口一样，都表现出一个战士的精神。来，把他送到军医那儿去。（侍从扶军曹下）

　　　　罗斯上。

邓肯 谁来啦？

马尔科姆 尊贵的罗斯爵士。

伦诺克斯 他的眼睛里露出多么慌张的神色！好像要说些什么古怪的事情似的。

罗斯 上帝保佑吾王！

邓肯 爵士，你从什么地方来？

罗斯 从法夫来，陛下。挪威的旌旗在那边的天空招展，把

5

一阵寒风扇进了我们人民的心里。挪威国君亲自率领了大队人马，靠着那个最奸恶的叛徒考特爵士的帮助，开始了一场残酷的血战；直到麦克白擐甲而前，和他奋勇交锋，方才挫折了他的傲气；胜利终于属我们所有。——

邓肯　好大的幸运！

罗斯　现在史威诺，挪威的国王，已经向我们求和了；我们责令他在圣戈姆小岛上缴纳一万块钱充入我们的国库，否则不让他把战死的将士埋葬。

邓肯　我们不能再让考特爵士窃取我们的厚爱。把他立刻宣布死刑，他的原来的爵位移赠麦克白。

罗斯　我就去执行陛下的旨意。

邓肯　他所失去的，也就是尊贵的麦克白所得到的。（同下）

第三场　荒野

雷鸣。三女巫上。

女巫甲　妹妹，你从哪儿来？

女巫乙　我刚杀了猪来。

女巫丙　姐姐，你从哪儿来？

女巫甲　一个水手的妻子坐在那儿吃栗子，唧呀唧呀唧呀地唧着。"给我，"我说。"滚开，妖巫！"那个吃人家剩下来的肉皮肉骨的贱人喊起来了。她的丈夫是"猛虎号"

6

的船长，到阿勒坡去了；可是我要坐在一张筛子里追上他去，像一头没有尾巴的老鼠，我要去，我要去，我要去。

女巫乙 我助你一阵风。

女巫甲 感谢你的神通。

女巫丙 我也助你一阵风。

女巫甲 驾风直到海西东。

到处狂风吹海立，

浪打行船无休息；

终朝终夜不得安，

骨瘦如柴血色干；

年年辛苦月月劳，

气断神疲精力销；

波涛汹涌鱼龙怒，

一叶漂流无定处。

瞧我有些什么东西？

女巫乙 给我看，给我看。

女巫甲 这是一个在归途覆舟殒命的舵工的拇指。（内鼓声。）

女巫丙 鼓声！鼓声！麦克白来了。

三女巫（合）手携手，三姊妹，

沧海高山弹指地，

朝飞暮返任游戏。

姊三巡，妹三巡，

7

三三九转蛊方成。

　　麦克白及班柯上。

麦克白　我从来没有见过这样阴郁而又这样光明的日子。

班柯　到福累斯还有多少路？这些是什么人，形容这样枯瘦，服装这样怪诞，不像是地上的居民，可是却在地上出现？你们是活人吗？你们能不能回答我们的问题？好像你们懂得我的话，每一个人都同时把她满是皱纹的手指按在她的干枯的嘴唇上。你们应当是女人，可是你们的胡须却使我不敢相信你们是女人。

麦克白　你们要是能够讲话，告诉我们你们是什么人？

女巫甲　万福，麦克白，祝福你，葛莱密斯爵士！

女巫乙　万福，麦克白，祝福你，考特爵士！

女巫丙　万福，麦克白，未来的君王！

班柯　将军，您为什么这样吃惊，好像害怕这种听上去很好的消息似的？用真理的名义回答我，你们是幻象呢，还是果然是像你们所显现的那样子的生物？你们向我的高贵的同伴致敬，并且预言他未来的尊荣和远大的希望，使他听得出了神；可是你们却没有对我说一句话。要是你们能够洞察时间所播的种子，知道哪一颗会长成，哪一颗不会长成，那么请对我说吧；我既不乞讨你们的恩惠，也不惧怕你们的憎恨。

女巫甲　祝福！

女巫乙　祝福！

女巫丙 祝福!

女巫甲 比麦克白低微,可是你的地位在他之上。

女巫乙 不像麦克白那样幸运,可是你比他更为有福。

女巫丙 你虽然不是君王,你的子孙将要君临一国。万福,
麦克白和班柯!

女巫甲 班柯和麦克白,万福!

麦克白 且慢,你们这些闪烁其词的预言者,明白一点告诉
我。西纳尔^①死了以后,我知道我已经晋封为葛莱密斯爵
士;可是怎么会做起考特爵士来呢?考特爵士现在还活
着,他的势力非常煊赫;至于说我是未来的君王,那正
像说我是考特爵士一样难以置信。说,你们这种奇怪的
消息是从什么地方来的?为什么你们要在这荒凉的旷野
用这种预言式的称呼使我们止步?说,我命令你们。(三
女巫隐去)

班柯 水上有泡沫,土地也有泡沫,这些便是大地上的泡沫。
她们消失到什么地方去了?

麦克白 消失在空气之中,好像是有形体的东西,却像呼吸
一样融化在风里了。我倒希望她们再多留一会儿。

班柯 我们正在谈论的这些怪物,果然曾经在这儿出现吗?
还是因为我们误食了令人疯狂的草根,已经丧失了我们
的理智?

---

① 西纳尔,麦克白的父亲。

9

麦克白 您的子孙将要成为君王。

班柯 您自己将要成为君王。

麦克白 而且还要做考特爵士；她们不是这样说的吗？

班柯 正是这样说的。谁来啦？

> 罗斯及安格斯上。

罗斯 麦克白，王上已经很高兴地接到了你的胜利的消息；当他听见你在这次征讨叛逆的战争中所表现的英勇的勋绩的时候，他简直不知道应当惊异还是应当赞叹，在这两种心理的交相冲突之下，他快乐得说不出话来。他又知道你在同一天之内，又在雄壮的挪威大军的阵地上出现，不因为你自己亲手造成的死亡的惨象而感到些微的恐惧。报信的人像密雹一样接踵而至，异口同声地在他的面前称颂你的保卫祖国的大功。

安格斯 我们奉王上的命令前来，向你传达他的慰劳的诚意；我们的使命只是迎接你回去面谒王上，不是来酬答你的功绩。

罗斯 为了向你保证他将给你更大的尊荣起见，他叫我替你加上考特爵士的称号；祝福你，最尊贵的爵士！这一个尊号是属于你的了。

班柯 什么！魔鬼居然会说真话吗？

麦克白 考特爵士现在还活着；为什么你们要替我穿上借来的衣服？

安格斯 原来的考特爵士现在还活着，可是因为他自取其咎，

10

犯了不赦的重罪，在无情的判决之下，将要失去他的生命。他究竟有没有和挪威人公然联合，或者曾经给叛党秘密的援助，或者同时用这两种手段来图谋颠覆他的祖国，我还不能确实知道；可是他的叛国的重罪，已经由他亲口供认，并且有了事实的证明，使他遭到了毁灭的命运。

麦克白 （旁白）葛莱密斯，考特爵士；最大的尊荣还在后面。（向罗斯、安格斯）谢谢你们的跋涉。（向班柯）她们叫我考特爵士，果然被她们说中了；您不希望您的子孙将来做君王吗？

班柯 您要是果然相信了她们的话，也许做了考特爵士以后，还想把王冠攫到手里。可是这种事情很奇怪；魔鬼为了要陷害我们起见，往往故意向我们说真话，在小事情上取得我们的信任，然后我们在重要的关头便会坠入他的圈套。两位大人，让我对你们说句话。

麦克白 （旁白）两句话已经证实，这是我有一天将会跻登王座的幸运的预告。（向罗斯、安格斯）谢谢你们两位。（旁白）这种神奇的启示不会是凶兆，可是也不像是吉兆。假如它是凶兆，为什么一开头就用一句灵验的预言保证我未来的成功呢？我现在不是已经做了考特爵士了吗？假如它是吉兆，为什么那句话会在我脑中引起可怖的印象，使我毛发森然，使我的心全然失去常态，怦怦地跳个不住呢？想象中的恐怖远过于实际上的恐怖；我的思想中不过偶然浮起了杀人的妄念，就已经使我全身震撼，心灵在疑似的猜测之中丧失了作用，把虚无的幻影认为真实了。

班柯　瞧，我们的同伴想得多么出神。

麦克白　（旁白）要是命运将会使我成为君王，那么也许命运会替我加上王冠，用不着我自己费力。

班柯　新的尊荣加在他的身上，就像我们穿上新衣服一样，在没有穿惯以前，总觉得有些不大适合身材似的。

麦克白　（旁白）无论事情怎样发生，最难堪的日子也是会过去的。

班柯　尊贵的麦克白，我们在等候着您的意旨。

麦克白　原谅我；我的迟钝的脑筋刚才偶然想起了一些已经忘记了的事情。两位大人，你们的辛苦已经铭刻在我的心版上，我每天都要把它翻开来诵读。让我们到王上那儿去。想一想最近发生的这些事情；等我们把一切仔细考虑过了以后，再把各人心里的意思彼此开诚相告吧。

班柯　很好。

麦克白　现在暂时不必多说。来，朋友们。（同下）

第四场　福累斯　王宫中的一室

　　喇叭奏花腔。邓肯、马尔科姆、道纳本、伦诺克斯
及侍从等上。

邓肯　考特的死刑有没有执行完毕？监刑的人还没有回
来吗？

马尔科姆　陛下，他们还没有回来；可是我曾经和一个亲眼
看见他死的人谈过话，他说他很坦白地供认他的叛逆，
请求您宽恕他的罪恶，并且表示深切的悔恨。他的一生
行事，从来不曾像他临终的时候那样值得钦佩；他抱着
视死如归的态度，抛弃了他的最宝贵的生命，就像它是
不足介意的琐屑一样。

邓肯　世上还没有一种方法，可以从一个人的脸上探察他的
居心；他是我所曾经绝对信任的一个人。

　　麦克白、班柯、罗斯及安格斯上。

邓肯　啊，贤卿！我的忘恩负义的罪恶，刚才还重压在我的
心头。你的功劳太超乎寻常了，飞得最快的报酬都追不
上你；要是它再微小一点，那么也许我可以按照适当的
名分，给你应得的感谢和酬劳；现在我只能这样说，一
切的报酬都不能抵偿你的伟大的勋绩。

麦克白　为陛下尽忠效命，它的本身就是一种酬报。接受我
们的劳力是陛下的名分；我们对于陛下和王国的责任，

13

正像子女和奴仆一样，为了尽我们的敬爱之忱，无论做什么事都是应该的。

邓肯　欢迎你回来；我已经开始把你栽培，我要努力使你繁茂。尊贵的班柯，你的功劳也不在他之下，让我把你拥抱在我的心头。

班柯　要是我能够在陛下的心头生长，那收获是属于陛下的。

邓肯　我的洋溢在心头的盛大的喜乐，想要在悲哀的泪滴里隐藏它自己。吾儿，各位国戚，各位爵士，以及一切最亲近的人，我现在向你们宣布封我的长子马尔科姆为肯勃兰亲王，他将来要继承我的王位；不仅仅是他一个人受到这样的光荣，广大的恩宠将要像繁星一样，照耀在每一个有功者的身上。陪我到因弗内斯去，让我再叨受你一次盛情的招待。

麦克白　这是一个莫大的光荣；让我做一个前驱者，把陛下光临的喜讯先去报告我的妻子知道；现在我就此告辞了。

邓肯　我的尊贵的考特！

麦克白　（旁白）肯勃兰亲王！这是一块横在我的前途上的阶石，我必须跳过这块阶石，否则就要颠仆在它的上面。星星啊，收起你们的火焰！不要让光亮照见我的黑暗幽深的欲望。眼睛啊，看着这双手吧；可是我仍要下手，就算干下的事会让眼睛不敢卒睹。（下）

邓肯　真的，尊贵的班柯；他真是英勇非凡，我已经饱听人家对他的赞美，那对我就像是一桌盛筵。他现在先去预备款待我们了，让我们跟上去。真是一个无比的国戚。

（喇叭奏花腔。众下）

第五场　因弗内斯　麦克白的城堡

麦克白夫人上，读信。

麦克白夫人　"她们在我胜利的那天迎接我；我根据最可靠的说法，知道她们是具有超越凡俗的知识的。当我燃烧着热烈的欲望，想要向她们详细询问的时候，她们已经化为一阵风不见了。我正在惊奇不止，王上的使者就来了，他们都称我为'考特爵士'；那一个尊号正是这些神巫用来称呼我的，而且她们还对我作这样的预示，说是'祝福，未来的君王！'我想我应该把这样的消息告诉你，我的最亲爱的有福同享的伴侣，好让你不至于因为对于你所将要得到的富贵一无所知，而失去你所应该享有的欢欣。把它放在你的心头，再会。"

你现在已经一身兼葛莱密斯和考特两个显爵，将来也会达到那预言所告诉你的那样高位。可是我却为你的天性忧虑：它充满了太多的人情的乳臭，使你不敢采取最近的捷径；你希望做一个伟大的人物，你不是没有野心，可是你却缺少和那种野心相联属的奸恶；你的欲望很大，但又希望用正直的手段，一方面不愿玩弄机诈，

15

一方面却又要作非分的攫夺；伟大的爵士，你想要的那东西正在喊："你要到手，就得这样干！"你也不是不肯这样干，而是怕干。赶快回来吧，让我把我的精神倾注在你的耳中；命运和玄奇的力量分明已经准备把黄金的宝冠罩在你的头上，让我用舌尖的勇气，把那阻止你得到那顶王冠的一切障碍驱扫一空吧。

　　　　一使者上。

麦克白夫人　你带了些什么消息来？

使者　王上今晚要到这儿来。

麦克白夫人　你在说疯话吗？主人是不是跟他在一起？要是在一起的话，一定会早就通知我们准备准备的。

使者　禀夫人，这话是真的。我们的爵爷快要来了；我的一个伙伴比他早到了一步，他奔得气都喘不过来，好容易告诉了我这个消息。

麦克白夫人　好好看顾他；他带来了重大的消息。（使者下）报告邓肯走进我这堡门来送死的乌鸦，它的叫声是嘶哑的。来，注视着人类恶念的魔鬼们！解除我的女性的柔弱，用最凶恶的残忍自顶至踵贯注在我的全身；凝结我的血液，不要让悔恨通过我的心头，不要让天性中的恻隐摇动我的狠毒的决意！来，你们这些杀人的助手，你们无形的躯体散满在空间，到处找寻为非作恶的机会，进入我妇人的胸中，把我的乳水当做胆汁吧！来，阴沉的黑夜，用最昏暗的地狱中的浓烟罩住你自己，让我的

16

锐利的刀瞧不见它自己切开的伤口，让青天不能从黑暗的重衾里探出头来，高喊"住手，住手！"

麦克白上。

麦克白夫人　伟大的葛莱密斯！尊贵的考特！比葛莱密斯更伟大，比考特更尊贵的未来的统治者！你的信使我飞越蒙昧的现在，我已经感觉到未来的搏动了。

麦克白　我的最亲爱的亲人，邓肯今晚要到这儿来。

麦克白夫人　什么时候回去呢？

麦克白　他预备明天回去。

麦克白夫人　啊！太阳永远不会见到那样一个明天。您的脸，我的爵爷，正像一本书，人们可以从那上面读到奇怪的事情。您要欺骗世人，必须装出和世人同样的神气；让您的眼睛里，您的手上，您的舌尖，随处流露着欢迎；让人家瞧您像一朵纯洁的花朵，可是在花瓣底下却有一条毒蛇潜伏。我们必须准备款待这位贵宾；您可以把今晚的大事交给我去办；凭此一举，我们今后就可以永远掌握君临万民的无上权威。

麦克白　我们还要商量商量。

麦克白夫人　泰然自若地抬起您的头来；脸上变色最易引起猜疑。一切都在我的身上。（同下）

第六场　同前　城堡之前

　　　　高音笛奏乐。火炬前导；邓肯、马尔科姆、道纳本、班柯、伦诺克斯、麦克达夫、罗斯、安格斯及侍从等上。

邓肯　这座城堡的位置很好；一阵阵温柔的和风轻轻地吹拂着我们微妙的感觉。

班柯　这一个夏天的客人，巡礼庙宇的燕子，也在这里筑下了它的温暖的巢居，这可以证明这里的空气有一种诱人的香味；檐下梁间，墙头屋角，都是这鸟儿安置它的吊床和摇篮的地方，凡是它们生息繁殖之处，空气总是很甘美的。

　　　　麦克白夫人上。

邓肯　瞧，瞧，我们的尊贵的主妇！到处跟随我们的挚情厚爱，有时候反而给我们带来麻烦，可是我们还是要把它当做厚爱来感谢；所以根据这个道理，我们给你带来了麻烦，你还应该感谢我们，祷告上帝保佑我们。

麦克白夫人　我们的犬马微劳，即使加倍报效，比起陛下赐给我们的深恩广泽来，也还是不足挂齿的；我们只有燃起一瓣心香，为陛下祷祝上苍，报答陛下过去和新近加于我们的荣宠。

邓肯　考特爵士呢？我们想要追在他的前面，趁他没有到家，先替他设筵洗尘；不料他的骑马的本领十分了得，他的一片忠心使他急如星火，帮助他比我们先到了一步。高贵贤淑的主妇，今天晚上我要做您的宾客了。

麦克白夫人 只要陛下吩咐，您的仆人们随时准备把他们自己和他们所有的一切开列清单，向陛下报账，把原来属于陛下的依旧呈献给陛下。

邓肯 把您的手给我；领我去见我的主人。我很爱重他，我还要继续眷顾他。请了，夫人。（同下）

第七场 同前 城堡中一室

高音笛奏乐；室中遍燃火炬。一司膳及若干仆人持着馔食具上，自台前经过。麦克白上。

麦克白 要是干了以后就完了，那么还是快一点干；要是凭着暗杀的手段，可以攫取美满的结果；要是这一刀砍下去，就可以完成一切、终结一切；要是我们可以在这里跳过时间的浅濑，展开生命的新页……可是在这种事情上，我们往往可以看见冥冥中的裁判；教唆杀人的人，结果反而自己被人所杀；把毒药投入酒杯里的人，结果也会自己饮鸩而死。他到这儿来是有两重的信任：第一，我是他的亲戚，又是他的臣子，按照名分绝对不能干这样的事；第二，他是我的客人，我应当保障他的身体的安全，怎么可以自己持刀行刺？而且，这个邓肯秉性仁

19

慈，处理国政，从来没有过失，要是把他杀死了，他的生前的美德，将要像天使一般发出喇叭一样清澈的声音，向世人昭告我的弑君重罪；"怜悯"像一个赤裸身体在狂风中飘荡的婴儿，又像一个御气而行的天婴，将要把这可憎的行为揭露在每一个人的眼中，使眼泪淹没了叹息。没有一种力量可以鞭策我前进，可是我的跃跃欲试的野心，却不顾一切地驱着我去冒颠踬的危险。

　　　麦克白夫人上。

麦克白　啊！什么消息？

麦克白夫人　他快要吃好了；你为什么跑了出来？

麦克白　他有没有问起我？

麦克白夫人　你不知道他问起过你吗？

麦克白　我们还是不要进行这一件事情。他最近给我极大的尊荣；我也好不容易从各种人的嘴里博到了无上的美誉，我的名声现在正在发射最灿烂的光彩，不能这么快就把它丢弃了。

麦克白夫人　难道你把自己沉浸在里面的那种希望，只是醉后的妄想吗？它现在从一场睡梦中醒来，因为追悔自己的孟浪而吓得脸色这样苍白吗？从这一刻起，我要把你的爱情看做同样靠不住的东西。你不敢让你在自己的行为和勇气上跟你的欲望一致吗？你宁愿像一只畏首畏尾的猫儿，顾全你所认为生命的装饰品的名誉，不惜让你在自己眼中成为一个懦夫，让"我不敢"永远跟随在"我想要"的后面吗？

麦克白　请你不要说了。只要是男子汉做的事，我都敢做；没有人比我有更大的胆量。

麦克白夫人　那么当初是什么畜生使你把这一种企图告诉我的呢？是男子汉就应当敢作敢为；要是你敢做你本不能做的事，那才更是一个男子汉。那时候，无论时间和地点都不曾给你下手的方便，可是你却居然会决意实现你的愿望；现在你有了大好的机会，你又失去勇气了。我曾经哺乳过婴孩，知道一个母亲是怎样怜爱那吮吸她乳汁的子女；可是我会在他看着我的脸微笑的时候，从他的柔软的嫩嘴里摘下我的乳头，把他的脑袋砸碎，要是我也像你一样，曾经发誓下这样的毒手的话。

麦克白　假如我们失败了，——

麦克白夫人　我们失败！只要你集中你的全副勇气，我们绝不会失败。邓肯赶了这一天辛苦的路程，一定睡得很熟；我再去陪他那两个侍卫饮酒作乐，灌得他们头脑模糊，记忆化成了一阵烟雾；等他们烂醉如泥，像死猪一样睡去以后，我们不就可以把那毫无防卫的邓肯随意摆布了吗？我们不是可以把这一件重大的谋杀罪案，推在他的酒醉的侍卫身上吗？

麦克白　愿你所生育的全是男孩子，因为你的无畏的精神，只应该铸造一些刚强的男性。要是我们在那睡在他寝室里的两个人身上涂抹一些血迹，而且就用他们的刀子，人家会不会相信真是他们干下的事？

麦克白夫人　等他的死讯传出以后，我们就假意装出号啕痛哭的样子，这样还有谁敢不相信？

麦克白　我的决心已定，我要用全身的力量，去干这件惊人的举动。去，用最美妙的外表把人们的耳目欺骗；奸诈的心必须罩上虚伪的笑脸。（同下）

第二幕

第一场　因弗内斯　堡中庭院

　　　　　班柯及弗里恩斯上，一仆人执火炬前行。

班柯　孩子，夜已经过了几更了？

弗里恩斯　月亮已经下去；我还没有听见打钟。

班柯　月亮是在十二点钟下去的。

弗里恩斯　我想它要到十二点钟以后方才下去呢，父亲。

班柯　等一下，把我的剑拿着。天上也讲究节俭，把灯烛一起熄灭了。把那个也拿着。催人入睡的疲倦，像沉重的铅块一样压在我身上，可是我却一点也不想睡。慈悲的神明！抑制那些罪恶的思想，不要让它们潜入我的睡梦之中。

　　　　　麦克白上，一仆人执火炬随从。

班柯　把我的剑给我。——那边是谁？

麦克白　一个朋友。

班柯　什么，爵爷！还没有安息吗？王上已经睡了；他今天非常高兴，赏了你家仆人许多东西。这一颗金刚钻是他送给尊夫人的，他称她为最殷勤的主妇。无限的愉快笼

23

罩着他的全身。

麦克白　我们因为事先没有准备，恐怕有许多招待不周的地方。

班柯　好说好说。昨天晚上我梦见那三个女巫；她们对您所讲的话倒有几分应验。

麦克白　我没有想到她们；可是等我们有了工夫，不妨谈谈那件事，要是您愿意的话。

班柯　悉如遵命。

麦克白　您听从了我的话，包您有一笔富贵到手。

班柯　为了觊觎富贵而丧失荣誉的事，我是不干的；要是您有什么见教，只要不毁坏我的清白的忠诚，我都愿意接受。

麦克白　那么慢慢再说，请安息吧。

班柯　谢谢，您也可以安息啦。（班柯、弗里恩斯同下）

麦克白　去对太太说要是我的睡前酒预备好了，请她打一下钟。你去睡吧。（仆人下）在我面前摇晃着，它的柄对着我的手的，不是一把刀子吗？来，让我抓住你。我抓不到你，可是仍旧看见你。不祥的幻象，你只是一件可视不可触的东西吗？或者你不过是一把想象中的刀子，从狂热的脑筋里发出来的虚妄的意匠？我仍旧看见你，你的形状正像我现在拔出的这一把刀子一样明显。你指示着我所要去的方向，告诉我应当用什么利器。我的眼睛倘不是受了其他知觉的愚弄，就是兼领了一切感官的机能。我仍旧看见你；你的刀上和柄上还流着一滴一滴刚

24

才所没有的血。没有这样的事！杀人的恶念使我看见这种异象。现在在半个世界上，大自然似乎已经死去，罪恶的梦境扰乱着平和的睡眠，作法的女巫在向惨白的赫卡忒献祭；形容枯瘦的杀人犯，听到了替他巡风的豺狼的嗥声，像一个鬼似的向他的目的地蹑足跨步前进。坚固结实的大地啊，不要听见我的脚步声音是向什么地方去的，我怕路上的砖石会泄露了我的行踪，打破这一片森然的死寂。我正在这儿威胁他的生命，他却在那儿活得好好的；在紧张的行动中间，言语是多么软弱无力。（钟声）我去，就这么干；钟声在招引我，不要听它，邓肯，这是召唤你上天堂或者下地狱的丧钟。（下）

第二场　同前

　　麦克白夫人上。

麦克白夫人　酒把他们醉倒了，却提起了我的勇气；浇熄了他们的馋焰，却燃起了我心头的烈火。听！不要响！这是夜枭的啼声，它正在鸣着丧钟，向人们道凄厉的晚安。他在那儿动手了。门都开着，那两个醉饱的侍卫用鼾声代替他们的守望；我曾经在他们的乳酒里放下麻药，瞧他们熟睡的样子，简直分别不出他们是活人还是死人。

麦克白　（在内）那边是谁？喂！

25

麦克白夫人　哎哟！我怕他们已经醒过来了，这件事情却还没有办好；不是行为的本身，是我们的企图扰乱了我们。听！我把他们的刀子都放好了；他不会找不到的。倘不是我看他睡着的样子活像我的父亲，我早就自己动手了。我的丈夫！

　　　麦克白上。

麦克白　我已经把事情办好了。你没有听见一个声音吗？

麦克白夫人　我听见枭啼和蟋蟀的鸣声。你没有讲过话吗？

麦克白　什么时候？

麦克白夫人　刚才。

麦克白　我下来的时候吗？

麦克白夫人　嗯。

麦克白　听！谁睡在隔壁的房间里？

麦克白夫人　道纳本。

麦克白　（视手）好惨！

麦克白夫人　别发傻，惨什么。

麦克白　一个人在睡梦里大笑，还有一个人喊"杀人啦！"他们把彼此惊醒了；我站定听他们；可是他们念完祷告，又睡过去了。

麦克白夫人　那一间是睡了两个。

麦克白　一个喊"上帝保佑我们！"一个喊"阿门！"好像他们看见我高举这一双杀人的血手似的。听着他们惊慌的口气，当他们说过了"上帝保佑我们"以后，我想要说"阿门"，却怎么也说不出来。

麦克白夫人　不要把它放在心上。

麦克白　可是我为什么说不出"阿门"两个字来呢？我才是最需要上帝垂恩的，可是"阿门"两个字却哽在我的喉间。

麦克白夫人　我们干这种事，不能尽往这方面想下去；这样想着是会使我们发疯的。

麦克白　我仿佛听见一个声音喊着："不要再睡了！麦克白已经杀害了睡眠。"那清白的睡眠，把忧虑的乱丝编织起来的睡眠，那日常的死亡，疲劳者的沐浴，受伤的心灵的油膏，大自然的最丰盛的肴馔，生命的盛筵上主要的营养，——

麦克白夫人　你这种话是什么意思？

麦克白　那声音继续向全屋子喊着："不要再睡了！葛莱密斯已经杀害了睡眠，所以考特将不再得到睡眠，麦克白将不再得到睡眠！"

麦克白夫人　谁喊着这样的话？唉，我的爵爷，您这样胡思乱想，是会妨害您的健康的。去拿些水来，把您手上的血迹洗洗干净。为什么您把这两把刀子带了来？它们应该放在那边。把它们拿回去，涂一些血在那两个熟睡的侍卫身上。

麦克白　我不高兴再去了；我不敢回想刚才所干的事，更没有胆量再去看它一眼。

麦克白夫人　意志动摇的人！把刀子给我。睡着的人和死了

27

的人不过和画像一样；只有小儿的眼睛才会害怕画中的魔鬼。要是他还流着血，我就把它涂在那两个侍卫的脸上；因为我们必须让人家瞧着是他们的罪恶。（下。内敲门声）

麦克白　那打门的声音是从什么地方来的？究竟是怎么一回事，一点点的声音都会吓得我心惊肉跳？这是什么手！嘿！它们要挖出我的眼睛。大洋里所有的水，能够洗净我手上的血迹吗？不，恐怕我这一手的血，倒要把一碧无垠的海水染成一片殷红呢。

　　　　麦克白夫人重上。

麦克白夫人　我的两手也跟你的同样颜色了，可是我的心却不像你这样惨白。（内敲门声）我听见有人打着南面的门；让我们回到自己房间里去；一点点的水就可以替我们泯除痕迹；不是很容易的事吗？你的魄力不知道到哪儿去了。（内敲门声）听！又在那儿打门了。披上你的睡衣，也许人家会来找我们，不要让他们看见我们还没有睡觉。别这样痴头痴脑地呆想了。

麦克白　要想到所干的事，最好还是不要知道我自己。（内敲门声）用你打门的声音把邓肯惊醒了吧！我希望你能够惊醒他！（同下）

28

第三场　同前

内敲门声。一司阍上。

门房　门打得这样厉害！要是一个人在地狱里做了管门人，就是拔闩开锁这一件事也够把他累老了。（内敲门声）敲，敲，敲！凭着魔鬼的名义，谁在那儿？一定是什么乡下人，想要来沾一点财主人家的光；赶快进来吧，多预备几方餐巾；这儿有的是大鱼大肉，你流着满身的臭汗都吃不完呢。（内敲门声）敲，敲！凭着还有一个魔鬼的名字，是谁在那儿？哼，一定是什么讲起话来暧昧含糊的家伙，他会同时站在两方面，一会儿帮着这个骂那个，一会儿帮着那个骂这个；他曾经为了上帝的缘故，干过不少亏心事，可是他那条暧昧含糊的舌头却不能把他送上天堂去。啊！进来吧，暧昧含糊的家伙。（内敲门声）敲，敲，敲！谁在那儿？哼，一定是什么英格兰的裁缝，他生前给人做条法国裤还要偷材料①，所以到了这里来。进来吧，裁缝；你可以在这儿烧你的烙铁。（内敲门声）敲，敲，敲个不停！你是什么人？你要进地狱，可是这儿太冷呢。我再也不想做这鬼看门人了。我倒很想放进几个各色各种的人来，让他们经过酒池肉林，一

---

① 当时法国裤很紧窄，在这种裤子上偷材料的裁缝，必是老手。

29

直到刀山火焰上去。（内敲门声）来了，来了！请你记着我这看门的人。（开门）

　　　　麦克达夫及伦诺克斯上。

麦克达夫　朋友，你是不是睡得太晚了，所以睡到现在还爬不起来？

司阍　不瞒您说，大人，我们昨天晚上喝酒，一直闹到第二遍鸡啼哩；喝酒这一件事，大人，最容易引起三件事情。

麦克达夫　是哪三件事情？

司阍　呃，大人，酒糟鼻、睡觉和撒尿。它也会挑起淫欲，可是喝醉了酒的人，干起这种事情来是一点不中用的。酒喝多了对这种事是两面的：先挑逗它，再打击它；闹得它上了火，又兜头一盆冷水；弄得它挺又挺不起来，趴又趴不下去；到最后让人睡着了，害他做了一场春梦，就溜走了。

麦克达夫　我看昨晚上杯子里的东西就叫你做了一场春梦吧。

司阍　可不是，大人，让我从来也没这么荒唐过。可我也不是好惹的，依我看，我比它强，我虽然不免给它揪住大腿，可我终究把它摔倒了。

麦克达夫　你的主人有没有起来？

　　　　麦克白上。

麦克达夫　我们的打门把他吵醒了；他来了。

伦诺克斯　早安，爵爷。

麦克白　两位早安。

30

麦克达夫　爵爷，王上有没有起来？

麦克白　还没有。

麦克达夫　他叫我一早就来叫他，我几乎误了时间。

麦克白　我带您去看他。

麦克达夫　我知道这是您所乐意干的事，可是有劳您啦。

麦克白　我们喜欢的工作，可以使我们忘记劳苦。这门里就是。

麦克达夫　那么我就冒昧进去了，因为我奉有王上的命令。

（下）

伦诺克斯　王上今天就要走吗？

麦克白　是的，他已经这样决定了。

伦诺克斯　昨天晚上刮着很厉害的暴风，我们住的地方，烟囱都给吹了下来；他们还说空中有哀哭的声音，有人听见奇怪的死亡的惨叫，还有人听见一个可怕的声音，预言着将要有一场绝大的纷争和混乱，降临在这不幸的时代。不知名的怪鸟整整地吵了一个漫漫的长夜；有人说大地都发热而战抖起来了。

麦克白　果然是一个可怕的晚上。

伦诺克斯　在我的年轻的经验里唤不起一个同样的回忆。

　　　　　麦克达夫重上。

麦克达夫　啊，可怕！可怕！可怕！不可言说、不可想象的恐怖！

麦克白、伦诺克斯　什么事？

麦克达夫　混乱已经完成了他的杰作！大逆不道的凶手打开

了王上的圣殿，把它的生命偷了去了！

麦克白　你说什么？生命？

伦诺克斯　你是说陛下吗？

麦克达夫　到他的寝室里去，让一幕惊人的惨剧昏眩你们的视觉吧。不要向我追问；你们自己去看了再说。（*麦克白、伦诺克斯同下*）醒来！醒来！敲起警钟来。杀了人啦！有人在谋反啦！班柯！道纳本！马尔科姆！醒来！不要贪恋温柔的睡眠，那只是死亡的假装，瞧一瞧死亡的本身吧！起来，起来，瞧瞧世界末日的影子！马尔科姆！班柯！像鬼魂从坟墓里起来一般，过来瞧瞧这一幕恐怖的景象吧！把钟敲起来！（*钟鸣*）

　　　　麦克白夫人上。

麦克白夫人　为什么要吹起这样凄厉的号角，把全屋子睡着的人唤醒？说，说！

麦克达夫　啊，好夫人！我不能让您听见我嘴里的消息，它一进到妇女的耳朵里，是比利剑还要难受的。

　　　　班柯上。

麦克达夫　啊，班柯！班柯！我们的主上给人谋杀了！

麦克白夫人　哎哟！什么！在我们的屋子里吗？

班柯　无论在什么地方，都是太惨了。好达夫，请你收回你刚才说过的话，告诉我们没有这么一回事。

　　　　麦克白及伦诺克斯重上。

麦克白　要是我在这件变故发生以前一小时死去，我就可以说是活过了一段幸福的时间；因为从这一刻起，人生已经失去它的严肃的意义，一切都不过是儿戏；荣名和美德已经死了，生命的美酒已经喝完，剩下来的只是一些无味的渣滓当做酒窖里的珍宝。

马尔科姆及道纳本上。

道纳本 出了什么乱子了？

麦克白 你们还没有知道你们重大的损失；你们的血液的源泉已经切断了，你们的生命的本根已经切断了。

麦克达夫 你们的父王给人谋杀了。

马尔科姆 啊！给谁谋杀的？

伦诺克斯 瞧上去是睡在他房间里的那两个家伙干的事；他们的手上脸上都是血迹；我们从他们枕头底下搜出了两把刀，刀上的血迹也没有揩掉；他们的神色惊惶万分；谁也不能把他自己的生命信托给这种家伙。

麦克白 啊！可是我后悔一时鲁莽，把他们杀了。

麦克达夫 你为什么杀了他们？

麦克白 谁能够在惊愕之中保持冷静，在盛怒之中保持镇定，在激于忠愤的时候，保持他的不偏不倚的精神？世上没有这样的人吧。我的理智来不及控制我的愤激的忠诚。这儿躺着邓肯，他的白银的皮肤上镶着一缕缕黄金的宝血，他的创巨痛深的伤痕张开了裂口，像是一道道毁灭的门户；那边站着这两个凶手，身上浸润着他们罪恶的颜色，他们的刀上凝结着刺目的血块；只要是一个尚有几分忠心的人，谁不要怒火中烧，替他的主子报仇雪恨？

麦克白夫人　啊，什么人来扶我进去！

麦克达夫　快来照料夫人。

马尔科姆　（向道纳本旁白）这是跟我们切身相关的事情，为什么我们一言不发？

道纳本　（向马尔科姆旁白）我们身陷危境，不可测的命运随时都会吞噬我们，还有什么话好说呢？去吧，眼下还不是掉眼泪的时候。

马尔科姆　（向道纳本旁白）也不是大放悲声的场合。

班柯　照料这位夫人。（侍从扶麦克白夫人下）等我们把自然流露出来的无遮饰的弱点收藏起来以后，让我们举行一次会议，详细彻查这一件最残酷的血案的真相。恐惧和疑虑使我们惊惶失措；站在上帝的伟大的指导之下，我一定要从尚未揭发的假面具下面，探出叛逆的阴谋，和它作殊死的奋斗。

麦克达夫　我也愿意作同样的宣告。

众人　我们也都抱着同样的决心。

麦克白　让我们赶快振起我们刚强的精神，大家到厅堂里商议去。

众人　很好。（除马尔科姆、道纳本外均下。）

马尔科姆　你预备怎么办？我们不要跟他们在一起。假装一副悲哀的脸，是每一个奸人的拿手好戏。我要到英格兰去。

道纳本 我到爱尔兰去；我们两人各奔前程，对于彼此都是
  比较安全的办法。我们现在所在的地方，人们的笑脸里
  都暗藏着利刃；越是跟我们血统相近的人，越是想喝我
  们的血。

马尔科姆 杀人的利箭已经射出，可是还没有落下，避过它
  的目标是我们唯一的活路。所以赶快上马吧；让我们不
  要拘于告别的礼貌，趁着有便就溜出去。明知没有网开
  一面的希望，就该及早逃避弋人的罗网。（同下）

第四场 同前 城堡外

  罗斯及一老翁上。

老翁 我已经活了七十个年头，惊心动魄的日子也经过得不
  少，稀奇古怪的事情也看到过不少，可是像这样可怕的
  夜晚，却还是第一次遇见。

罗斯 啊！好老人家，你看上天好像恼怒人类的行为，在向
  这流血的舞台发出恐吓。照钟上现在应该是白天了，可
  是黑夜的魔手却把那盏在天空中运行的明灯遮蔽得不露
  一丝光亮。难道黑夜已经统治一切，还是因为白昼不好
  意思抬起头来，所以在这应该有阳光遍吻大地的时候，
  地面上却被无边的黑暗所笼罩？

老翁 这种现象完全是反常的，正像那件惊人的血案一样。

在上星期二那天，有一头雄踞在高岩上的猛鹰，被一只吃田鼠的鸱鸮飞来啄死了。

罗斯 还有一件非常怪异可是十分确实的事情，邓肯有几匹躯干俊美、举步如飞的骏马，的确是不可多得的良种，忽然野性大发，撞破了马棚，冲了出来，倔强得不受羁勒，好像要向人类挑战似的。

老翁 据说它们还彼此相食。

罗斯 是的，我亲眼看见这种事情，简直不敢相信自己的眼睛。麦克达夫来了。

麦克达夫上。

罗斯 情况现在变得怎么样啦？

麦克达夫 啊，您没有看见吗？

罗斯 有没有知道谁干了这件残酷得超乎寻常的行为？

麦克达夫 就是那两个给麦克白杀死了的家伙。

罗斯 唉！他们干了这件事可以希望得到什么好处呢？

麦克达夫 他们一定受人的教唆。马尔科姆和道纳本，王上的两个儿子，已经偷偷地逃走了，这使他们也蒙上了嫌疑。

罗斯 那更加违反人情了！反噬自己的命根，这样的野心会有什么好结果呢？看来大概王位要让麦克白登上去了。

麦克达夫 他已经受到推举，现在到斯贡即位去了。

罗斯 邓肯的尸体在什么地方？

麦克达夫 已经抬到戈姆基尔，他的祖先的陵墓上。

罗斯 您也要到斯贡去吗？

麦克达夫　不，大哥，我还是到法夫去。

罗斯　好，我要到那边去看看。

麦克达夫　好，但愿您看见那边的一切都是好好儿的，再会！怕只怕我们的新衣服不及旧衣服舒服哩！

罗斯　再见，老人家。

老翁　上帝祝福您，也祝福那些把恶事化成善事，把仇敌化为朋友的人们！（各下）

第三幕

第一场　福累斯　王宫中一室

　　班柯上。

班柯　你现在已经如愿以偿了：国王、考特、葛莱密斯，一切符合女巫们的预言。你得到这种富贵的手段恐怕不大正当，可是据说你的王位不能传及子孙，我自己却要成为许多君王的始祖。她们的话既然已经在你麦克白身上应验，那么难道不也会成为对我的启示，使我对未来发生希望吗？可是闭口！不要多说了。

　　喇叭奏花腔。麦克白王冠王服；麦克白夫人后冠后服；伦诺克斯、罗斯、贵族、贵妇、侍从等上。

麦克白　这儿是我们主要的上宾。

麦克白夫人　要是忘记了请他，那就要成为我们盛筵上绝大的遗憾，一切都要显得寒碜了。

麦克白　将军，我们今天晚上要举行一次隆重的宴会，请你千万出席。

班柯　谨遵陛下命令；我的忠诚永远接受陛下的使唤。

38

麦克白　今天下午你要骑马去吗？

班柯　是的，陛下。

麦克白　否则我很想请你参加我们今天的会议，贡献我们一些良好的意见，你的老谋深算，我是一向佩服的；可是我们明天再谈吧。你要骑到很远的地方吗？

班柯　陛下，我想尽量把从现在起到晚餐时候为止这一段时间在马上消磨过去；要是我的马不跑得快一些，也许要到天黑以后一两小时才能回来。

麦克白　不要误了我们的宴会。

班柯　陛下，我一定不失约。

麦克白　我听说我那两个凶恶的王侄已经分别到了英格兰和爱尔兰，他们不承认他们的残酷的弑父重罪，却到处向人传播离奇荒谬的谣言；可是我们明天再谈吧，有许多重要的国事要等候我们两人共同处理呢。请上马吧；等你晚上回来的时候再会。弗里恩斯也跟着你去吗？

班柯　是，陛下；时间已经不早，我们就要去了。

麦克白　愿你快马飞驰，一路平安，再见。（班柯下）大家请便，各人去干各人的事，到晚上七点钟再聚首吧。为要更能领略到嘉宾满堂的快乐起见，我在晚餐以前，预备一个人独自静息静息；愿上帝和你们同在！（除麦克白及侍从一人外均下）喂，问你一句话。那两个人是不是在外面等候着我的旨意？

侍从　是，陛下，他们就在宫门外面。

39

麦克白　带他们进来见我。（侍从下）单单做到了这一步还不算什么，总要把现状确定巩固起来才好。我对于班柯怀着深切的恐惧，他的高贵的天性中有一种使我生畏的东西；他是个敢作敢为的人，在他的无畏的精神上，又加上深沉的智虑，指导他的胆勇在确有把握的时机行动。除了他以外，我什么人都不怕，只有他的存在却使我惴惴不安；据说安东尼在恺撒的手下，他的天才完全被恺撒所埋没，我在他的雄才大略之下，情形也是这样。当那些女巫们最初称我为王的时候，他呵斥她们，叫她们对他说话；她们就像先知似的说他的子孙将相继为王，她们把一顶没有后嗣的王冠戴在我的头上，把一根没有人继承的御杖放在我的手里，然后再从我的手里夺去，我的子孙得不到继承。要是果然是这样，那么我玷污了我的手，只是为了班柯后裔的好处；我为了他们暗杀了仁慈的邓肯；为了他们良心上负着重大的罪疚和不安；我把我的永生的灵魂给了人类的公敌，只是为了使他们可以登上王座，使班柯的种子登上王座！不，我不能忍受这样的事，宁愿接受命运的挑战！是谁？

　　　　侍从率二刺客重上。

麦克白　你现在到门口去，等我叫你再进来。（侍从下）我们不是在昨天谈过话吗？

刺客甲　回陛下的话，正是。

麦克白　那么好，你们有没有考虑过我的话？你们知道从前

40

都是因为他的缘故，使你们屈身微贱，虽然你们却错怪到我的身上。在上一次我们谈话的中间，我已经把这一点向你们说明白了，我用确凿的证据，指出你们怎样被人操纵愚弄、怎样受人牵制压抑、人家对你们是用怎样的手段、这种手段的主动者是谁，以及一切其他的种种，都可以使一个半痴的疯癫的人恍然大悟地说："这些都是班柯干的事。"

刺客甲 我们已经蒙陛下开示过了。

麦克白 是的，而且我还要更进一步，这就是我们今天第二次谈话的目的。你们难道有那样的好耐性，能够忍受这样的屈辱吗？他的铁手已经快要把你们压下坟墓里去，使你们的子孙永远做乞丐，难道你们所受到的教诲，还要叫你们替这个好人和他的子孙祈祷吗？

刺客甲 陛下，我们是人总有人气。

麦克白 嗯，你们也是算作人类的，正像家狗、野狗、猎狗、巴儿狗、狮子狗、杂种狗、癞皮狗，统称为狗一样；它们有的灵敏，有的迟钝，有的狡猾，有的可以看门，有的可以打猎，各自按照造物赋予它们的本能而分别价值的高下，在广泛的总称之上，得到特殊的名号；人类也是一样。要是你们在人类的行列之中，并不属于最卑劣的一级，那么说吧，我就可以把一件事情信托你们，你们照我的话干了以后，不但可以除去你们的仇人，而且还可以永远受我的眷宠；他一天活在世上，我的心病一

41

天不能痊愈。

刺客乙 陛下，我久受世间无情的打击和虐待，为了向这世界发泄我的怨恨起见，我什么事都愿意干。

刺客甲 我也是这样，一次次的灾祸逆运使我厌倦于人世，我愿意拿我的生命去赌博，或者从此交上好运，或者了结我的一生。

麦克白 你们两人都知道班柯是你们的仇人。

刺客乙 是的，陛下。

麦克白 他也是我的仇人；而且他是我的肘腋之患，他的存在每一分钟都威胁着我生命的安全。虽然我可以老实不客气地动用我的权力，把他从我的眼前扫去，而且这样做在我的良心上并没有使我不安的地方，可是我却还是不能就这么干，因为他有几个朋友同时也是我的朋友，我不能招致他们的反感，即使我亲手把他打倒，也必须假意为他的死亡悲泣；所以我只好借重你们两人的助力，为了许多重要的理由，把这件事情遮过一般人的眼睛。

刺客乙 陛下，我们一定照您的命令做去。

刺客甲 即使我们的生命——

麦克白 你们的勇气已经充分透露在你们的神情之间。最迟在这一小时之内，我就可以告诉你们在什么地方埋伏，在什么时间动手；因为这件事情一定要在今晚干好，而且要离开王宫远一些，你们必须记住不能把我牵涉在内；同时为了免得留下形迹起见，你们还要把跟在他身边的他的儿子弗里恩斯也一起杀了，他们父子两人的死，对于我是同样重要的，必须让他们同时接受黑暗的命运。你们先下去决定一下，我就来看你们。

刺客乙 我们已经决定了，陛下。

麦克白 我立刻就会来看你们；你们进去等一会儿。（二刺客下）班柯，你的命运已经决定，你的灵魂要是找得到天堂的话，今天晚上你就该去找起来了。（下）

第二场　同前　王宫中另一室

麦克白夫人及一仆人上。

麦克白夫人 班柯已经离开宫廷了吗？

仆人 是，娘娘，可是他今天晚上就要回来的。

麦克白夫人 你去对王上说，我要请他允许我跟他说几句话。

仆人 是，娘娘。（下）

麦克白夫人 费尽了一切，结果还是一无所得，我们的目的虽然达到，却一点不感觉满足。要是用毁灭他人的手段，使自己置身在充满忧疑的欢娱里，那么还不如那被我们所害的人，倒落得无忧无虑。

麦克白上。

麦克白夫人 啊！我的主！您为什么一个人孤零零的，让最悲哀的幻想做您的伴侣，把您的思想念念不忘地集中在一个已死者的身上？没有挽回的事，只好听其自然；事情干了就算了。

麦克白 我们不过刺伤了蛇身，却没有把它杀死，它的伤口会慢慢平复过来，再用它的原来的毒牙向我们复仇。可是让一切秩序完全解体，让活人死人都去受罪吧，为什么我们要在忧虑中进餐，在每夜使我们惊恐的噩梦的虐弄中睡眠呢？我们为了希求自身的平安，把别人送下坟墓里去享受永久的平安，可是我们的心灵却把我们折磨得没有一刻平静的安息，使我们觉得还是跟已死的人在一起，倒要幸福得多了。邓肯现在睡在他的坟墓里；经过了一场人生的热病，他现在睡得好好的，叛逆已经对他施过最狠毒的伤害，再没有刀剑、毒药、内乱、外患，可以加害于他了。

麦克白夫人 算了算了，我的好丈夫，把您的烦恼的面孔收起；今天晚上您必须和颜悦色地招待您的客人。

麦克白 正是，爱人；你也要这样。尤其请你对班柯曲意殷勤，用你的眼睛和舌头给他特殊的荣宠。我们的地位现在还没有巩固，必须把我们的尊严濡染在这种谄媚的流水里，用我们的外貌遮掩着我们的内心，不要给人家窥破。

麦克白夫人 您不要多想这些了。

麦克白 啊！我的头脑里充满着蝎子，亲爱的妻子，你知道班柯和他的弗里恩斯尚在人间。

麦克白夫人　可是他们并不是长生不死的。

麦克白　那还可以给我几分安慰，他们是可以侵害的；所以你快乐起来吧。在蝙蝠完成它黑暗中的飞翔以前，在振翅而飞的甲虫应答着赫卡忒的呼唤，用嗡嗡的声音摇响催眠的晚钟以前，将要有一件可怕的事情干完。

麦克白夫人　是什么事情？

麦克白　你暂时不必知道，最亲爱的宝贝，等事成以后，你再鼓掌称快吧。来，使人盲目的黑夜，遮住可怜的白昼的温柔的眼睛，用你的无形的毒手，撕毁那使我畏惧的重大的束缚吧！天色在朦胧起来，乌鸦都飞回到昏暗的林中；一天的好事开始沉沉睡去，黑夜的罪恶的使者却在准备攫捕他们的猎物。我的话使你惊奇，可是不要说话；以不义开始的事情，必须用罪恶巩固。跟我来。

（同下）

第三场　同前　苑囿，有一路通王宫

三刺客上。

刺客甲　可是谁叫你来帮我们的？

刺客丙　麦克白。

刺客乙　他不必不信任我们，他已经把我们的任务和怎样动手的方法都指示给我们了。

刺客甲　那么就跟我们站在一起吧。西方还闪耀着一线白昼的余晖；晚归的行客现在快马加鞭，要来找寻宿处了；我们守候的目标已经在那儿向我们走近。

刺客丙　听！我听见马蹄声。

班柯　（在内）喂，给我们一个火把！

刺客乙　一定是他；别的客人们都已经到了宫里了。

刺客甲　他的马在兜圈子。

刺客丙　差不多有一英里路；可是他正像许多人一样，常常把从这儿到宫门口的这一条路作为他们的走道。

刺客乙　火把，火把！

刺客丙　是他。

刺客甲　准备好。

　　　　班柯及弗里恩斯持火炬上。

班柯　今晚恐怕要下雨。

刺客甲　让它下吧。（刺客等向班柯攻击）

班柯　啊，阴谋！快逃，好弗里恩斯，逃，逃，逃！你也许可以替我报仇。啊，奴才！（死。弗里恩斯逃去）

刺客丙　谁把火灭了？

刺客甲　不应该灭火吗？

刺客丙　只有一个人倒下；那儿子逃去了。

刺客乙　我们工作的重要的一部分失败了。

刺客甲　好，我们回去报告我们工作的结果吧。（同下）

第四场　同前　王宫中的大厅

　　　　厅中陈设筵席。麦克白、麦克白夫人、罗斯、伦诺克斯、群臣及侍从等上。

麦克白　大家按着各人自己的品级坐下来；总而言之一句话，我竭诚欢迎你们。

群臣　谢谢陛下的恩典。

麦克白　我自己将要跟你们在一起，做一个谦恭的主人，我们的主妇现在还坐在她的宝座上，可是我就要请她对你们殷勤招待。

麦克白夫人　陛下，请您替我向我们所有的朋友们表示我的欢迎的诚意吧。

　　　　刺客甲上，至门口。

麦克白　瞧，他们用诚意的感谢答复你了；两方面已经各得其平。我将要在这儿中间坐下来。大家不要拘束，乐一个畅快；等会儿我们就要合席痛饮一巡。（至门口）你的脸上有血。

刺客甲　那么它是班柯的。

麦克白　我宁愿你站在门外，不愿他置身室内。你们已经把他结果了吗？

刺客甲　陛下，他的咽喉已经割破了；这是我干的事。

麦克白　你是一个最有本领的杀人犯；可是谁杀死了弗里恩

斯，也一样值得夸奖；要是你也把他杀了，那你才是一个无比的好汉。

刺客甲　陛下，弗里恩斯逃走了。

麦克白　我的心病本来可以痊愈，现在它又要发作了；我本来可以像大理石一样完整，像岩石一样坚固，像空气一样广大自由，现在我却被恼人的疑惑和恐惧所包围拘束。可是班柯已经死了吗？

刺客甲　是，陛下；他安安稳稳地躺在一条泥沟里，他的头上刻着二十道伤痕，最轻的一道也可以致他死命。

麦克白　谢天谢地。大蛇躺在那里；那逃走了的小虫，将来会用它的毒液害人，可是现在它的齿牙还没有长成。走吧，明天再来听候我的旨意。（刺客甲下）

麦克白夫人　陛下，您还没有劝过客人；宴会上倘没有主人的殷勤招待，那就不是在请酒，而是在卖酒了；这倒不如在自己家里吃饭来得舒适呢。既然出来作客，在席面上最让人开胃的就是主人的礼节，缺少了它，那就会使合席失去了兴致的。

麦克白　亲爱的，不是你提起，我几乎忘了！来，请放量醉饱吧，愿各位胃纳健旺，身强力壮！

伦诺克斯　陛下请安坐。

　　　　班柯鬼魂上；坐在麦克白座上。

麦克白　要是班柯在座，那么全国的英俊，真可以说是汇集于一堂了；我宁愿因为他的疏怠而嗔怪他，不愿因为他遭到什么意外而为他惋惜。

罗斯 陛下，他今天失约不来，是他自己的过失。请陛下上坐，让我们叨陪末席。

麦克白 席上已经坐满了。

伦诺克斯 陛下，这儿是给您留着的一个位置。

麦克白 什么地方？

伦诺克斯 这儿，陛下。什么事情使陛下这样变色？

麦克白 你们哪一个人干了这件事？

群臣 什么事，陛下？

麦克白 你不能说是我干的事；别这样对我摇着你的染着血的头发。

罗斯 各位大人，起来，陛下病了。

麦克白夫人 坐下，尊贵的朋友们，王上常常这样，他从小就有这种毛病。请各位安坐吧；他的癫狂不过是暂时的，一会儿就会好起来。要是你们太注意了他，他也许会动怒，发起狂来更加厉害；尽管自己吃喝，不要理他吧。你是一个男子吗？

麦克白 哦，我是一个堂堂男子，可以使魔鬼胆裂的东西，我也敢正眼瞧着它。

麦克白夫人 啊，这才说得不错！这不过是你的恐惧所描绘出来的一幅图画；正像你所说的那柄引导你去行刺邓肯的空中的匕首一样。啊！要是在冬天的火炉旁，听一个妇女讲述她的老祖母告诉她的故事的时候，那么这种情绪的冲动、恐惧的伪装，倒是非常合适的。不害羞吗？
你为什么扮这样的怪脸？你瞧着的不过是一张凳子罢了。

麦克白　你瞧那边！瞧！瞧！瞧！你怎么说？哼，我什么都
不在乎。要是你会点头，你也应该会说话。要是殡舍和
坟墓必须把我们埋葬了的人送回世上，那么我们的坟墓
要变成鸢鸟的胃囊了。（鬼魂隐去）

麦克白夫人　什么！你发了疯，把你的男子气都失掉了吗？

麦克白　要是我现在站在这儿，那么刚才我明明瞧见他。

麦克白夫人　啐！不害羞吗？

麦克白　在人类不曾制定法律保障公众福利以前的古代，杀
人流血是不足为奇的事；即使在有了法律以后，惨不忍
闻的谋杀事件，也随时发生。从前的时候，一刀下去，
当场毙命，事情就这样完结了；可是现在他们却会从坟
墓中起来，他们的头上戴着二十件谋杀的重罪，把我们
推下座位。这种事情是比这样一件谋杀案更奇怪的。

麦克白夫人　陛下，您的尊贵的朋友们都因为您不去陪他们
而十分扫兴哩。

麦克白　我忘了。不要对我惊诧，我的最尊贵的朋友们；我
有一种怪病，认识我的人都知道那是不足为奇的。来，
让我们用这一杯酒表示我们的同心永好，祝各位健康！
你们干了这一杯，我就坐下。给我拿些酒来，倒得满满
的：我为今天在座众人的快乐，还要为我们亲爱的缺席
的朋友班柯尽此一杯；要是他也在这儿就好了！来，为

大家、为他，请干杯。

群臣　敢不从命。

　　　　鬼魂重上。

麦克白　去！离开我的眼前！让土地把你藏匿了！你的骨髓已经枯竭，你的血液已经凝冷；你那向人瞪着的眼睛也已经失去了光彩。

麦克白夫人　各位大人，这不过是他的旧病复发，没有什么别的缘故；害各位扫兴，真是抱歉得很。

麦克白　别人敢做的事，我都敢；无论你用什么形状出现，像粗暴的俄罗斯大熊也好，像披甲的犀牛、舞爪的猛虎也好，只要不是你现在的样子，我的坚定的神经绝不会起半分战栗；或者你现在死而复活，用你的剑向我挑战，要是我会惊惶胆怯，那么你就可以宣称我是一个少女怀抱中的婴孩。去，可怕的影子！虚妄的揶揄，去！（鬼魂隐去）吓，他一去，我的勇气又恢复了。请你们安坐吧。

麦克白夫人　你这样疯疯癫癫的，已经打断了众人的兴致，扰乱了今天的良会。

麦克白　世上会有这种事情，像一朵夏天的黑云遮在我们的头上，怎么不叫人吃惊呢？我吓得面无人色，你们眼看着这样的怪象，你们的脸上却仍然保持着天然的红润，这才怪哩。

罗斯　什么怪象，陛下？

麦克白夫人　请您不要对他说话；他越来越疯了；你们多问

了他，他会动怒的。对不起，请各位还是散席了吧；大家不必推先让后，请立刻就去，晚安！

伦诺克斯　晚安；愿陛下早复健康！

麦克白夫人　各位晚安！（群臣及侍从等下）

麦克白　他们说，流血是免不了的；流血必须引起流血。据说石块曾经自己转动，树木曾经开口说话；鸦鹊的鸣声里已经预示着阴谋作乱的人。夜过去了多少了？

麦克白夫人　差不多到了黑夜和白昼的交界，分别不出谁是谁来。

麦克白　麦克达夫藐视王命，拒不奉召，你看怎么样？

麦克白夫人　你有没有差人去叫过他？

麦克白　我在路上听人这么说；可是我要差人去唤他。他们这一批人家里谁都有一个被我买通的仆人，替我窥探他们的动静。我明天就要去访那三个女巫，听她们还有什么话说；因为我现在非得从最妖邪的恶魔口中知道我的最悲惨的命运不可。为了我自己的好处，只好把一切置之不顾。我已经两足深陷于血泊之中，要是不再涉血前进，那么回头的路也是同样使人厌倦的。我想起了一些非常的计谋，必须在不曾被人家觉察以前迅速实行。

麦克白夫人　一切有生之伦，都少不了睡眠的调剂，可是你还没有好好睡过。

麦克白　来，我们睡去。我的疑鬼疑神、出乖露丑，都是因为未经历练、心怀恐惧的缘故；我们在行事上太缺少经验了。（同下）

第五场　荒野

雷鸣。三女巫上，与赫卡忒相遇。

女巫甲　哎哟，赫卡忒！您在发怒哩。

赫卡忒　我不应该发怒吗，你们这些放肆大胆的丑婆子？你
们怎么敢用哑谜和有关生死的秘密和麦克白打交道；我
是你们魔法的总管，一切的灾祸都由我主持支配，你们
却不通知我一声，让我也来显一显我们的神通？而且你
们所干的事，都只是为了一个刚愎自用、残忍狂暴的人；
他像所有的世人一样，只知道自己的利益，一点不是对
你们存着什么好意。可是现在你们必须补赎你们的过失；
快去，天明的时候，在阿克戎①的地坑附近会我，他将
要到那边来探询他的命运；把你们的符咒、魔蛊和一切
应用的东西预备齐整，不得有误。我现在乘风而去，今
晚我要用整夜的工夫，布置出一场悲惨的结果；在正午
以前，必须完成大事。月亮角上挂着一颗湿淋淋的露珠，
我要在它没有坠地以前把它摄取，用魔术提炼以后，就
可以凭着它呼灵召鬼，让种种虚妄的幻影迷乱了他的本
性；他将要藐视命运，唾斥死生，超越一切的情理，排
弃一切的疑虑，执著他的不可能的希望；你们都知道自

---

① 阿克戎（Acheron），本为希腊神话中的一条冥河，这里借指地狱。

信是人类最大的仇敌。（内歌声，"来吧，来吧……"）听！他们在叫我啦；我的小精灵们，瞧，他们坐在云雾之中，在等着我呢。（下）

女巫甲 来，我们赶快；她就要回来的。（同下）

第六场　福累斯　王宫中一室

伦诺克斯及另一贵族上。

伦诺克斯 您现在才想起我从前的话，那些话是还可以进一步解释的；我只觉得事情有些古怪。仁厚的邓肯被麦克白所哀悼；邓肯是已经死去的了。勇敢的班柯不该在深夜走路，您也许可以说，要是您愿意这么说的话，他是被弗里恩斯杀死的，因为弗里恩斯已经逃匿无踪；人总不应该在夜深的时候走路。哪一个人不以为马尔科姆和道纳本杀死他们仁慈的父亲，是一件多么惊人的巨变？万恶的行为！麦克白为了这件事多么痛心；他不是乘着一时的忠愤，把那两个酗酒贪睡的溺职卫士杀了吗？那件事干得不是很忠勇的吗？嗯，而且也干得很聪明；因为要是人家听见他们抵赖他们的罪状，谁都会怒从心起的。所以我说，他把一切事情处理得很好；我想要是邓肯的两个儿子也给他拘留起来——上天保佑他们不会落在他的手里——他们就会知道向自己的父亲行弑，必须受到怎样的报应；弗里恩斯也是一样。可是这些话别提啦，我听说麦克达夫因为出言不逊，又不出席那暴君的宴会，已经受到贬辱。您能够告诉我他现在在什么地方吗？

贵族 被这暴君篡逐出亡的邓肯世子现在寄身在英格兰宫廷之中，谦恭的爱德华对他非常优待，一点不因为他处境颠危而减削了敬礼。麦克达夫也到那里去了，他的目的是要请求贤明的英王协力激励诺森伯兰和好战的西沃德，使他们出兵相援，凭着上帝的意旨帮助我们恢复已失的自由，使我们仍旧能够享受食桌上的盛馔和酣畅的睡眠，不再畏惧宴会中有沾血的刀剑，让我们能够一方面输忠效信，一方面安受爵赏而心无疑虑；这一切都是我们现在所渴望而求之不得的。这一个消息已经使我们的王上大为震怒，他正在那儿准备作战了。

伦诺克斯 他有没有差人到麦克达夫那儿去？

贵族 他已经差人去过了；得到的话是很干脆的一句："大人，我不去。"那恼怒的使者就转过身哼了两声，好像说："你给我这样的答复，看着吧，你一定会自食其果。"

伦诺克斯 那很可以叫他留心留心远避当前的祸害。但愿什么神圣的天使飞到英格兰的宫廷里，预先把他的信息带来给我们，让上天的祝福迅速回到我们这一个在毒手压制下备受苦难的国家！

贵族 我愿意为他祈祷。（同下）

第四幕

第一场　山洞　中置沸釜

雷鸣。三女巫上。

女巫甲　斑猫已经叫过三声。

女巫乙　刺猬已经啼了四次。

女巫丙　怪鸟在鸣啸：时候到了，时候到了。

女巫甲　绕釜环行火融融，

毒肝腐脏置其中。

蛤蟆蛰眠寒石底，

三十一日夜相继；

汗出淋漓化毒浆，

投之鼎釜沸为汤。

三女巫　（合）不惮辛劳不惮烦，

釜中沸沫已成澜。

女巫乙　沼地蟒蛇取其肉，

脔以为片煮至熟；

蝾螈之目青蛙趾，

56

蝙蝠之毛犬之齿，

蝮舌如叉蚯蚓刺，

蜥蜴之足枭之翅，

炼为毒蛊鬼神惊，

扰乱人世无安宁。

三女巫 （合）不惮辛劳不惮烦，

釜中沸沫已成澜。

女巫丙 豺狼之牙巨龙鳞，

千年巫尸貌狰狞；

海底抉出鲨鱼胃，

夜掘毒芹根块块；

杀犹太人摘其肝，

剖山羊胆汁潺潺；

雾黑云深月食时，

潜携斤斧劈杉枝；

娼妇弃儿死道间，

断指持来血尚殷；

土耳其鼻鞑靼唇，

烈火糜之煎作羹；

猛虎肝肠和鼎内，

炼就妖丹成一味。

三女巫 （合）不惮辛劳不惮烦，

釜中沸沫已成澜。

女巫乙 炭火将残盅将成，

猩猩滴血盅方凝。

赫卡忒上。

赫卡忒 善哉尔曹功不浅，

颁赏酬劳利泽遍。

于今绕釜且歌吟，

大小妖精成环形，

摄人魂魄荡人心。（音乐，众巫唱幽灵之歌）

女巫乙 拇指怦怦动，

必有恶人来；

既来皆不拒，

洞门敲自开。

麦克白上。

麦克白 啊，你们这些神秘的幽冥的夜游的妖婆子！你们在干什么？

众巫 一件没有名义的行动。

麦克白 凭着你们的职业，我吩咐你们回答我，不管你们的知识是从哪里得来的。即使你们的嘴里会放出狂风，让它们向教堂猛击；即使汹涌的波涛会把航海的船只颠覆吞噬；即使谷物的叶片会倒折在田亩上，树木会连根拔起；即使城堡会向它们的守卫者的头上倒下；即使宫殿和金字塔都会倾圮；即使大自然所孕育的一切灵奇完全归于毁灭，我也要你们回答我的问题。

女巫甲　说。

女巫乙　你问吧。

女巫丙　我们可以回答你。

女巫甲　你愿意从我们嘴里听到答复呢，还是愿意让我们的
　　　　主人们回答你？

麦克白　叫他们出来；让我见见他们。

女巫甲　母猪九子食其豚，

　　　　血浇火上焰生腥；

　　　　杀人恶犯上刑场，

　　　　汗脂投火发凶光。

众　巫　（合）鬼王鬼卒火中来，

　　　　现形作法莫惊猜。

　　　　　雷鸣，第一鬼魂出现，为一戴盔之头。

麦克白　告诉我，你这不知名的力量——

女巫甲　他知道你的心事；听他说，你不用开口。

第一鬼魂　麦克白！麦克白！麦克白！留心麦克达夫；留心
　　　　法夫爵士。放我回去。够了。（隐入地下）

麦克白　不管你是什么精灵，我感谢你的忠言警告；你已经
　　　　一语道破了我的忧虑。可是再告诉我一句话——

女巫甲　他是不受命令的。这儿又来了一个，比第一个法力
　　　　更大。

　　　　　雷鸣。第二鬼魂出现，为一流血之小儿。

第二鬼魂　麦克白！麦克白！麦克白！——

59

麦克白 我要是有三只耳朵，我的三只耳朵都会听着你。

第二鬼魂 你要残忍、勇敢、坚决；你可以把人类的力量付之一笑，因为没有一个妇人所生下的人可以伤害麦克白。

（隐入地下）

麦克白 那么尽管活下去吧，麦克德夫；我何必惧怕你呢？可是我要使确定的事实加倍确定，从命运手里接受切实的保证。我还是要你死，让我可以斥胆怯的恐惧为虚妄，在雷电怒作的夜里也能安心睡觉。

　　雷鸣。第三鬼魂出现，为一戴王冠之小儿，手持一树枝。

麦克白 这是什么，他的模样像是一个王子，他的幼稚的头上还戴着统治的荣冠？

众巫 静听，不要对它说话。

第三鬼魂 你要像狮子一样骄傲而无畏，不要关心人家的怨怒，也不要担忧有谁在算计你。麦克白永远不会被人打败，除非有一天勃南的树林会向邓斯纳恩高山移动。（隐入地下）

麦克白 那是绝不会有的事；谁能够命令树木，叫它从泥土之中拔起它的深根来呢？幸运的预兆！好！勃南的树林不会移动，叛徒的举事也不会成功，我们巍巍高位的麦克白将要尽其天年，在他寿数告终的时候奄然物化。可是我的心还在跳动着想要知道一件事情；告诉我，要是你们的法术能够解释我的疑惑，班柯的后裔会不会在这

60

一个国土上称王？

众巫 不要追问下去了。

麦克白 我一定要知道究竟；要是你们不告诉我，愿永久的诅咒降在你们身上！告诉我。为什么那口釜沉了下去？这是什么声音？（吹高音笛）

女巫甲 出来！

女巫乙 出来！

女巫丙 出来！

众巫 （合）一见惊心，魂魄无主；

如影而来，如影而去。

着国王装束者八人次第上；最后一人持镜；班柯鬼魂随其后。

麦克白 你太像班柯的鬼魂了；下去！你的王冠刺痛了我的眼球。怎么，又是一个戴着王冠的，你的头发也跟第一个一样。第三个又跟第二个一样。该死的鬼婆子！你们为什么让我看见这些人？第四个！跳出来吧，我的眼睛！什么！这一连串戴着王冠的，要到世界末日才会完结吗？又是一个？第七个！我不想再看了。可是第八个又出现了，他拿着一面镜子，我可以从镜子里面看见许许多多戴王冠的人；有几个还拿着两重的宝球，三头的御杖。可怕的景象！啊，现在我知道这不是虚妄的幻象，因为血污的班柯在向我微笑，用手指点着他们，表示他们就是他的子孙。（众幻影消灭）什么！真是这样吗？

女巫甲 嗯，这一切都是真的；可是麦克白为什么这样呆若木鸡？来，姊妹们，让我们鼓舞鼓舞他的精神，用最好的歌舞替他消愁解闷。我先用魔法使空中奏起乐来，你们就挽成一个圈子团团跳舞，让这位伟大的君王知道，我们并没有怠慢了他。（音乐。众女巫跳舞，舞毕与赫卡忒俱隐去）

麦克白 她们在哪儿？去了？愿这不祥的时辰在日历上永远被人诅咒！外面有人吗？进来！

　　　　　伦诺克斯上。

伦诺克斯 陛下有什么命令？

麦克白 你看见那三个女巫吗？

伦诺克斯 没有，陛下。

麦克白 她们没有打你身边过去吗？

伦诺克斯 确实没有，陛下。

麦克白 愿她们所驾乘的空气都化为毒雾，愿一切相信她们言语的人都永堕沉沦！我方才听见奔马的声音，是谁经过这地方？

伦诺克斯 启禀陛下，刚才有两三个使者来过，向您报告麦克达夫已经逃奔英格兰去了。

麦克白 逃奔英格兰去了！

伦诺克斯 是，陛下。

麦克白 时间，你早就料到我的狠毒的行为；无远弗至的恶念，一旦见之事实，就容易被人所乘，从这一刻起，我心里一想到什么，便要把它立刻实行，没有迟疑的余地；
我现在就要用行动表示我的意志：我要去突袭麦克达夫
的城堡；把法夫攫取下来；把他的妻子儿女和追随他的
不幸的人们一起杀死。我不能像一个傻瓜似的只会空口
说大话；我必须趁着我这一个目的还没有冷淡下来把这
件事干好。可是我不想再看见什么幻象了！那几个使者
呢？来，带我去见见他们。（同下）

第二场　法夫　麦克达夫城堡

麦克达夫夫人、麦克达夫子及罗斯上。

麦克达夫夫人　他干了什么事，要逃亡国外？

罗斯　您必须安心忍耐，夫人。

麦克达夫夫人　他可没有一点忍耐；他的逃亡全然是发疯。
我们的行为本来是光明坦白的，可是我们的疑虑却使我
们成为叛徒。

罗斯　您还不知道他的逃亡究竟是明智的行为还是无谓的
疑虑。

麦克达夫夫人　明智的行为！他自己高飞远走，把他的妻子
儿女、他的宅第尊位，一齐丢弃不顾，这算是明智的行
为吗？他不爱我们；他没有天性之情；鸟类中最微小的
鹪鹩也会奋不顾身，和鸱鸮争斗，保护它巢中的众雏。

他心里只有恐惧没有爱；也没有一点智慧，因为他的逃亡是完全不合情理的。

罗斯　好嫂子，请您抑制一下自己；讲到尊夫的为人，他是高尚明理而有识见的，他知道应该怎样见机行事。我不敢多说什么；现在这种时世太冷酷无情了，我们自己还不知道，就已经蒙上了叛徒的恶名；一方面恐惧流言，一方面却不知道为何而恐惧，就像在一个风波险恶的海上漂浮，全没有一定的方向。现在我必须向您告辞；不久我会再到这儿来。最恶劣的事态总有一天告一段落，或者逐渐恢复原状。我的可爱的侄儿，祝福你！

麦克达夫夫人　他虽然有父亲，却和没有父亲一样。

罗斯　我要是再逗留下去，才真是不懂事的傻子，既会叫人家笑话我不像个男子汉，还要连累您心里难过；我现在立刻告辞了。（下）

麦克达夫夫人　小子，你爸爸死了；你现在怎么办？你预备怎样过活？

麦克达夫子　像鸟儿一样过活，妈妈。

麦克达夫夫人　什么！吃些小虫儿、飞虫儿吗？

麦克达夫子　我的意思是说，我得到些什么就吃些什么，正像鸟儿一样。

麦克达夫夫人　可怜的鸟儿！你从来不怕有人在张起网儿，布下陷阱，捉了你去哩。

麦克达夫子　我为什么要怕这些，妈妈？他们是不会算计可怜的小鸟的。我的爸爸并没有死，虽然您说他死了。

麦克达夫夫人　不，他真的死了。你没了父亲怎么好呢？

麦克达夫子　您没了丈夫怎么好呢？

麦克达夫夫人　嗨，我可以到随便哪个市场上去买二十个丈夫回来。

麦克达夫子　那么您买了他们回来，还是要卖出去的。

麦克达夫夫人　这刁钻的小油嘴；可也亏你想得出来。

麦克达夫子　我的爸爸是个反贼吗，妈妈？

麦克达夫夫人　嗯，他是个反贼。

麦克达夫子　怎么叫做反贼？

麦克达夫夫人　反贼就是起假誓扯谎的人。

麦克达夫子　凡是反贼都是起假誓扯谎的吗？

麦克达夫夫人　起假誓扯谎的人都是反贼，都应该绞死。

麦克达夫子　起假誓扯谎的都应该绞死吗？

麦克达夫夫人　都应该绞死。

麦克达夫子　谁去绞死他们呢？

麦克达夫夫人　那些正人君子。

麦克达夫子　那么那些起假誓扯谎的都是些傻瓜，他们有这许多人，为什么不联合起来打倒那些正人君子，把他们绞死了呢？

麦克达夫夫人　哎哟，上帝保佑你，可怜的猴子！可是你没了父亲怎么好呢？

麦克达夫子　要是他真的死了，您会为他哀哭的；要是您不哭，那是一个好兆，我就可以有一个新的爸爸了。

麦克达夫夫人　这小油嘴真会胡说!

　　　　一使者上。

使者　祝福您，好夫人!您不认识我是什么人，可是我久闻夫人的令名，所以特地前来，报告您一个消息。我怕夫人目下有极大的危险，要是您愿意接受一个微贱之人的忠告，那么还是离开此地，赶快带着您的孩子们避一避的好。我这样惊吓着您，已经是够残忍的了;要是有人再要加害于您，那真是太没有人道了，可是这没人道的事儿快要落到您头上了。上天保佑您!我不敢多耽搁时间。（下）

麦克达夫夫人　叫我逃到哪儿去呢?我没有做过害人的事。可是我记起来了，我是在这个世上，这世上做了恶事才会被人恭维赞美，做了好事反会被人当做危险的傻瓜;那么，唉!我为什么还要用这种婆子气的话替自己辩护，说是我没有做过害人的事呢?

　　　　刺客等上。

麦克达夫夫人　这些是什么人?

众刺客　你的丈夫呢?

麦克达夫夫人　我希望他是在光天化日之下，你们这些鬼东西不敢露脸的地方。

刺客　他是个反贼。

麦克达夫子　你胡说，你这蓬头的恶人!

刺客　什么！你这叛徒的孽种！（刺麦克达夫之子）

麦克达夫子　他杀死我了，妈妈，您快逃吧！（死）（麦克达夫夫人呼"杀了人啦！"下，众刺客追下）

第三场　英格兰　王宫前

马尔科姆及麦克达夫上。

马尔科姆　让我们找一处没有人踪的树荫，在那里把我们胸中的悲哀痛痛快快地哭个干净吧。

麦克达夫　我们还是紧握着利剑，像好汉子似的卫护我们被蹂躏的祖国吧。每一个新的黎明都听得见新媚的寡妇在哭泣，新失父母的孤儿在号啕，新的悲哀上冲霄汉，发出凄厉的回声，就像哀悼苏格兰的命运，替她奏唱挽歌一样。

马尔科姆　我要为我所知道的一切痛哭，我还要等待机会报复我的仇恨。您说的话也许是事实。一提起这个暴君的名字，就使我们切齿腐舌，可是他曾经有过正直的名声，您对他也有很好的交情，他也还没有加害于您。我虽然年轻识浅，可是您也许可以利用我向他邀功求赏，把一头柔弱无罪的羔羊向一个愤怒的天神献祭，不失为一件聪明的事。

麦克达夫　我不是一个奸诈小人。

67

马尔科姆　麦克白却是的。在尊严的王命之下，忠实仁善的人也许不得不背着天良行事。可是我必须请您原谅；您的忠诚的人格绝不会因为我用小人之心去测度它而发生变化。最光明的天使也许会堕落，可是天使总是光明的；虽然丑恶的东西总要做出一副美德的表象来，但美德自身的样子还是美德。

麦克达夫　我已经失去我的希望。

马尔科姆　也许正是这一点刚才引起了我的怀疑。您为什么不告而别，丢下您的妻子儿女，那些生活中的宝贵的原动力，爱情的坚强的联系，让她们担惊受险呢？请您不要把我的多心引为耻辱，为了我自己的安全，我不能不这样顾虑。不管我心里怎样想，也许您真是一个忠义的汉子。

麦克达夫　流血吧，流血吧，可怜的国家！不可一世的暴君，奠下你的安若泰山的基业吧，因为正义的力量不敢向你诛讨！忍受你的屈辱吧，这是你的已经确定的名分！再会，殿下。即使把这暴君掌握下的全部土地一起给我，再加上富庶的东方，我也不愿做一个像你所猜疑我那样的奸人。

马尔科姆　不要生气；我说这样的话，并不是完全为了不放心您。我想我们的国家呻吟在虐政之下，流泪，流血，每天都有一道新的伤痕加在旧日的疮痍之上；我也想到一定有许多人愿意为了我的权利奋臂而起，就在友好的

68

英格兰这里，也已经有数千义士愿意给我助力；可是虽然这样说，要是我有一天能够把暴君的头颅放在足下践踏，或者把它悬挂在我的剑上，我的可怜的祖国却要在一个新的暴君的统治之下，滋生更多的罪恶，忍受更大的苦痛，造成更分歧的局面。

麦克达夫 这新的暴君是谁?

马尔科姆 我的意思就是说我自己。我知道在我的天性之中，深植着各种的罪恶，要是有一天暴露出来，黑暗的麦克白在相形之下，将会变成白雪一样纯洁。我们的可怜的国家看见了我的无限的暴虐，将会把他当做一头羔羊。

麦克达夫 踏遍地狱也找不出一个比麦克白更万恶不赦的魔鬼。

马尔科姆 我承认他嗜杀、骄奢、贪婪、虚伪、欺诈、狂暴、凶恶，一切可以指名的罪恶他都有。可是我的淫逸是没有止境的：你们的妻子、女儿、妇人、处女，都不能填满我的欲壑；我的猖狂的欲念会冲决一切节制和约束。与其让这样一个人做国王，还是让麦克白统治的好。

麦克达夫 人性中无限制的纵欲是一种虐政，它曾经颠覆了不少王位，推翻了无数君主。可是您还不必担心，谁也不能禁止您满足您的分内的欲望。您可以一方面尽情欢乐，一方面在外表上装出庄重的神气，世人的耳目是很容易遮掩过去的。我们国内尽多自愿献身的女子，无论您怎样贪欢好色，也应付不了这许多求荣献媚的娇娥。

马尔科姆　除了这一种弱点以外，在我的邪僻的心中还有一种不顾廉耻的贪婪，要是我做了国王，我一定要诛除贵族，侵夺他们的土地；不是向这个人索取珠宝，就是向那个人索取房屋；我所有的越多，我的贪心越不知道餍足，我一定会为了图谋财富的缘故，向善良忠贞的人无端寻衅，把他们陷于死地。

麦克达夫　这一种贪婪比起少年的情欲来，它的根是更深而更有毒的，我们曾经有许多过去的国王死在它的剑下。可是您不用担心，苏格兰有足够您享用的财富，它都是属于您的；只要有其他的美德，这些缺点都不算什么。

马尔科姆　可是我一点没有君主之德，什么公平、正直、节俭、镇定、慷慨、坚毅、仁慈、谦恭、诚敬、宽容、勇敢、刚强，我全没有；各种罪恶却应有尽有，在各方面表现出来。嘿，要是我掌握了大权，我一定要把和谐的甘乳倾入地狱，扰乱世界的和平，破坏地上的统一。

麦克达夫　啊，苏格兰，苏格兰！

马尔科姆　你说这样一个人是不是适宜于统治？我正是像我所说那样的人。

麦克达夫　适宜于统治！不，这样的人是不该让他留在人世的。啊，多难的国家，一个篡位的暴君握着染血的御杖高踞在王座上，你的最合法的嗣君又亲口吐露了他是这样一个可诅咒的人，辱没了他的高贵的血统，那么你几时才能重见天日呢？你的父王是一个最圣明的君主；生养你的母后每天都在死中过活，她朝夕都在屈膝跪求上天的垂怜。再会！你自己供认的这些罪恶，已经把我从苏格兰放逐。啊，我的胸膛，你的希望永远在这儿埋葬了！

马尔科姆　麦克达夫，只有一颗正直的心，才会有这种勃发的忠义之情，它已经把黑暗的疑虑从我的灵魂上一扫而空，使我充分信任你的真诚。魔鬼般的麦克白曾经派了许多说客来，想要把我诱进他的罗网，所以我不得不着意提防；可是上帝鉴临在你我二人的中间！从现在起，我委身听从你的指导，并且撤回我刚才对我自己所讲的坏话，我所加在我自己身上的一切污点，都是我的天性中所没有的。我还没有近过女色，从来没有背过誓，即使是我自己的东西，我也没有贪得的欲念；我从不曾失信于人，我不愿把魔鬼出卖给他的同伴，我珍爱忠诚不亚于生命；刚才我对自己所作的诽语，是我第一次的说谎。那真诚的我，是准备随时接受你和我的不幸的祖国的命令的。在你还没有到这儿来以前；年老的西沃德已经带领了一万个战士，装备齐全，向苏格兰出发了。现在我们就可以把我们的力量合并在一起；我们堂堂正正的义师，一定可以克奏肤功。您为什么不说话？

麦克达夫　好消息和恶消息同时传进了我的耳朵里，使我的喜怒都失去了自主。

　　一医生上。

马尔科姆　好，等会儿再说。请问一声，王上出来了吗？

医生　出来了，殿下；有一大群不幸的人们在等候他的医治，他们的疾病使最高明的医生束手无策，可是上天给他这样神奇的力量，只要他的手一触，他们就立刻痊愈了。

马尔科姆　谢谢您的见告，大夫。（医生下）

麦克达夫　他说的是什么疾病？

马尔科姆　他们都把它叫做恶病①；自从我来到英格兰以后，我常常看见这位善良的国王显示他的奇妙无比的本领。除了他自己以外，谁也不知道他是怎样祈求着上天；可是害着怪病的人，浑身肿烂，惨不忍睹，一切外科手术所无法医治的，他只要嘴里念着祈祷，用一枚金章亲手挂在他们的颈上，他们便会霍然痊愈；据说他这种治病的天能，是世世相传永袭罔替的。除了这种特殊的本领以外，他还是一个天生的预言者，福祥环拱着他的王座，表示他具有各种美德。

麦克达夫　瞧，谁来啦？

马尔科姆　是我们国里的人；可是我还认不出他是谁。

　　　　　罗斯上。

麦克达夫　我的贤弟，欢迎。

马尔科姆　我现在认识他了。好上帝，赶快除去使我们成为陌路之人的那一层隔膜吧！

---

① 指淋巴结核。——编者注

72

罗斯 阿门，殿下。

麦克达夫 苏格兰还是原来那样子吗？

罗斯 唉！可怜的祖国！它简直不敢认识它自己。它不能再称为我们的母亲，只是我们的坟墓；除了浑浑噩噩、一无所知的人以外，谁的脸上也不曾有过一丝笑容；叹息、呻吟、震撼天空的呼号，都是日常听惯的声音，不能再引起人们的注意；剧烈的悲哀变成一般的风气；葬钟敲响的时候，谁也不再关心它是为谁而鸣；善良人的生命往往在他们帽上的花朵还没有枯萎以前就化为朝露。

麦克达夫 啊！太巧妙，也是太真实的描写！

马尔科姆 最近有什么令人痛心的事情？

罗斯 一小时以前的变故，在叙述者的嘴里就已经变成陈迹了；每一分钟都产生新的祸难。

麦克达夫 我的妻子安好吗？

罗斯 呃，她很安好。

麦克达夫 我的孩子们呢？

罗斯 也很安好。

麦克达夫 那暴君还没有毁坏他们的平静吗？

罗斯 没有；当我离开他们的时候，他们是很平安的。

麦克达夫 不要吝惜你的言语；究竟怎样？

罗斯 当我带着沉重的消息，预备到这儿来传报的时候，一路上听见谣传，说是许多有名望的人都已经纷纷起义；这种谣言照我想起来是很可靠的，因为我亲眼看见那暴

73

君的肆虐。现在是应该出动全力，挽救祖国沦夷的时候了；你们要是在苏格兰出现，可以使男人们个个变成兵士，使女人们愿意从她们的困苦之下获得解放而奋斗。

马尔科姆 我们正要回去，让这消息作为他们的安慰吧。友好的英格兰已经借给我们西沃德将军和一万兵士，所有基督教的国家里找不出一个比他更老练、更优秀的军人。

罗斯 我希望我也有同样好的消息给你们！可是我所要说的话，是应该把它在荒野里呼喊，不让它钻进人们耳中的。

麦克达夫 它是关于哪方面的？是和大众有关的呢，还是一两个人单独的不幸？

罗斯 天良未泯的人，对于这件事谁都要觉得像自己身受一样伤心，虽然你是最感到切身之痛的一个。

麦克达夫 倘然那是与我有关的事，那么不要瞒过我；快让我知道了吧。

罗斯 但愿你的耳朵不要从此永远憎恨我的舌头，因为它将要让你听见你有生以来所听到的最惨痛的声音。

麦克达夫 哼，我猜到了。

罗斯 你的城堡受到袭击；你的妻子和儿女都惨死在野蛮的刀剑之下；要是我把他们的死状告诉你，那么不但他们已经成为猎场上被杀害的驯鹿，就是你也要痛不欲生的。

马尔科姆 慈悲的上天！什么，朋友！不要把你的帽子拉下来遮住你的额角；用言语把你的悲伤倾泻出来吧；无言的哀痛是会向那不堪重压的心低声耳语，叫它裂成片片的。

麦克达夫　我的孩子也都死了吗？

罗斯　妻子、孩子、仆人，凡是被他们找得到的，杀得一个不存。

麦克达夫　我却必须离开那里！我的妻子也被杀了吗？

罗斯　我已经说过了。

马尔科姆　请宽心吧；让我们用壮烈的复仇做药饵，治疗这一段残酷的悲痛。

麦克达夫　他自己没有儿女。我的可爱的宝贝们都死了吗？你说他们一个也不存吗？啊，地狱里的恶鸟！一个也不存？什么！我的可爱的鸡雏们和他们的母亲一起葬送在毒手之下了吗？

马尔科姆　拿出男子汉的气概来。

麦克达夫　我要拿出男子汉的气概来；可是我不能抹杀我的人类的感情。我怎么能够把我所最珍爱的人置之度外，不去想念他们呢？难道上天看见这一幕惨剧，而不对他们抱同情吗？罪恶深重的麦克达夫！他们都是为了你的缘故而死于非命。我真该死，他们没有一点罪过，只是因为我自己不好，无情的屠戮才会降临到他们的身上。愿上天给他们安息！

马尔科姆　把这一桩仇恨作为磨快你的剑锋的砺石；让哀痛变成愤怒；不要让你的心麻木下去，激起它的怒火来吧。

麦克达夫　啊！我可以一方面让我的眼睛里流着妇人之泪，一方面让我的舌头发出豪言壮语。可是，仁慈的上天，求你撤除一切中途的障碍，让我跟这苏格兰的恶魔正面相对，使我的剑能够刺到他的身上；要是我放他逃走了，那么上天饶恕他吧！

马尔科姆　这几句话说得很像个汉子。来，我们见国王去；我们的军队已经调齐，一切齐备，只待整装出发。麦克白气数将绝，天诛将至；黑夜无论怎样悠长，白昼总会到来。（同下）

第五幕

第一场　邓斯纳恩　城堡中一室

一医生及一侍女上。

医生　我已经陪着你看守了两夜，可是一点不能证实你的报
　　　告。她最后一次晚上起来行动是在什么时候？

侍女　自从王上出征以后，我曾经看见她从床上起来，披上
　　　睡衣，开了橱门上的锁，拿出信纸，把它折起来，在上
　　　面写了字，读了一遍，然后把信封好，再回到床上去；
　　　可是在这一段时间里，她始终睡得很熟。

医生　这是心理上的一种重大的纷乱，一方面入于睡眠的状
　　　态，一方面还能像醒着一般做事。在这种睡眠不安的情
　　　形之下，除了走路和其他动作以外，你有没有听见她说
　　　过什么话？

侍女　大夫，那我可不能背着她告诉您。

医生　你不妨对我说，而且应该对我说。

侍女　我不能对您说，也不能对任何人说，因为没有一个见
　　　证可以证实我的话。

麦克白夫人持烛上。

侍女 您瞧！她来啦。这正是她往常的样子；凭着我的生命起誓，她现在睡得很熟。留心看着她；站近一些。

医生 她怎么会有那支蜡烛？

侍女 那就放在她的床边；她的寝室里通宵点着灯火，这是她的命令。

医生 你瞧，她的眼睛睁着呢。

侍女 嗯，可是她的视觉却关闭着。

医生 她现在在干什么？瞧，她在擦她的手。

侍女 这是她的一个惯常的动作，好像在洗手似的。我曾经看见她这样擦了足有一刻钟的时间。

麦克白夫人 可是这儿还有一点血迹。

医生 听！她说话了。我要把她的话记下来，免得忘记。

麦克白夫人 去，该死的血迹！去吧！一点、两点，啊，那么现在可以动手了。地狱里是这样幽暗！呸，我的爷，呸！你是一个军人，也会害怕吗？既然谁也不能奈何我们，为什么我们要怕被人知道？可是谁想得到这老头儿会有这么多血？

医生 你听见没有？

麦克白夫人 法夫爵士从前有一个妻子；现在她在哪儿？什么！这两只手再也不会干净了吗？算了，我的爷，算了；你这样大惊小怪，把事情都弄糟了。

医生 说下去，说下去；你已经知道你所不应该知道的事。

侍女　我想她已经说了她所不应该说的话；天知道她心里有些什么秘密。

麦克白夫人　这儿还是有一股血腥气；所有阿拉伯的香科都不能叫这只小手变得香一点。啊！啊！啊！

医生　这一声叹息多么沉痛！她的心里蕴蓄着无限的凄苦。

侍女　我不愿为了身体上的尊荣，而让我的胸膛里装着这样一颗心。

医生　好，好，好。

侍女　但愿一切都是好好的，大夫。

医生　这种病我没有法子医治。可是我知道有些曾经在睡梦中走动的人，都是很虔敬地寿终正寝。

麦克白夫人　洗净你的手，披上你的睡衣；不要这样面无人色。我再告诉你一遍，班柯已经下葬了，他不会从坟墓里出来的。

医生　有这等事？

麦克白夫人　睡去，睡去；有人在打门哩。来，来，来，来，让我搀着你。事情已经干了就算了。睡去，睡去，睡去。

（下）

医生　她现在要上床去吗？

侍女　就要上床去了。

医生　外边很多骇人听闻的流言。反常的行为引起了反常的纷扰；良心负疚的人往往会向无言的衾枕泄露他们的秘密；她需要教士的训诲甚于医生的诊视。上帝，上帝饶

79

恕我们一切世人！留心照料她；避免一切足以使她烦恼的根源，随时看顾着她。好，晚安！她扰乱了我的心，迷惑了我的眼睛。我心里所想到的，却不敢把它吐出嘴唇。

侍女 晚安，好大夫。（各下）

第二场 邓斯纳恩附近乡野

　　旗鼓前导，门蒂思、凯恩尼斯、安格斯、伦诺克斯及兵士等上。

门蒂思 英格兰军队已经迫近，领军的是马尔科姆、他的叔父西沃德和麦克达夫三人，他们的胸头燃起复仇的怒火；即使心如死灰的人，这种痛入骨髓的仇恨也会激起他溅血的决心。

安格斯 在勃南森林附近，我们将要碰上他们；他们正在从那条路上过来。

凯恩尼斯 谁知道道纳本是不是跟他的哥哥在一起？

伦诺克斯 我可以确实告诉你，将军，他们不在一起。我有一张他们军队里高级将领的名单，里面有西沃德的儿子，还有许多初上战场、乳臭未干的少年。

门蒂思 那暴君有什么举动？

凯恩尼斯 他把邓斯纳恩防御得非常坚固。有人说他疯了；

对他比较没有什么恶感的人，却说那是一个猛士的愤怒；可是他不能自己约束住他的惶乱的心情，却是一件无疑的事实。

安格斯 现在他已经感觉到他的暗杀的罪恶紧粘在他的手上；每分钟都有一次叛变，谴责他的不忠不义；受他命令的人，都不过奉命行事，并不是出于对他的忠诚；现在他已经感觉到他的尊号罩在他的身上，就像一个矮小的偷儿穿了一件巨人的衣服一样拖手绊脚。

门蒂思 他自己的灵魂都在谴责它本身的存在，谁还能怪他的昏乱的知觉怔忡不安呢。

凯恩尼斯 好，我们整队前进吧；我们必须认清谁是我们应该服从的人。为了拔除祖国的沉疴，让我们准备和他共同流尽我们的最后一滴血。

伦诺克斯 否则我们也愿意喷洒我们的热血，灌溉这一朵国家主权的娇花，淹没那凭陵它的野草。向勃南进军！（众列队行进下）

第三场　邓斯纳恩　城堡中一室

麦克白、医生及侍从等上。

麦克白 不要再告诉我什么消息；让他们一个个逃走吧；除非勃南的森林会向邓斯纳恩移动，我是不知道有什么事情值得害怕的。马尔科姆那小子算得什么？他不是妇人所生的吗？预知人类死生的精灵曾经这样向我宣告："不要害怕，麦克白；没有一个妇人所生下的人可以加害于你。"那么逃走吧，不忠的爵士们，去跟那些饕餮的英格兰人在一起吧。我的头脑，永远不会被疑虑所困扰，我的心灵永远不会被恐惧所震荡。

一仆人上。

麦克白　魔鬼罚你变成炭团一样黑，你这脸色惨白的狗头！你从哪儿得来这么一副呆鹅的蠢相？

仆人　有一万——

麦克白　一万只鹅吗，狗才？

仆人　一万个兵，陛下。

麦克白　去刺破你自己的脸，把你那吓得毫无血色的两颊染一染红吧，你这鼠胆的小子。什么兵，蠢材？该死的东西！瞧你吓得脸像白布一般。什么兵，不中用的奴才？

仆人　启禀陛下，是英格兰兵。

麦克白　不要让我看见你的脸。（仆人下）西登！——我心里很不舒服，当我看见——喂，西登！——这一次的战争也许可以使我从此高枕无忧，也许可以立刻把我倾覆。我已经活得够长久了；我的生命已经日就枯萎，像一片凋谢的黄叶；凡是老年人所应该享有的尊荣、敬爱、服从和一大群的朋友，我是没有希望再得到的了；代替这一切的，只有低声而深刻的诅咒，口头上的恭维和一些违心的假话。西登！

　　　　西登上。

西登　陛下有什么吩咐？

麦克白　还有什么消息没有？

西登　陛下，刚才所报告的消息，全都证实了。

麦克白　我要战到我的全身不剩一块好肉。给我拿战铠来。

西登　现在还用不着哩。

麦克白　我要把它穿起来。加派骑兵，到全国各处巡回视察，要是有谁嘴里提起了一句害怕的话，就把他吊死。给我拿战铠来。大夫，你的病人今天怎样？

医生　回陛下，她并没有什么病，只是因为思虑太过，继续不断的幻想扰乱了她的神经，使她不得安息。

麦克白　替她医好这一种病。你难道不能诊治一个病态的心理，从记忆中拔去一桩根深蒂固的忧郁，拭掉那写在脑筋上的烦恼，用一种使人忘却一切的甘美的药剂，把那堆满在胸间、重压在心头的积毒扫除干净吗？

医生　那还是要仗病人自己设法的。

麦克白　那么把医药丢给狗子吧；我不要仰仗它。来，替我穿上战铠；给我拿指挥杖来。西登，把我的命令传出去。——大夫，那些爵士们都背了我逃走了。——来，快去。——大夫，要是你能够替我的国家验一验小便，查明她的病根，使她回复原来的健康，我一定要使太空之中充满着我对你的赞美的回声。——喂，把它脱下了。——什么大黄肉桂，什么清泻的药剂，可以把这些英格兰人驱走呢？你听见关于他们的消息吗？

医生　是的，陛下；您的森严的防卫告诉了我们一些消息。

麦克白　给我把铠甲带着。除非勃南森林会向邓斯纳恩移动，我对死亡和毒害都没有半分惊恐。

医生　（旁白）要是我能够从邓斯纳恩远远离开，高官厚禄再也诱不动我回来。（同下）

第四场　勃南森林附近的乡野

　　旗鼓前导，马尔科姆、西沃德父子、麦克达夫、门蒂思、凯恩尼斯、安格斯、伦诺克斯、罗斯及兵士等列队行进上。

马尔科姆　诸位贤卿，我希望大家都能够安枕而寝的日子已经不远了。

门蒂思　那是我们一点也不疑惑的。

西沃德　前面这一座是什么树林？

门蒂思　勃南森林。

马尔科姆　每一个兵士都砍下一根树枝来，把它举起在各人的面前；这样我们可以隐匿我们全军的人数，让敌人无从知道我们的实力。

兵士等　得令。

西沃德　我们所得到的情报，都说那自信的暴君仍旧在邓斯纳恩深居不出，等候我们兵临城下。

马尔科姆　这是他的唯一的希望；因为在他手下的人，不论地位高低，一找到机会都要叛弃他，他们接受他的号令，都只是出于被迫，并不是自己心愿。

麦克达夫　等我们看清了真情实况再下准确的判断吧，眼前让我们发扬战士的坚毅的精神。

西沃德　我们这一次的胜败得失，不久就可以分晓。口头的推测不过是一些悬空的希望，实际的行动才能够产生决定的结果。大家奋勇前进吧！（众列队行进下）

第五场　邓斯纳恩　城堡内

旗鼓前导，麦克白、西登及兵士等上。

麦克白　把我们的旗帜挂在城墙外面；到处仍旧是一片"他们来了"的呼声；我们这座城堡防御得这样坚强，还怕他们围攻吗？让他们到这儿来，等饥饿和瘟疫来把他们收拾了去吧。倘不是我们自己的军队也倒了戈跟他们联合在一起，我们尽可以挺身出战，把他们赶回老家去。（内妇女哭声）那是什么声音？

西登　是妇女们的哭声，陛下。（下）

麦克白　我简直已经忘记了恐惧的滋味。从前一声晚间的哀

85

叫，可以把我吓出一身冷汗，听着一段可怕的故事，我的头发会像有了生命似的竖起来。现在我已经饱尝无数的恐怖；我的习惯于杀戮的思想，再也没有什么悲惨的事情可以使它惊悚了。

　　西登重上。

麦克白　那哭声是为了什么事？

西登　陛下，王后死了。

麦克白　迟早总是要死的，总要有听到这个噩耗的一天。明天，明天，再一个明天，一天接着一天地蹑步前进，直到最后一秒钟的时间；我们所有的昨天，不过替傻子们照亮了到死亡的土壤中去的路。熄灭了吧，熄灭了吧，短促的烛光！人生不过是一个行走的影子，一个在舞台上指手画脚的拙劣的伶人，登场了片刻，就在无声无臭中悄然退下；它是一个愚人所讲的故事，充满着喧哗和骚动，却找不到一点意义。

　　一使者上。

麦克白　你要来拨弄你的唇舌；有什么话快说。

使者　陛下，我应该向您报告我以为我所看见的事，可是我不知道应该怎样说起。

麦克白　好，你说吧。

使者　当我站在山头守望的时候，我向勃南一眼望去，好像那边的树木都在开始行动了。

麦克白　说谎的奴才！

使者　要是没有那么一回事，我愿意悉听陛下的惩处；在这三英里路以内，您可以看见它向这边过来；一座活动的树林。

麦克白　要是你说了谎话，我要把你活活吊在树上，让你饥饿而死；要是你的话是真的，我也希望你把我吊死了吧。我的决心已经有些动摇，我开始怀疑起那魔鬼所说的似是而非的暧昧的谎话了："不要害怕，除非勃南森林会到邓斯纳恩来。"现在一座树林真的到邓斯纳恩来了。披上武装，出去！他所说的这种事情要是果然出现，那么逃走固然逃走不了，留在这儿也不过坐以待毙。我现在开始厌倦白昼的阳光，但愿这世界早一点崩溃。敲起警钟来！吹吧，狂风！来吧，灭亡！就是死我们也要捐命沙场。（同下）

第六场　同前　城堡前平原

　　旗鼓前导，马尔科姆、老西沃德、麦克达夫等率军队各持树枝上。

马尔科姆　现在已经相去不远；把你们树叶的幕障抛下，现出你们威武的军容来。尊贵的叔父，请您带领我的兄弟，您的英勇的儿子，先去和敌人交战；其余的一切统归尊贵的麦克达夫跟我两人负责部署。

西沃德　再会。今天晚上我们只要找得到那暴君的军队，一定要跟他们拼个你死我活。

麦克达夫　把我们所有的喇叭一齐吹起来；鼓足了你们的中气，把流血和死亡的消息吹进敌人的耳里。（同下）

第七场　同前　平原上的另一部分

　　　　号角声。麦克白上。

麦克白　他们已经缚住我的手脚；我不能逃走，可是我必须像熊一样挣扎到底。哪一个人不是由妇人生下来的？除了这样一个人以外，我还怕什么人。

　　　　小西沃德上。

小西沃德　你叫什么名字？

麦克白　我的名字说出来会吓坏你。

小西沃德　即使你给自己取了一个比地狱里的魔鬼更炽热的名字，也吓不倒我。

麦克白　我就叫麦克白。

小西沃德　魔鬼自己也不能向我的耳中说出一个更可憎恨的名字。

麦克白　他也不能说出一个更可怕的名字。

小西沃德　胡说，你这可恶的暴君；我要用我的剑证明你的说谎。（二人交战，小西沃德被杀）

麦克白　你是妇人所生的；我瞧不起一切妇人之子手里的刀剑。（下）

　　　　号角声。麦克达夫上。

麦克达夫　那喧声是在那边。暴君，露出你的脸来；要是你已经被人杀死，等不及我来取你的性命，那么我的妻子儿女的阴魂一定不会放过我。我不能杀害那些被你雇用的倒霉的士卒；我的剑倘不能刺中你，麦克白，我宁愿让它闲置不用，保全它的锋刃，把它重新插回鞘里。你应该在那边；这一阵高声的呐喊，好像是宣布什么重要的人物上阵似的。命运，让我找到他吧！我没有此外的奢求了。（下。号角声）

　　　　马尔科姆及老西沃德上。

西沃德　这儿来，殿下；那城堡已经拱手纳降。暴君的人民有的帮这一面，有的帮那一面；英勇的爵士们一个个出力奋战；您已经胜算在握，大势就可以决定了。

马尔科姆　我们也碰见了敌人，他们只是虚晃几枪罢了。

西沃德　殿下，请进堡里去吧。（同下。号角声）

　　　　麦克白重上。

麦克白　我为什么要学那些罗马人的傻样子，死在我自己的剑上呢？我的剑是应该为杀敌而用的。

　　　　麦克达夫重上。

麦克达夫　转过来，地狱里的恶狗，转过来！

麦克白　我在一切人中间，最不愿意看见你。可是你回去吧，我的灵魂里沾着你一家人的血，已经太多了。

麦克达夫　我没有话说；我的话都在我的剑上，你这没有一个名字可以形容你的狠毒的恶贼！（二人交战）

麦克白　你不过白费了气力；你要使我流血，正像用你锐利的剑锋在空气上划一道痕迹一样困难。让你的刀刃降落在别人的头上吧；我的生命是有魔法保护的，没有一个妇人生产下来的人可以把它伤害。

麦克达夫　不要再信任你的魔法了吧；让你所信奉的神告诉你，麦克达夫是没有足月就从他母亲的腹中剖出来的。

麦克白　愿那告诉我这样的话的舌头永受诅咒，因为它使我失去了男子汉的勇气！愿这些欺人的魔鬼再也不要被人相信，他们用模棱两可的话愚弄我们，听来好像大有希望，结果却完全和我们原来的期望相反。我不愿跟你交战。

麦克达夫　那么投降吧，懦夫，我们可以饶你活命，可是要叫你在众人的面前出丑：我们要把你当做一头稀有的怪物一样，把你缚在柱上，涂上花脸，下面写着："请看暴君的原形。"

麦克白　我不愿投降，我不愿低头吻那马尔科姆小子足下的泥土，被那些下贱的民众任意唾骂。虽然勃南森林已经到了邓斯纳恩，虽然今天和你狭路相逢，你偏偏不是妇人所生下的，可是我还要擎起我的雄壮的盾牌，尽我最后的力量。来，麦克达夫，谁先喊"住手，够了"的，

让他永远在地狱里沉沦。（二人且战且下）

　　吹退军号。喇叭奏花腔。旗鼓前导，马尔科姆、老西沃德、罗斯、众爵士及兵士等重上。

马尔科姆　我希望我们所失去的朋友都能够安然到来。

西沃德　总有人免不了牺牲；可是照我看见眼前这些人说起来，我们这次重大的胜利所付的代价是很小的。

马尔科姆　麦克达夫跟您的英勇的儿子都失踪了。

罗斯　老将军，令郎已经尽了一个军人的责任；他刚刚活到成人的年龄，就用他的勇往直前的战斗精神证明了他的勇力，像一个男子汉似的死了。

西沃德　那么他已经死了吗？

罗斯　是的，他的尸体已经从战场上搬走。他的死是一桩无价的损失，您必须勉抑哀思才好。

西沃德　他的伤口是在前面的吗？

罗斯　是的，在他的胸前。

西沃德　那么愿他成为上帝的兵士！要是我有像头发一样多的儿子，我也不希望他们得到一个更光荣的结局；这就作为他的丧钟吧。

马尔科姆　他是值得我们更深的悲悼的，我将向他致献我的哀思。

西沃德　他已经得到他最大的酬报；他们说，他死得很英勇，他的责任已尽；愿上帝与他同在！又有好消息来了。

　　麦克达夫携麦克白首级重上。

麦克达夫 祝福，吾王陛下！您已经是王上了。瞧，篡贼的万恶的头颅已经取来；无道的虐政从此推翻了。我看见全国的英俊拥绕在你的周围，他们心里都在发出跟我同样的敬礼；现在我要请他们陪着我高呼：祝福，苏格兰的国王！

众人 祝福，苏格兰的国王！（喇叭奏花腔）

马尔科姆 多承各位拥戴，论功行赏，在此一朝。各位爵士国戚，从现在起，你们都得到了伯爵的封号，在苏格兰你们是最初享有这样封号的人。在这去旧布新的时候，我们还有许多事情要做；那些因为逃避暴君的罗网而出亡国外的朋友们，我们必须召唤他们回来；这个屠夫虽然已经死了，他的魔鬼一样的王后，据说也已经亲手杀害了自己的生命，可是帮助他们杀人行凶的党羽，我们必须一一搜捕，处以极刑；此外一切必要的工作，我们都要按照上帝的旨意，逐一处理。现在我要感谢各位的相助，还要请你们陪我到斯贡去，参与加冕大典。（喇叭奏花腔。众下）